Corruption in the O.R.

The Outlander Physician Series

Corruption in the O.R.

by Barbara Ebel, M.D.

The Outlander Physician Series

Book One: Corruption in the O.R.
Book Two: Wretched Results

Copyright © 2019 by Barbara Ebel, M.D.

Paperback ISBN-13: 978-1-7324466-6-3
eBook ISBN-13: 978-1-7324466-7-0

This book is a work of fiction. Names, characters, places and events are the product of the author's imagination or are used fictitiously. Any resemblance to actual events, persons, or locations is coincidental.

CHAPTER 1

"Hi, I'm Dr. Viktoria Thorsdottir. Sometimes I go by 'Doctor Viktoria.' Makes it easier on everyone."

Helen Grant popped her head up from the glowering stare she gave the IV in her hand. A nurse had stuck her five times to make a catheter spear into a feeble vein, and she was ready to call all health care workers incompetent. Her sullen annoyance intensified when she laid eyes on the thirty-nine-year-old physician.

"I'd like to see the male, silver-haired attending, please."

"That doctor you spoke to is the emergency room physician. He doesn't practice anesthesia."

"Of course, you do?" She shook her head as if to eject lice crawling around in her scalp. "Just my luck."

"Yes, Ma'am. I'm the anesthesiologist."

The woman yanked the sheet up on the hospital gown covering her breasts. "Humph," she interjected, barely audible. "Just so you know, I'm no novice. I've been through this before. Damn diabetes causes the skin on my foot to disintegrate and pus-out like some rancid scene in a horror movie."

"That can't be easy on you."

"You're damn right."

"May I ask you some questions?

"My husband's not here right now."

"Do you need him around in order to talk to me? Your surgeon has put you on the OR schedule before his first patient who is late to arrive. I would hate for your case to be delayed. Apparently, you have a nasty infection in your foot which needs attention."

Mrs. Grant pondered the question while Viktoria continued a more thorough visual summary of the woman's appearance. Along with being an aged sixty-two years old, the patient was bordering on morbid obesity and her exposed skin was tough and dry, like a reptile who basked in the hot Florida sun.

Helen Grant shoved her cursed right foot out from the side of the sheet,

1

as if showing off a trophy. "All right then. Go ahead. Same old questions, I'm sure."

Viktoria asked the woman the pertinent questions she needed answered, but she didn't learn any surprises from Mrs. Grant's health history and physical exam. She surmised that her patient was a bit of a rarity because Type II diabetics nowadays were, in general, under better control than years ago.

Mrs. Grant, however, lived her days the way she wanted, chugging down canned sodas, sugary snacks, and TV dinners. She expected her oral hypoglycemic medication and recent insulin prescription to manage her glucose all by themselves, and she had grown a huge wall of denial that her own lifestyle was to blame.

The ER record noted that the woman was found eating a bag of pretzels after she'd been evaluated, but it didn't stop Viktoria from redundantly asking the relevant question. "When did you last eat or drink?"

"I don't know."

"Mrs. Grant, if you're a frequent flier, any anesthesiologist in the past would have told you that recent food in your stomach is always a concern to us."

"My husband took away the pretzels at 3 a.m. It's boring spending the middle of the night in an ER waiting for all the tests, and watching people come in and out and poke on you. But I ain't ate nothing since then. The snacks gave me something to do. But you've never been on the other side of hospital care. You're just a baby. How long you been working here anyway?"

"This is my first day."

Helen's eyes shot wide open. "You're joking."

"No. I provide staffing assistance for anesthesia departments that are short-handed, especially in under-served areas. Don't worry, I'm an experienced anesthesiologist."

"Get out!" Helen rolled her eyes. "Like I said, just my luck. Not only are you a woman doctor, but you wouldn't know where the life-saving oxygen is."

"The tanks are green and I'm not color blind. They're the same everywhere and in the usual places, like hooked into anesthesia machines. But I can ask the person in charge of the anesthesia schedule today to turn over your case to someone else if you're uncomfortable with me."

"That'll delay my surgery?"

"Most certainly."

Helen pouted her lips. "Never mind. Let's get on with it."

"A general anesthetic would be preferable for your case," Viktoria said. She explained the risks and benefits as she scrutinized Helen's IV. It was a small-bore catheter and was only seeded halfway in the vein. By the looks of the woman's arms, the nursing staff had done as good a job as possible.

Mrs. Grant withdrew her hand. "Over my dead body. Not again. Don't even think about making me your pin cushion."

"Your veins have seen better days. For your case and your postop care, chances are you will need something bigger. I'll do my best to put you to sleep with this one, but I may need better access after you're asleep, such as a central line."

"They told me that need would come someday."

"Those lines carry a greater risk of infection, injury to a lung, or bleeding."

Helen twisted her dry lips. "But you said you're experienced."

"Every medical procedure carries a risk no matter who does it."

"All right. Be careful, in particular since you don't like me."

"I didn't like vegetables when I was growing up. Tasteless vegetables and people are two different things."

Much to Dr. Thorsdottir's intent, Helen's face went blank as she tried to sort that out, so Viktoria took the opportunity to slip out. She took an elevator upstairs, made her way past the OR front desk, and rechecked the day's schedule.

Written in magic marker on a white board in the hallway, the changing schedule was the gospel itinerary for the OR staff, anesthesia department, and surgeons. Same as earlier, Helen Grant had been written into Room 7, taking the place of a "no show" elective case. With the help of the anesthetic tech, Viktoria had previously set up her room with the necessary anesthetic equipment and drugs, but now she added a central line kit.

Her first patient had been correct, however, about the need to find out where everything was. Since it was Viktoria's first day at the community hospital in northern Pennsylvania, she still needed to check out the preop area and recovery room. She noted the open door to the preop area where elective patients were waiting to go back to the OR, and then she strolled into the recovery room and sat behind the long counter. Several nurses were preparing for the day, but two of them were at the bedside of a patient being checked in. One nurse swiftly applied monitors to a male adult while the other one listened to the report from the CRNA who had just done his case.

The pretty woman holding an anesthetic record was a CRNA, or certified registered nurse anesthetist. She did not wear a plastic name badge like the anesthesiologists Viktoria had already seen in the hallway. The woman wore a deep red unisex three-pocket scrub jacket and from where she sat, Viktoria could make out, "CRNA" embroidered after her name.

A nurse leaned over for a pen and Viktoria smiled. "Is that case from the middle of the night?"

"Yes," the woman said. "Car accident. Lucky guy to only suffer an arm fracture. Are you this week's hired help in the anesthesia department?"

"I signed on for a month."

After glancing at her name tag, Viktoria wondered if Sally was going to welcome her. It was always a crap shoot what strangers on the job told her: "This is a great place to work for stable people," or "Everyone here is so nice, but we are a close-knit bunch." Sometimes it was more like, "Are you not board certified to work for a permanent group?" or "What makes you not settle down in a real job?"

Of course, what they were normally thinking was *"She must be a terrible anesthesiologist or something's wrong with her. No stable anesthesia group would dare hire her because she must be no good at what she does."*

Sally's attention drifted to the stretcher across from them, and she ignored Viktoria. The male patient contorted his face with pain. His blood pressure reading popped up on the screen as 152/86 and the nurse pushed more contents of a syringe into his IV.

The nurse anesthetist beside him pulled off her OR bonnet and silky, dark shoulder-length hair fell to her shoulders. As she added the final notes to her record, the automatic doors opened, another CRNA entered, and he sauntered straight over to his colleague. Viktoria realized the woman was leaving after night call and the young man was fresh on duty for a regular day schedule. After pleasantries at the patient's bedside, the CRNA pulled out a thick tissue from her pocket, but changed her mind about using it.

She shoved it back in as the male nurse nodded. After good-bye smiles, they both left through different doors.

"You must be the temporary hired help, the locum tenens anesthesiologist." A man with thin lips and a hawkish nose leaned against the counter and gave her intermittent eye contact. "I'm Dr. Berry, the surgeon for your morning cases. The anesthesiologist running the schedule, Dr. Huff, told me to find you here. No doubt you met my patient who qualifies for a loyalty-hospital program discount. However, she has earned a reputation for being 'difficult.' The internal medicine service will also be caring for her in the postop period for her out-of-control diabetes. We'll need dependable access for antibiotics." On second thought, he added, "What's your name?"

"Viktoria Thorsdottir. Sounds like a central line would be helpful for everyone involved."

"And no better time to put it than when she's asleep. She can't complain, and we won't have to hear about it."

Viktoria nodded as Dr. Berry tapped the counter top.

"Do you do central lines with what you do," he asked, "going around to different places and avoiding big cases? I can ask Dr. Huff to make himself available for a few minutes during the case and put it in."

"That would be a shame. The group wouldn't be getting their money's worth out of me if he did that."

"Suit yourself."

The nurse overseeing the recovery room patient stepped next to Dr. Berry and scowled across the counter. "Don't mean to interrupt, but you must be the temporary anesthesiologist. Can you give me an additional order for pain for my patient over there, over and above the standing order? He's had ten of morphine."

The man across from them grimaced and wiggled uncomfortably on the bed and his blood pressure had scarcely improved.

"Is he allergic to any medications?"

"No."

"Give him 15 MGS of ketorolac IV."

"Thanks. What's your name for the order?"

"Dr. Thorsdottir."

"Ugh. How do you spell that?"

"T-H-O-R-S-D-O-T-T-I-R."

She grabbed a notepad on the desk, wrote it down, and glanced at Dr. Berry.

He spoke for the both of them. "That's an unusual name."

Viktoria rose. He'd be one angry surgeon if she wasn't ready for his patient upon her arrival in Room 7. She pushed in the rolling chair. "See you back there."

The stainless-steel double doors to Room 7 clunked open and the stretcher carrying Helen Grant rolled in. "Let's get this over," the patient mumbled. "I don't want to be here anymore than any of you. I'm a born southerner. Made the mistake of coming here to this God-forsaken town because one of our kids moved here."

Viktoria supported Helen's shoulders and head while a nurse and orderly each grabbed the sheet from both sides and at the end of the stretcher. They all lifted her over to the OR table. Viktoria had injected one mg of midazolam into her patient's IV, but it seemed to have little effect.

"If you don't care," Helen barked, "I'll take a blanket."

"I'll fetch you one. That's not that doctor's job," the nurse responded, flicking her head towards Viktoria.

The nurse's name tag said "Alice Coleman, RN." She threw Dr. Thorsdottir another look, making Victoria wonder if the stethoscope draped around her own neck resembled a snake.

Viktoria methodically attached her patient to all the necessary monitors and secured the oxygen mask over her mouth. After a bit more sedation to her patient, she said, "Nurse Coleman, please apply some cricoid pressure on Mrs. Grant's neck as she drifts off to sleep. She's a full stomach and a diabetic. Let's try to prevent any possible food regurgitation during induction to slip down into her airway."

Alice drew in her lips and her eyes rolled to the side. Viktoria said good-night to Mrs. Grant and slid the diprivan and succinylcholine into her IV. After she verified the endotracheal tube's correct placement and secured it in place, Alice let out a huff and stepped away to prepare the patient's leg.

Dr. Berry stood nearby as he watched his patient go to sleep, and then he stepped out to scrub. As if on cue, Dr. Jay Huff came in and stood between the door and the anesthesia machine.

Since Helen's vital signs were stable, Viktoria prepared the central line kit and her patient for the procedure. Since Dr. Huff was also available, she figured there was an extra set of anesthesia hands in the room in case the woman's anesthetic needed to be adjusted.

She palpated her patient's carotid artery and felt the internal jugular vein next to it. Skillfully, the seeker needle and then the guide wire went in smoothly. She inserted the large bore IV, removed the guide wire, and sutured it in. Next, she dressed the area with a sterile cover. Fluids began dripping into the new access and she de-gloved.

Viktoria glanced at the head physician of the anesthesia department. He was a stocky man with narrow shoulders and a wrinkled forehead. If the anesthesia machine had not been the barrier between them, his breath would have been right down her neck into her scrubs. *No doubt,* she thought, *he wasn't really there to help, but to offensively oversee what she was doing.*

She tucked a piece of stray hair into her patient's head bonnet as the bellows of the anesthesia machine whisked up and down. "Dr. Huff," she said, "didn't the locum tenens agency advise you of my credentials?"

"I believe so."

"I'm a board-certified anesthesiologist just like you."

"I'll remember that," he said over his shoulder as he left.

Dr. Huff held one side of the door open for Dr. Berry. The surgeon had intermittently gazed through the windows over the scrub sink, and now held his clean, scrubbed hands in the air while coming in.

"Holler if you need me," Dr. Huff said softly to Darryl Berry as they passed each other.

"If you ask me," Dr. Berry said, "this Dr. Thors-something-or-other inserted the patient's central line and made the procedure look like the apotheosis of how it should be done."

CHAPTER 2

Helen Grant's case quieted down to a steady pace with little to no chit chat. For a Monday morning, Viktoria found that strange. Didn't these people do anything over the weekend that they talked about on resuming work for the new week? That's how it went in most ORs on Monday mornings: banter about some daughter's soccer game on Saturday; or some new restaurant that opened up; or the worst local wanna-be pop group performance at the local community center. Sometimes it would be the male surgeon making jabs at his wife's weekend honey-do list, and he wished he'd been on call instead of being home.

She jotted down a new set of vital signs on the iPad anesthetic record. It was fortunate the woman was under a general anesthetic. Had she qualified for sedation and a regional block on her lower extremity, Mrs. Grant may have kept up the negative innuendos like Viktoria being a 'woman' doctor. Where she came from, gender equality was the highest in the world, even going as far as electing the world's first female president back in 1980. Viktoria grimaced. Although the United States had been her home for a long time, the country still had a long way to go.

She glanced again at the time. The case was deep into its third hour and, rather than being close to being finished, the surgeon was slower than a box turtle deciding which direction to take. In Viktoria's experience, the slowest surgery cases took place in teaching institutions, not by attending physicians in private practice who were accountable to multiple facets of healthcare oversights and reimbursement policies.

Dr. Darryl Berry handed the scrub tech his scalpel and swayed his neck like he had a cramp. Upon seeing Viktoria over the drape between the surgical field and the anesthesia work area, he stared at her for a moment.

"Your patient is doing fine," she said.

"Did you treat her high glucose level and did you think to send off a new blood sample after we got started?"

"Yes. She's much better. Sugar is one hundred twenty."

His eyes didn't blink, and he held his glance.

"Is there something else?" Viktoria asked, prompting a disapproving stare from the scrub tech and Alice Coleman.

"I'm not used to seeing an anesthesiologist or CRNA standing up so much during a case and peering over the ether screen to watch what I'm doing. Makes me wonder if you're paying attention to anesthetic care."

"During a case, I don't sit much. Makes me more alert to oversee the patient, the surgical procedure, and the anesthetic. Because I'm not planted on the stool most of the time, I don't read as many books or check my iPhone as much as other anesthesia caretakers do."

Viktoria immediately regretted speaking her private thoughts aloud. It was not her style to chastise the few less diligent anesthesia care providers.

Dr. Berry gasped. "I harbor a love-hate relationship with anesthesia personnel and you just confirmed my thoughts about their diversions at the head of the table. And just like you were out of line, my love-hate comment can stay in this room." He pointed his bird-like nose at the tech and then the RN. They both looked the other way like they didn't hear a thing.

With a sigh, Viktoria turned around and tidied up the syringes on top of the anesthesia cart. She licked her dry lips under her mask and was overdue for something to drink, even if it wasn't coffee.

In addition, she thought, she needed a bathroom break. Since Dr. Huff was running the schedule, he should have allocated one or two anesthesiologists or CRNAs to go around from OR to OR and give colleagues a morning break. Anesthesia providers couldn't just leave a room. Someone needed to stand in for the patient's care after a thorough report on the case.

She glanced at the double doors hoping to see someone enter and wondered about this department's policy for short respites to use the bathroom and to grab food and drink. Ten minutes later, someone showed up at the scrub sink outside. They didn't wash their hands, but inclined their head over their phone and became immersed in tapping their thumbs a mile a minute. He looked familiar – the male CRNA who earlier greeted the other CRNA at the patient's bedside in the recovery room.

"You may get a break yet," the scrub tech said nodding towards the window.

"I'm in the homestretch," Dr. Berry said. "Hand me some dressings and I'll wrap her wound and finish this case."

Viktoria began easing off on the volatile anesthetic, pulled a pair of disposable gloves out from the box on the cart, and made sure any drugs she needed were drawn up. The CRNA from outside sauntered in and stood between the door and the OR table.

"Hey, Dr. Berry," he said. "Are you finished?"

"Sure am."

The nurse sidled closer to the head of the bed. "I'm Casey Johnston, one of the CRNAs. I can see it's not a good time to give you a break." Thankful for his well-timed arrival, he grinned under his mask. He had dark blue eyes, like the color of the deep northern Atlantic, and a pleasant voice, definitely radio-worthy. Viktoria figured him to be in his late twenties.

"Too true," she said. "Now is not the appropriate time to switch Mrs. Grant's care. I'm already reversing her anesthetic."

"Dr. Huff has you slotted to do Dr. Berry's next case as well. Who knows? Maybe I'll be relieving you for lunch later or for an afternoon break."

Dr. Berry patted the sterile white gauze he'd wrapped around Mrs. Grant's leg and looked only at Casey. "When is Jay going to make her supervise CRNAs and oversee a couple of rooms at once? Like the anesthesia care team model your group mostly works by?"

Casey chuckled. "Ask him. Maybe it depends on whether your patient makes it to the recovery room." He leaned his elbow on the plastic enclosure to the bellows. "Only kidding," he said to Viktoria.

Dr. Thorsdottir untaped her patient's eyes and turned off the sevoflurane vaporizer. The CRNA withdrew his arm and stepped away.

As she glanced at the doors closing behind him, she mumbled something in Danish. Under her breath.

Alice Coleman reached up and turned on the recovery room EKG machine above the stretcher and it came alive with electronic beeps. She lowered her arms aside her plump breasts, slid a pen off her top pocket, and waited for Dr. Thorsdottir's report.

For the second time, Helen opened her eyes after her surgery and tried to make sense of her situation.

"Helen," Viktoria said, "you did fine. You're in the recovery room."

"That's not funny."

"Seriously, your surgery is finished."

Helen fought to keep her eyes open, glanced around in the curtained cubicle, and accepted her whereabouts. "Dr. Berry should get a medal for getting me through another weed whacking."

"You can slumber off again," Alice said. "Dr. Thorsdottir will finish giving me report."

"Ask radiology to slip in and grab a chest X-ray on Mrs. Grant," Viktoria said after her full report. "They just need to confirm my central line placement and lack of complications."

Alice nodded and Viktoria stepped away to sign off on her paperwork. She passed Casey sitting idly behind the desk or taking a break which should have been hers.

Jay Huff ambled in, bouncing with authority, and positioned himself midway in front of Viktoria and Casey. Dr. Viktoria, how'd it go?"

"How did Mrs. Grant do or how did I do?"

"She seems no worse for wear," he said throwing his glance over his shoulder. "And you, well, you can take a quick lunch before your next patient … the usual deal, thirty minutes. Casey will set your room up and check out your drugs and I'll do the preanesthetic assessment on the patient. However, you need to stop by Jeff Appleton's office. He's the Director of Surgical Services. His office is down the hallway from the OR."

"What is Dr. Berry's next case?"

"A cholecystectomy on a forty-two-year-old female."

Viktoria nodded. She signed the intraoperative record and went into the anesthesia office, a room with counters facing one and a half walls and a full couch on one side. Two rolling chairs were available, bookshelves with mostly paperwork, and a plastic tray for the anesthesia records. Besides the electronic record, each intraoperative case with anesthesia start and end times went into it for reimbursement purposes. She dropped in Helen Grant's sheet.

Foremost, she needed to hit the restroom before hunting down the Surgical Services Director, so she deviated into where she had changed and stored her things in a locker earlier in the day. As opposed to many hospitals, especially newer ones, the female locker room was the same for all female OR staff whether a person was a doctor, nurse, or tech.

A woman in scrubs crouched over her sneaker and was tying a knot while she was in full conversation with a nurse next to her. "I couldn't care less about the wedding. It's the reception that'll be worth our while. Jennie never does anything half-assed."

The adjacent nurse glimpsed at Viktoria and shut her locker. "I hope she doesn't invite any last-minute strays," she said softly.

The other woman planted her sneaker on the floor, stood up straight, and turned her back to the entrance. Viktoria turned into the bathroom area. When she left, the two women exited the locker room in front of her without holding the door open.

Dr. Thorsdottir walked the quiet corridor outside the OR and found the Director's office only three doors down. She rapped on the door and heard a firm, pleasant "Come in."

A man immediately stood up from behind his desk. He was around Viktoria's age; tall and fit like a winter athlete who modeling ski clothes. Although his mouth registered a smile, his light brown eyes conveyed most of his social friendliness. He wore dark pants and a blue-pressed shirt with an open-top button.

"You must be Dr. Thorsdottir. I hope I'm pronouncing your name correctly. Please have a seat."

Viktoria stood between two dark red chairs. She lowered herself into the right one as a stack of booklets littered the one to her left. "I settle for most attempts at my last name, but that was almost spot on."

"Glad to hear it."

She eyed a copper name plate on the edge of the desk; Jeffrey Appleton, RN, MS, Director of Surgical Services. A laptop computer stood open nearby and stacks of paperwork and binders dotted the rest of the desk.

"Even though you're only 'passing through,' I wanted to welcome you to our two-hundred thirty-seven bed hospital. We're not exactly a tiny community hospital, but we're not a huge regional center either. However, from these small towns around the south-eastern area of Lake Erie, we pull in a lot of patients."

"Since you're a full-time person on the business side of running an OR, thank you for the welcome. I am so far removed from the operational side of an operating room."

"For sure. Anymore, in your field, there are a dozen models of how the departments are run and get paid. The anesthesia group here is not independent. The hospital employs them. We pay everyone's salaries. In your case, my department's budget has paid the locum tenens agency to find you and to pay you. The bottom line is to let you know that my door is open in case the stipulations of your four-week stint here do not meet what you were promised. Such as a forty-hour week etc."

"Appreciate that." She inched to the end of her chair, ready to spring up, but Jeffrey leaned back more comfortably into his.

"Jay Huff and the other anesthesiologists have been working like dogs. That's why they begged for help. The only female anesthesiologist in the group went out on maternity leave two weeks ago, and they puffed out their chests and said they could handle the extra work load and call. I think they all wanted a little extra cash in their pockets."

"There's something to be said about keeping sane nine-to-five work days. Or seven-to-three as the case may be."

"I would be ecstatic to put in forty hours in four days and then have a three-day weekend, but that'll never happen."

"Well, it was nice meeting you," she said and rose.

He came around the desk and stepped behind her as she left. "I detect an accent, not from the Lake Erie region, but we knew that. However, you don't sound like a typical Long Islander from New York, which is listed as your residence on your paperwork. Where you from originally?" He stopped in the doorway and let the question hang in the air.

She turned and faced him. "I'm originally from Iceland. I'm an Icelander."

Viktoria flicked her hand as a good-bye, and scurried away before Jeffrey Appleton bombarded her with questions about her origins. He still stood open-mouthed, and only when she reached the staircase, did she hear his door close.

Now she was in a time jam. Half her allotted "lunchtime" was over, and she still needed to eat, let alone find the cafeteria. She took the stairs and, in the main lobby, she saw the coffee shop. Grabbing something there would be her best option, so she bought a yogurt, banana, and a hot, strong Americano. Like a stray dog, she gobbled down her small lunch, and finished the coffee on the elevator back to the OR. She deviated to the recovery room first and went on a hunt for Helen Grant's X-ray to confirm her central line placement. It proved fine and there was no pneumothorax. Viktoria had not "dropped" the patient's lung.

She raced out and contemplated her next patient as she headed to the preop area to see her—a female for a gallbladder removal. Chances were that her forty-two-year-old patient, if statistics were correct, would be female, fat, and forty.

Viktoria read Dr. Huff's preop assessment first and then swung open the drapes. "Tina Parker?"

"That's me," replied a woman of more than average girth. For someone about to undergo a surgical procedure, she carried a happy disposition like she'd just eaten a piece of chocolate cake. Which made Viktoria realize her NPO status, or nothing per mouth status, would be her most important question.

"I will be doing your anesthesia today. I'm Dr. Thorsdottir."

"Oh, okay, I guess. After you give me a bunch of drugs, I'll never remember that when I wake up."

"Not to worry. Most people don't remember my name even if they don't go under anesthesia."

"That makes me feel better."

"That's the intent of your surgery today, Mrs. Parker. And when did you last eat or drink?"

"Yesterday. Not a blasted thing today."

"Perfect. I have Dr. Huff's notes about you. Nothing else you want to tell me about your medical background?"

"We covered it."

"He told you the risks and benefits of your anesthetic?"

"Yes, ma'am."

Viktoria checked Tina's IV. "I'll give you sedation when they wheel you back to the OR. And someone is here to take you home today?"

"Oh yes. He went downstairs to eat. Without me!"

Viktoria nodded and peeled away to go back to OR 7. Sure enough, Casey had set up her work area for the case. She scanned through the machines, equipment, and laid-out syringes. Controlled substances had been checked out as well. He'd drawn up a five-cc syringe labeled with midazolam, for sedation, and a five-cc syringe labeled as fentanyl, a narcotic. There was a second unopened vial of fentanyl lying beside it. That was overkill, she thought. For a straightforward cholecystectomy, the probability of her opening the second vial was slim.

The double doors pushed open and in came the stretcher with Tina

Parker, who glanced around and made small talk with Alice Coleman and the tech. Viktoria sighed. At least her second patient was cheery compared to most of the people who had come across her path since she arrived at the Masonville, Pennsylvania hospital.

However, there was one other person who qualified as cheerful— Jeffrey Appleton.

CHAPTER 3

Viktoria should have guessed it. Aside from again being slow doing a case, Dr. Berry was far from adept at laparoscopy. The scope was a narrow tube with a camera, and he had the hardest time inserting it through the incision he made, which delayed him from seeing Tina Parker's gallbladder on the screen.

Since Dr. Berry and his assistant were not stimulating his patient like some critical, painful surgical case, Viktoria kept her anesthetic on the "light" side. The two women in the room expertly listened to Dr. Berry's gripes as they discussed their jobs before working in an OR.

"Did I ever tell you that I'm an ex-barista?" Alice asked.

"Less challenging than what you're doing now," the tech said. "Where'd you work?"

"The coffee shop on Hospital Road. Half the people working here stop in there. I figured I heard so much hospital talk, I might as well go into nursing."

"That was a mindless, uninteresting job," Dr. Berry chimed in. "Now you have responsibility."

"However, I carry the inside secrets of the most major mainstream coffee franchise."

"Like what?" the tech asked.

"I bet you think that a Venti hot drink carries three shots of espresso."

"Why would we think that?" the surgeon asked.

"Because there are three cup sizes; a Tall, a Grande, and a Venti. So, you'd think that a Tall comes with one shot of espresso, a Grande with two, and a Venti with three. But if you order a Venti, it comes with only the same two shots as the Grande."

"Rip off," the tech said.

"Yeah. The few folks in-the-know would order a Venti and ask for an extra shot of espresso, but then they'd be charged for it."

"Double rip off," the tech said.

"You can get your java buzz another way, however. Three shots of espresso are included in a Venti iced drink."

"What?" Dr. Berry said, holding the scope handle stationery.

"You heard me," Alice said. "Order a Venti iced mocha on the way home tonight and you'll stay awake for a midnight movie."

"I'm on call, so maybe I'll run over there whenever, between cases."

Viktoria noted another set of her patient's vital signs. It would be no sweat off her back if he disappeared for coffee between his cases.

One of the doors inched open and Casey stepped in. Alongside the surgeon, he viewed the screen to watch Dr. Berry try to define the gallbladder with his instruments. "One more gallbladder bites the dust," Casey said and laughed at his own joke.

He kept his smile and stepped into Viktoria's space between the OR table, the anesthesia machine, and her drug and equipment cart. "Ready for an afternoon break or should I go on to the next room?"

"Depends on if you'll return."

"Don't give up your only chance now," he said eyeing her cart.

"I'll take it. Mrs. Parker is a forty-two-year old with a recent history of right upper abdominal pain and nausea. Dr. Berry's doing a laparoscopic cholecystectomy, and she does have gallstones. No other significant medical history, and she's only allergic to sulfa drugs. I'm running her on isoflurane and very little diprivan as an infusion. She took three ccs of fentanyl in the beginning and a little midazolam. Vitals are stable, and she's all yours while I'm gone. By the way, thanks for setting up my room while I ate lunch."

"No trouble."

Viktoria slipped past him and slipped off her OR jacket.

"Hey, Casey," Alice said. "I just told our clueless surgeon and tech the difference between coffee cup sizes at the local coffee shop. Want to hear about it?"

"Sure."

Viktoria draped her jacket on the back of the cart and walked out. She hated to admit it to herself because she immensely loved her career in anesthesia, but she looked forward to later when her exit from OR 7 would be the last one for the day.

With his feet widened out in an authoritative stance, Jay Huff studied the OR white board like he was playing a game of chess. The goal was to maximize the usage of his anesthesia personnel before the elective surgery cases were finished and the OR went down to one room with the potential to run an emergency case.

Jay cluttered the middle of the hallway, so Viktoria stopped for small talk with him. "The locum agency mentioned that this group is a nice size. Not too big, not too little."

"With the hospital's blessing, I run this place with nine CRNAs and seven MDs. A nurse and a doctor are always on vacation, and one each are always off postcall. Leaves me with six CRNAs in a room daily and one to give breaks. Three docs supervise the CRNAs daily, one doc runs the schedule, and one of them does their own cases. Of course, a female doc is on maternity leave and you're making my fifth MD."

Viktoria nodded. "Feel free to put me in a room or supervise the nurses. I'm flexible."

"Since you are a gypsy anesthesiologist, I don't doubt it." Thinking his comment was original and clever, he patted his thigh twice. "Are you a vagabond in your personal life too?"

"Absolutely. My footloose lifestyle came about after watching the stagnant anesthesia chiefs who count personnel and cases in front of OR schedule boards and lose their hands-on-anesthesia skills. A superior skill set comes from working in brand-new places with unknown geographic situations and healthcare personnel. Sometimes I spot things about patients, surgeons, and hospital employees that staff doesn't admit is right under their noses or are blinded by denial."

Jay spun forty-five degrees and exaggerated his already wrinkled forehead. "Did you just denigrate me?"

Viktoria held her gaze at the OR schedule. "I never, ever do that to anyone. Unless, of course, I am criticized first."

Jay held his tongue. This anesthesiologist was a lot more spirited than he gave her credit for, and so much different from his pliable colleague who was at home nursing a newborn. *This one is confident with a capital "C,"* he thought. "Good. Verbally sparring with the scheduler is not a wise idea."

"I clock out soon, regardless. At three o'clock. One of the perks of being a gypsy anesthesiologist."

Dr. Huff glanced at his wrist watch as she hastened away. After a bathroom break, she went down from Jeffrey Appleton's office where she'd previously seen a sign for the doctor's lounge. Two men were inside, absorbed with charts. The coffee pot was empty, so she chugged down a small bottle of water and then her ten minutes was up.

Back in OR 7, Viktoria noted the enthusiasm of the caretakers in the room when she arrived. Whatever they'd been talking about simmered down to a muffled few words as she went around the anesthesia equipment to Casey.

"How is she doing?" Viktoria asked.

"One little spike in blood pressure, so I gave her two more ccs of fentanyl. That Dr. Berry stimulated her too much."

Dr. Berry shook his head. "Hey, what I do must hurt patients sometimes otherwise I wouldn't be doing my job."

"Other than that, all is well."

"Thanks for the break."

"You're welcome."

They changed position as Viktoria scanned the top of her cart. "I don't see the other vial of fentanyl that you checked out."

"Contents are right here. I snapped open the vial and drew it up." He pointed to a labeled syringe with the five ccs. "It's ready in case you need to use it."

"Okay, thanks."

Casey left and Viktoria frowned at the syringe. For a laparoscopic cholecystectomy, her patient had had enough narcotics and, unless she didn't know anything about anesthesia, she wouldn't need to be dosing out anymore. The drawn-up contents of the syringe would go to waste, the patient would have to be charged, and she would need to chart and corroborate dumping it with someone at the end of the case.

After relentless manipulation of the laparoscopic instruments while looking at the monitor, Dr. Berry finally slithered Mrs. Parker's gallbladder out from the main incision. "Another bile sac bites the dust. You can close the incisions," he said to his assistant. He shed his blue gown at the door before leaving.

After returning the OR table flat from the Trendelenburg position and with the anesthesia turned off, Viktoria's patient soon breathed adequately on her own, and she removed the endotracheal tube. While she was preoccupied with her patient, the door opened again, and Casey tapped her on the shoulder.

"Dr. Huff sent me in to relieve you because the time is three o'clock. I can take her to recovery room and give report."

"I'm fine. Relief right now would be too disruptive and not in my patient's best interest. I'll bring her over myself."

"Suit yourself."

Viktoria picked up the five-cc syringe of narcotics. "Initial the wastage," she said and squirted the liquid into the garbage can. Casey cosigned her chart note and left.

After settling her patient in the recovery room, Viktoria went to the locker room and changed out of scrubs. Since it was half past three, the seven to three shift OR workers had left and the afternoon shift was already on the job. She clutched her shoulder bag and was free for the rest of the day.

A grove of trees stood just outside the entrance of the hospital and Viktoria stopped beside them to take in the sunshine and a big, fresh breath of air. It was a conscious thing she did every time she left any hospital, like someone who was programmed to chant a meditation mantra. It psychologically cleansed her of the confinement of being in an OR and helped balance her with the great outdoors for the remainder of any day. Even if she was stationed in a larger city, nature was somewhere. She only had to look for it.

Her commitment at Masonville General Hospital was for four weeks—the whole month of September. She had driven the almost five-hundred miles from Long Island; a no-brainer straight-shot along I-80 of eight and a half hours. Provisions with the agency allowed her to rent a car, but she preferred to take her own. It afforded a little familiarity with something of her own away from home.

She scurried off the curb and went to find her white Honda Accord. Visitors, patients, and health care workers came and went. Most were dressed in long sleeves and a few wore light jackets. She wore a crisp checkered blouse with the collar open, and she was aware that the temperature seemed no different from Long Island's. There, the Atlantic or the Long Island Sound was not too far away, and here they had Lake Erie to contend with. The giant body of water created a lake effect which influenced the weather patterns most times of the year, especially winter.

Arriving beside her car, she threw in her bag and jumped in. It was time to learn the layout of the land, especially between the hospital and her hotel. The initial scouting around was how she always did it. By the time she was ready to leave an assignment, she had figured out her favorite places. Today, however, she had a heads up after listening to Alice Coleman's conversation which did not include her.

She drove down Hospital Road and kept her eyes peeled for the coffee franchise. With a tall sign over the top of the building, she couldn't miss it. It was smack between the ten-minute drive to where she was staying, so it would be an easy walk in the next few weeks. She parked, went inside, and stood at the counter. The decision was whether to grab the iced mocha Venti with the three-shot espresso or skip coffee all together.

A double-braided barista waited.

"On the recommendation of Nurse Alice Coleman who used to work here, I'll take a Venti iced mocha."

"Don't know her, but that's a decent stepping stone from barista to nurse."

"What's yours going to be?"

"I'm in college and want to be a veterinarian. I also put in a few hours at a vet's office."

"Hard worker. Good for you." She read "Linda" on the girl's name tag.

Viktoria slipped to the end of the counter and was going to carry the drink back to her car, but her phone rang with a call from the locum tenens agency.

"Dr. Thorsdottir here."

"So, did they 'hold your place?'"

Viktoria knew the voice of Regina, the head agent she always dealt with, and smiled. The woman had recently told her that 'locum tenens' was a term based on a loose Latin translation that meant "hold your place."

"The anesthesia department at Masonville General Hospital waited for my arrival with bated breath. Although I'm saving their butts by helping them out, they applied a new term to my locum tenens work."

"I sense it may not be complementary."

"They called me a gypsy."

"I like the term you use for yourself instead."

"Doc on the road. Yes, I am a 'Doc on the Road.' I don't qualify as a gypsy. Not yet, anyway. My understanding is that gypsies dress more

21

flamboyantly than I do."

"I haven't met you personally to comment one way or the other, but I suspect anesthesiologists dress drab like an extension of being outside the OR."

"For me, it's quite the opposite. Since I'm in a strict 'uniform' all day, I beef up my personal attire. But I don't qualify as dramatic."

"Sounds reasonable. Anyway, I'm calling to make sure the first day worked out. Persons, place, time etc. was what all parties agreed on?"

"All in order. Even met the hospital director. This is another anesthesia group that lost their independence and is paid a salary by the hospital."

"Such a pity."

"It's one of the nice things about doing locums. I'm not involved with the politics and financial downfalls of either being in a private, self-billing group, or a minion physician paid directly by a hospital."

"True. Although there may be some downfalls to doing locums but I can't think of any."

"Now, now, Rebecca. It's a doc-on-the road lifestyle and it isn't for everyone."

"The alternative to a traditional anesthesiologist's job does work for you."

"For a person at a desk job, you possess intuition about people."

"I'm less at a desk than you think. Here's something you're not aware of. I'm in a wheelchair, so this job really suits me. I'm also in my fifties in case you were wondering."

"I wasn't wondering. So, your job is right for you too. Glad to hear it."

"By the way, that Dr. Huff called here an hour ago. Wanted to know if you might want to work a night shift or two if they needed that coverage."

"I must have been tolerable enough for him to request that, despite being treated like some second-class citizen."

"I don't know how you put up with the occasional prejudiced 'outsider' mentality from others that comes with the job."

"That mentality is one of the downsides and, like I said, there are pluses and minuses. Tell Jeff Huff to make the request again if a dire need for night coverage arises." She set a straw in her drink and headed to the car.

CHAPTER 4

Viktoria parked in front of the railing at her "Stay Long Hotel." It was a three building, single floor complex, and she was in the first building which was closest to the front desk. When available at a destination, she chose to stay with the franchise. The spacious suites offered a lot more than a standard hotel or motel room. She liked the fully equipped kitchens, Wi-Fi, flat-screen TV, and laundry facilities. Besides being pet-friendly, the office area even offered a few breakfast items, and the locums agency paying the bill loved the long-term budget rates.

Viktoria unlocked the door and went into the large, clean room with plenty of leg room to be comfortable. First, there was the kitchen and bathroom on either side after walking in, next was a desk with her computer, and then came the spacious bedroom and sitting area. The shiny gold bed scarf matched the material on the headboard and the gold/brown indoor/outdoor carpeting.

She placed her bag on the counter and enjoyed a cold drink without so much as a glance at her cell phone. No text messages, or emails, or apps blaring unwanted information at her. Now was her time. The rest of the September day would not go to waste. She would get her blood moving by going for a run.

Viktoria finished the drink and changed into striped running pants and a purple long-sleeved cotton shirt. In front of the mirror, she took a long look. She had a full face with a wide forehead and dark eyebrows, almost as black as her shiny hair which she usually wore back with an elastic hair tie. Her lips were full and wide, as distinctive as what a fine artist would paint on an impressive canvas portrait.

All told, she looked rugged—which was what she was. All one hundred and thirty-five pounds of her. Her DNA was handed down from the Viking age when a mixed Norse and Celtic population explored and settled Iceland. Viktoria's upbringing on the island nation was shades easier than the people who founded the continent one thousand years ago, but it was still fraught with hard-work and a laborious childhood. Her hands and body had always toiled away at outdoor chores and now she used her firm and able hands in the very physical surgical field of anesthesia that she had chosen.

Although she was rugged, Viktoria was handsomely pretty, and her five-foot seven body was toned and firm. She tried to maintain her physique; a doable task since she did not work fifty hours a week like most doctors.

Viktoria stepped back, sat on the bed, and pulled on a top-line pair of running sneakers. Now she was ready to pound the ground. Outside, she decided to head north on Hospital Road. She cut across the parking lot between scattered areas with landscaping and past the other two hotel buildings.

On purpose, Viktoria's pace was medium-slow, allowing her to get the lay of the land. She passed a small gas station convenience store, a waffle joint, a "Loans, Loans, Loans" place, and a do-it-yourself car wash. The breakfast joint made her smile. She could live on breakfast food and often did.

Viktoria stayed on the sidewalk and at the half-to-one-mile mark, the white stripes on the traffic road disappeared and the road assumed a name change to "Erie Trail." At that point, a concrete three-foot wall was on both sides as the road formed a small overpass across a creek. She slowed and gazed down at only two inches of water trickling its way underneath. Approaching the other side, something below caught her eye.

She grasped the top of the concrete wall. Her eyes focused on a barely perceptible movement. An animal on its back? Her heart sped and her pulse quickened. *Horrors!* she thought. How atrocious.

The incline appeared to be about six feet and not steep enough that she couldn't manage going down. She eyed the heavy cover of old leaves, creek rocks, and the scattering of human trash and calculated the risk of falling. If she hurt herself, she'd be of no help to the helpless life left to die below her.

The importance of rescuing an animal far outweighed the small peril to herself. She grabbed the edge of the overpass, slipped to the other side, and carefully chose her footing.

One step at a time, Viktoria changed her opinion. It wasn't as soggy as she had assumed, but she still focused on her balance and the placement of her attractive footwear. *Regardless of how trashed they get, to hell with my sneakers,* she thought.

She put her legs astride a helpless dog. Belly up, he now saw her above him but no relief registered on his wide-open, terrified eyes. If a human being had done this to him, why would the next human being who showed up be less of a Hitler than the last one?

Viktoria's face contorted with a multitude of wrinkles filled with sorrow. Tossed like the surrounding garbage, he'd been thrown out of sight from the road, left to suffer a horrific fate and left to die.

Several inches wide, silver duct tape secured the dog's mouth shut and went back as far as his snout.

She sniffled and wiped her eyes. The dog's back paws were also brought together. More adhesive tape spiraled around them. He was bound into a terminal captivity by some torturing masochist.

At the core of who she was, Viktoria was a caretaker. On top of that, her physician common sense kicked into gear. She squatted down and evaluated the security of the tape. Whoever had secured it, made sure it would hold. Trying to peel it off could be disastrous. She was too afraid it would pull off whiskers and hair and possibly peel off skin.

Maybe because she was an anesthesiologist, she considered the pain to the dog. Whoever did this to him had at least not occluded his nostrils, so that he was still able to breathe. She figured they didn't know any better because they wanted him dead, and yet left his nostrils open.

She should get him to a vet where he could be sedated to remove the duct tape and evaluate him for other injuries. He seemed like a pup, not quite a year old, and still had growing to do. Certainly, he appeared too lean.

Viktoria couldn't waste any more time. Her heart would not allow her to leave him there while she went back for her car. She felt the ground for two smooth areas to rest her knees, positioned herself, and wrapped her arms under him. Belly up, limber, and practically cooperative, she braved the incline holding the grubby dog.

Clasping him like a beloved baby, she walked the sidewalk back to the hotel. She figured him to be around thirty-five or forty pounds, and she stopped only once to take a break. A handful of vehicles passed. She almost wished someone would stop and give them a lift. Perhaps the situation looked too strange, perhaps people had no time in their schedule, or perhaps they didn't notice the bundle in her arms. Lucky for her, the dog was lanky and his weight was distributed nicely in her arms. Although he was dirty and his hair soiled, he appeared to be only black and white, so she wondered if he was a border collie.

Viktoria arrived back at the Stay Long Hotel clenching the dog. At the third building, there were three pickup trucks she did not pay attention to before. A ladder extended over the top of one of them and an open cargo bed of another displayed worker's tool boxes, planks of wood, and cans of paint.

The door to one of the units was open, and she saw two men inside. She passed the vehicles and zigzagged between the furniture which had been placed outside. A stringy looking man wearing blue jeans lit up a cigarette in the doorway and saw her coming.

"Excuse me," she said. "Can you tell me where the nearest veterinarian's office is located?"

The worker uncrossed his legs and stared like he saw a mirage. After tilting his head backwards, he said, "Can't help you, lady."

Beyond him, his coworker sat on the floor against the wall. He raised his head, but lowered it again. *Maybe they were taking a deserved break,* she thought, *but the man inside could use the bed situated behind him.*

She quit trying to extract any information out of them and went over to her unit #1. After putting the dog down, she opened the door. Inside, she grabbed her purse and keys. When she was ready, she gently put the dog on the back seat of her car.

Viktoria drove a bit too quickly back to the coffee shop, raced inside, and spotted the double-braided young woman by the pick-up counter. She spoke softly to not draw attention.

"Linda, please tell me where the vet's office is where you work. I have a taped-up dog that was discarded by some vile person. He's in my car, and he needs help."

Linda nodded. "Go past the hospital on Hospital Road. At the first intersection, make a right, and Masonville Animal Clinic is not even a mile down the road. The last doc usually hangs around with the latest appointments and sees to those hospitalized overnight, but you better hurry just in case."

"Thanks," Viktoria said, already turning around.

Viktoria's heart bled when she checked on the dog again before starting her car. Now she felt like a part of his ongoing abuse because she hadn't untaped him, but sometimes, she knew, you have to allow a wrong thing to continue before you can turn it around into the correct thing.

She found Masonville Animal Clinic with no problem and first checked that the front door was open. There were no customers in the waiting room but a woman was at the front desk.

"I have an emergency with a dog I just found," she said. "Any vets still available to help out?"

"Dr. Price is here. Our after hours are beginning so you'll qualify for an emergency visit, if that's okay."

"Absolutely." Viktoria turned and came back in with her bundle.

"Oh brother," the woman said, shaking her head. She picked up the intercom and called into the back. "Go in that first exam room," she pointed.

Viktoria slipped into the room and placed the dog on the table while the back door opened and a man with gray hair and a limp ambled in. He previewed the dog and Viktoria with his eyes and then said, "You're not a regular. I'm not as old a vet as you think. I'm just in need of a new hip but I'm putting it off as long as I can. Taking care of situations like this is the reason why."

"I found him in a ditch. Taped and thrown to die. I'm a medical doctor and sure want a vet to humanely remove his duct tape, and give him a thorough evaluation."

Dr. Price signaled her to place the dog on the scale. The numbers settled on thirty-eight pounds. While he drew up sedation in a syringe, Viktoria stroked the dog on the table. With the vet's one intramuscular shot, he became sleepy and his whole body relaxed. With two instruments, and going slowly and gently, the vet and Viktoria first undid the tape on his mouth. Whiskers were pulled out and the foremost part of his mouth lost some skin and bled.

The two adults kept quiet and went to his back legs. The tape went around twice before getting to his paws. Again, he did his best to prevent any injury to the dog, but blood was already on the tape. With the tape off, he scrutinized his legs. The inside right leg had a five-inch gash, a straight slice, and open to tissue below.

"This'll need stitches," he said. He cleaned the area and reached in the back cabinet and pulled down a sterile surgical set. After donning sterile gloves, he laced in five stitches.

"Maybe the dog sliced his leg open and the owner didn't want to mess with getting him stitches for whatever reason and decided to dump him. Or the owner or caretaker cut the dog themselves as part of their sadistic behavior before taping him up. Who knows? I can never figure this stuff out."

"Only madmen or madwomen who deserve the same treatment do stuff like this. It's all about wielding power over living things that can't fight back. I shudder to think of the things you must see."

"It's routine. Two weeks ago, some couple was out hiking and found a plastic grocery bag tied to a tree. Had six newborn puppies in it. All left to die. Brought them in here. Thank God they kept one, but they brought the rest of them to the shelter. I heard they were all euthanized. Nobody adopted any of the puppies the size of your hand."

"Don't tell me anymore or I'll be sick."

"You have any dogs?"

"No. I'm a doctor who moves around to where I'm needed. Be difficult to keep a pet. But they're no stranger to me. I grew up with animals all around me. Learned responsibility and how to be a caretaker all because of them."

"I don't want to date myself, but kids don't learn that stuff anymore. All they know how to do is wiggle their fingers on electronic screens."

"With the dog, you have two choices," he added. "Either he wears a cone on his head, so he can't mess with the stitches or I can bandage it. I can give you extra gauze in case he pulls it off."

"Wrap it and how about doing everything else? Shots appropriate for his age, any blood work you think is necessary?"

Dr. Price leaned against the counter. "Why? Are you going to keep him?"

"I guess I must. No sense in saving his life only to send him to that shelter where he'll lose it for good."

"You just made my day. No, made my week. You are my reward for hanging on and not getting my hip done and be absent on medical leave."

"Dr. Price, better yet, you are the dog's guardian angel."

"No, you are."

"That's the nicest compliment I've had in no telling how long."

"Your job is that underappreciated?"

She frowned and he nodded.

"What do you think he is? A border collie?"

"Oh yeah. No doubt as far as I'm concerned. They are extremely active. That might be another factor in why someone got fed up with him. They bit off more than they could chew. Also, these dogs are bright as hell. Probably a lot smarter than the ass hole who did this to him. Excuse my language. Since you're a doctor too, I'll speak my mind."

Viktoria finally sat on the one chair in the room. She took a deep breath and let her muscles relax while Dr. Price did what was needed. The dog began to respond to their voices and his touch.

"Another thing," Viktoria thought of. "Can you microchip him?"

"Sure thing," he said with the biggest smile yet.

Slipping the chip into the dog's neck was the last needed poke to make him snap out of his slumber. His legs kicked into gear and he stood wobbly on his feet. With Dr. Price's okay, she placed him on the floor.

"Even being a dirty puppy," she said, "you're still beautiful."

Dr. Price patted his head.

"How old do you think he is?" she asked.

"All his baby teeth are gone and those are all adult, permanent teeth. My estimate is about eight months old. For his stature, he's behind on his weight a bit, so he has some catching up to do and then some further growing in the next few months."

"God help us both," she said. "I'll grab the dog food you sell out in the waiting room, so I don't have to go on a shopping expedition tonight."

"We've got slip leashes too. That'll hold you until you get to a pet store."

Dr. Price opened the door and the puppy addled around the waiting room like he was drunk. The vet finished up the paperwork with the girl at the front desk.

Viktoria swiped her credit card.

"Bring him back in seven to ten days and I'll remove the sutures," Dr. Price said as the girl stapled all the papers together.

Viktoria slipped the leash over the dog's head. "See you then."

The woman handed her the papers. "You're not from around here, are you?"

"No."

"Are you from another country?"

"Pretty much, but everyone is from somewhere."

Dr. Price stood behind the woman's chair. "What are you going to name him?"

"Don't have a clue. Thanks, doc."

Outside, she lifted the big pup into her car where he curled up and fell asleep.

CHAPTER 5

More cars were parked at the hotel when Viktoria drove back. It was dark but well lit in front of her door. She first bused the dog supplies inside along with the chicken sandwich and drink she purchased at a fast food drive-thru. There had been no time to pick up the basic groceries she routinely stocked up on, so she scoffed at the otherwise empty counter.

Exiting her room, the door opened to the unit next to her and a man began unpacking his car trunk. They nodded at each other and Viktoria lifted the dog out from the back seat.

"Hope he's not a barker and keeps me up tonight," the man scowled.

"I wish the same thing for myself." She slipped on the leash, and walked the dog beside the sidewalk.

The man glared as she left. "Some people," he mumbled.

She walked to the corner. The doors to the last building were all closed and the workers and their vehicles had left. After turning around, the puppy did his business, and she didn't want to stir him up anymore. After his traumatic and frightening day, she wanted nothing more for the dog to be hugged and petted and have a full, comfortable night's sleep.

Inside, she offered him a small bowl of food, put down water, and opened her own dinner. He came straight to her feet and laid down. His eyes closed and when she was finished eating, she stepped over him and got ready for bed.

Making sure to add extra time before her early wake up time, she set her phone alarm. She slipped under the bed covers, and opened her phone again. One text had come in a few hours ago from her husband.

"New hospital first day over? How'd it go?"

"The usual, but got myself a dog." Her eyes wandered over to the border collie—the picture of innocence and beauty. A smile grew on her lips as she realized that someday the dog may qualify as her best buddy.

She typed another line. *"I'm naming him 'Buddy.'"*

She did not expect to hear back from him, so she placed the phone on the adjacent nightstand and faded off to sleep.

An old rock song woke Viktoria up. She was on her side with an arm draped around a pillow, and opened her eyes. Two dark eyes surrounded by black fur stared in front of her. Above them, on either side, two silvery colored clumps of hair poked straight out from his head like antennae. And down the center of his face and wrapped around his muzzle, his hair was pure white like fresh snow. His jet-black nose inched forward as if testing the scent from the bed.

"Hello there, Buddy. That's your new name. I'm popping up right now to walk you." She kept the rest of her thoughts to herself, especially one that worried her. At eight months old, he should be physically capable of being housetrained, but what if he wasn't? That would throw a wrench in her return every day. House training, if needed, would be difficult as well since she would not be at her Stay Long Hotel suite most of the day.

She dressed into wrinkle-free tan slacks, a cream-colored scooped neck top, and slip-on shoes. It was early enough that the air outside was cool and refreshing, reminding her that Fall weather was around the bend. She walked the collie for ten minutes and shuttled him back to the room. While he gobbled up dog food, she inspected his back-leg bandage, which seemed fine.

Viktoria checked her phone. No messages. She scoured the entire room for anything important that may grab a puppy's attention. Maybe it was all up for grabs, and she made a mental note to buy the dog toys and things to chew on. The room could be a disaster upon her return later in the day. She crouched down and gave the dog a solid hug and a kiss.

"Buddy, please be a good dog and keep us both from getting into trouble with the hotel manager."

She clicked the door shut. The coffee shop stop was as important as the dog's prior walk and, without time to spare, she pulled through the drive-thru line and placed her order. With a dark roast in hand, she kept time and entered Masonville General Hospital for her second day.

Viktoria changed into blue scrubs and stashed her clothes and purse in a locker. The benches in the two aisles were cluttered with clothing and other women who had nothing to say to her.

The tempo of the OR was in full swing when Viktoria emerged. She grabbed a paper schedule, and stopped at the board. Jay Huff was not standing guard over it, but another anesthesiologist with glasses as thick as pancakes.

The stocky, round MD turned toward her. "I saw you yesterday. You must be Dr. Thorsdottir. I'm Phillip Nettle."

"Nice to meet you."

"If you need help with anything, just holler. You're in Room 7 by yourself again; first case is a vascular procedure, a fem pop bypass graft. Who knows? One of these days, we may let you supervise CRNAs."

Viktoria shrugged. She didn't care one way or the other and either way carried its own set of benefits. If they thought they were giving her the short end of the stick by stashing her away in a room for most of the time, they were mistaken. She went into anesthesia because she picked it out from every other specialty and sub-specialty available. Sometimes she wondered if some anesthesiologists had forgotten that it's called the "practice of anesthesia," which included doing your own cases *or* supervising and medically directing nurse anesthetists.

Doing anesthesia ranged from sitting through an uncomplicated case while managing a patient's medical problems and delivering a safe and effective anesthetic, all the way through to the hair-raising, acute life-threatening emergencies when every medical, surgical, and resuscitation skill came into play … all the while using the tremendous knowledge of anesthetic drugs and pharmacology that a doctor had been taught.

Viktoria first set up her room, checked out the narcotics and anxiolytics from the drug dispenser machine, and then went to see her patient, Mr. Quinn, a sixty-five-year-old man nervously jerking his legs around under the sheet.

His wife poked at his arm. "Can you quit acting like the stretcher has bed bugs?"

"Sorry to interrupt," Viktoria said. "I'm the anesthesiologist and I'll be taking care of Mr. Quinn today."

Mr. Quinn forced a smile and, after answering all her questions, mentioned the most important thing on his mind. "I'm waiting for you to stick something into my IV, so I don't change my mind about surgery and get up and leave."

She reached into her pocket and whipped out a labeled syringe. "No real second thoughts?"

"No, please. Let's get this over with."

After drawing it up, Viktoria slowly injected two ccs of midazolam and stopped with that. As she walked away, she considered the case. Besides his significant peripheral vascular disease, Mr. Quinn was a smoker and a drinker and on pain medication at home. She had checked out a two-cc vial of fentanyl, but now went back to the machine and ordered another two ccs.

Viktoria stood ready when the door opened and Mr. Quinn was wheeled into the OR. His wiggling had stopped, and he vaguely paid attention to being hoisted over to the table. The vascular surgeon followed and nodded at her while she prepared the patient for his anesthesia.

"Good night, Mr. Quinn," she said after the induction dose of propofol raced into his vein.

"Hi, I'm Tom Parker," the surgeon said. He spoke with a northern accent and retied the back of his OR mask.

"Viktoria Thorsdottir." She focused on the patient and smoothly intubated him and secured his tube. With a polite gesture, Dr. Parker handed her the used endotracheal tube wrapper for the garbage.

In the room was the same OR nurse and tech as yesterday and Viktoria hoped she'd learn more about Masonville by listening to their conversations. After all, the franchise coffee shop had already proved useful.

She logged all the details into her iPad since the patient rolled into the room, and she lingered over the cart to tidy up her syringes. The assortment of drugs was either needed for the case or ready in case a hemodynamic need arose.

In addition, she had used only one cc of narcotic on the patient during induction and, so far, had not needed the other cc. Instead of leaving the other fentanyl vial in plain sight like yesterday, she stuck it in the second drawer with other drugs. If the need arose, she wanted to be the one to crack it open and not someone giving her a break.

Viktoria swung around and peered over the drapes. Dr. Parker streamed his own music choice from a personal device he left on the shelf but seemed oblivious to the beat, whereas Alice Coleman and the tech occasionally took a stab at bobbing their heads.

"You buy them anything yet?" the tech asked Alice.

"She put up a wish list on some online wedding registry, but I'm skipping that. The two of them have damn near everything a person or a couple could want. I'm giving them a card and a check. What about you?"

"Had a formal China dinner plate shipped to them from the set she listed online."

"Maybe you got off cheaper than me."

"Doesn't matter. You know the reception will be the best damn party in Masonville."

"What are you two talking about?" Tom asked.

The tech plucked a pair of scissors from the instrument set and handed it to him. "Are you living under a mattress in a call room?"

"Like Dr. Winter?!" Alice asked and laughed.

"People are starting to notice him, huh?" the surgeon said.

Alice scrunched her forehead like it was an off-limit topic. "Forget about him. We're talking about Jennie Shaw and Casey Johnston. They're getting married on Saturday. Did they skip you on the invite list? They struck me as being liberal with their invitations."

Tom rested his hands on the patient's leg and frowned. "Guess not. Most of my case load is up north in the next hospital, so I can understand why I wasn't on their radar. My name didn't roll onto some hospital list of physicians and OR folks."

"Too bad," Alice said.

"I don't know why they're getting married anyway," the tech said. "They've been living together for six months. Why not keep it that way?"

"Together they turn ashes to gold. Think what they can do if they're Mr. and Mrs." Alice relaxed her forearm on her right breast like resting it on a table. She went to the shelf and double-checked the patient's OR paperwork. The room silenced except for the drone of contemporary music.

Maintenance fluid dripped into Mr. Quinn's IV and when the bag almost emptied, Viktoria grabbed a new one from the bottom drawer of her cart. She spiked it open and hung it on the pole as the OR door swung open.

A female CRNA walked in and Viktoria recognized her from the day before with Casey Johnston in the recovery room. The young woman briefly flanked the surgeon's right shoulder, glancing at his procedure.

"Another roto rooter, Dr. Parker?"

35

Tom glanced up. "You bet. I only learned today that you're getting married this weekend to a fellow CRNA."

"Someone's got to do it. Say, you want to come?"

"I can't imagine you have that much flexibility with your guest list. Thanks, but I'm accounted for this weekend. Too much I need to do around the house."

She shrugged her shoulders and stepped around the equipment and into Viktoria's space. "Hi, I'm Jennie Shaw. You must be the anesthesia locum doc. I'm giving morning breaks if you want one." The young woman had alert, round eyes like a puppy dog, which made Viktoria think of Buddy.

"Sure," Viktoria said slowly. "The patient's a sixty-five-year old undergoing a fem pop bypass procedure or a roto-rooter, as you mentioned. He's a big smoker and drinker, but no other significant medical history besides his vascular insufficiency, that we know about anyway. I'm running him on sevoflurane, a little nitrous with oxygen, and a muscle relaxant and, so far, he only needed fentanyl and midazolam up front. I just hung this second bag of Lactated Ringers. Any questions?"

"No. I can handle it."

"Thanks." Viktoria glanced at Mr. Quinn's vital signs one more time, a habit to assure her that there was no sudden change in her patient's hemodynamics.

She stepped to the door while switching her thoughts to Buddy. Hopefully, he was faring well in the confines of her hotel suite or, better yet, she hoped the room and its furnishings were not undergoing major puppy reconstruction. In actuality, she realized, she needed to buy him a dog crate, not only for the safety of the room, but also for wise dog crate training.

"So, what kind of music do you have planned for your wedding?" Alice asked Jennie as the door closed behind Viktoria.

Viktoria walked to the main hallway where Dr. Nettle squinted his eyes through his glasses as he noticed her coming. "I see you're out on a break. Already?"

It was too early to be the dart board for snide innuendos, so she couldn't help herself. "Why? Is that a problem? Isn't that what Jennie Shaw is supposed to be doing? Giving breaks?"

"Yeah, sure. I didn't think she'd get you out first, that's all."

"I'm off to the doctor's lounge in case you need me back."

In the hallway she opened the door, and unlike the day before, there was the fresh smell of coffee. The big room had recently undergone a half facelift. The kitchen area was spanking new, but on the other side, two walls needed repainting. Three single computer desks were against one old painted wall. The middle of the room was dotted with three round tables and chairs. A long couch was to the side as well as two recliners.

A man wearing a long, wrinkled doctor's coat looked up from the couch. He was half slumped against the armrest and tried to fake the fact that he'd been lying further spread out as Viktoria came in. "Hey," he said.

"Good morning. I'm grabbing a cup of coffee. Can I pour you one?"

He inched his hand along his hair, trying to make sense of it. "Why not?"

Viktoria filled two Styrofoam cups and eyed the flavored creamers. "I'm doctoring mine up. Want yours black?"

"Sure."

She dumped in two vanilla baby containers, stirred her own, and handed him his cup.

"You must be new," he said. "Didn't know any new docs were in the pipeline."

"I'm not permanent. Just passing through."

He took a sip and nodded. "The anesthesia department, I bet. Their female is out on maternity leave. Sometimes I wish I'd chosen to pass gas."

There was no name tag over his top pocket, so she ventured on. "What's your specialty?"

"OB/GYN."

"Were you on call last night?"

He flinched at the question. "Not exactly. By the way, I'm Jessy Winter."

"Viktoria Thorsdottir," she said, not extending her hand. His appearance made her think he had delivered a baby twelve hours ago and had yet to wash his hands. "Glad to meet you."

Jessy stood, showing off his lanky six-foot-three frame. He tipped his hand in a salute and ambled out of the lounge with his coffee.

Viktoria settled in one of the plush recliners to enjoy the coffee and realized where she heard Dr. Winter's name before. In the OR, someone said something about him being "noticeable." *Maybe there was some truth to that*, she thought.

She plucked her iPhone out of her pocket. It was time to check if her husband had texted her about the news she told him last night.

About the dog named Buddy.

CHAPTER 6

Viktoria took a big swig of coffee and pressed her iPhone to wake up. She went to text messages and read the back and forth between her and her husband, Rick, the night before.

"New hospital first day over? How'd it go?"

"The usual, but got myself a dog. I'm naming him 'Buddy.'"

She scrolled down and saw that he had responded at 9 a.m., a time which didn't say much about what he was doing. Then or now, was he still lounging in bed? Was he making coffee and watching local weather? Or was he at his small insurance company's office or working on his second business? All told, both "jobs" didn't quite fill a normal person's full-time job and, during the last year, she was well aware that each of them filled up less and less of his time.

"A dog?" his text said, followed by six question marks and a flutter of ridiculous dog emojis. *"I could do with a dog, but what are you going to do with one?"*

She half agreed with him, at least the part about her. *"Can't help it,"* she responded. *"The dog was abusively dumped. Maybe you can keep him some of the time."*

As she turned again to her coffee her phone dinged, so she knew the subject matter was of interest to him. *"I can do that. What does he look like? How old?"*

"Short of a year. He's a Border Collie, capable of inexhaustible energy."

"I can do stuff with him."

I bet you can, she thought. *"All right. We're settled. What are you doing today?"*

There was a long delay, so she crimped the foam cup and dropped it in a can on the way to the counter.

"Going to a customer's house to evaluate a new claim. Roof damage from a fallen tree."

That will fill his whole day, she sarcastically thought. *"Out on break. Going back to the OR,"* she responded and her phone went quiet. She retraced her steps to the counter, peeled a banana, and ate it as quick as she could. After a rest room stop, she weaved her way back to the OR.

Viktoria walked around the bottom of the operating room table, taking in the entire surgical field and lap sponges. Evaluating the whole area gave her an idea of the patient's blood loss. In this case, it was reasonably minimal. Dr. Parker was also making good progress, his head bent, his hands busy.

"How's Mr. Quinn doing?" she asked Jennie.

"He's stable as a rock. I didn't tamper with the anesthetic at all."

"Perfect. I appreciated the break."

"Don't mention it." She rammed her hands in her scrub jacket and slipped between the equipment. "Bye, everyone. Dr. Parker, if you change your mind …"

The wrinkles around Dr. Parker's eyes smiled, but he shook his head. Another half-liter of crystalloid dripped into her patient for the rest of the case, and the surgeon later announced he was closing Mr. Quinn's incisions.

Viktoria injected the other one cc of narcotic which would make for a smooth awakening without pain. With the surgeon totally finished, she backed off all the other anesthetics and soon had the patient breathing on his own through the endotracheal tube. When he opened his eyes and squeezed her hand on command, she pulled out the tube.

Mr. Quinn gasped a big breath and then settled back down. Viktoria logged in his last vital signs and her last remarks about extubation. With the OR staff and an orderly, they all moved him to a stretcher.

Viktoria placed her iPad on the mattress, turned around, and opened the drug drawer. She needed to return the two-cc unused vial of fentanyl into the drug dispenser machine.

Her heart skipped a beat. She was sure she had slipped the vial in the empty compartment next to the vasodilators and vasopressors. But that space was empty.

Staff began to move the stretcher and someone held open the doors. "Dr. Thorsdottir," Alice said, "we're waiting on you."

Viktoria's eyes scanned each drug compartment and, as panic set in, she opened the top drawer and glanced carefully there as well. Seeing nothing resembling a fentanyl vial on the top of the cart, she peered into the sharps' container.

Shit, she thought. *This is a "first."*—A schedule II narcotic signed out to her patient, under her name, and she couldn't account for it.

Mr. Quinn opened his eyes back up in the recovery room and spoke softly after Viktoria gave the nurse a report. "I'm counting on Dr. Parker to make my leg good as new. Maybe even better."

"He's all finished," Viktoria said, "so time will tell."

The man forced his eyes open wider and grinned. "You're pulling my leg. My surgery is over?"

"Yes, sir."

"That man is a magician."

Viktoria patted him on the shoulder and raced back to the OR. She checked the anesthesia drawers from top to bottom, poked around in the sharps' container, and moved every item on top. The ventilator, inhalational agents, and monitor set-up machine had two drawers as well, and she rummaged through both.

She grimaced and admonished herself over her apparent mistake. Especially in a new place, not accounting for a narcotic would be a scar on her personal and professional record. She headed to the anesthesia scheduler for the day, Phillip Nettle.

The round man barreled out of the anesthesia office with his hands in the air. "We have to wait until a room comes down," he told the OR nurse scheduler, "before Dr. Berry adds on a case and opens another room."

Viktoria waited until he had his say.

"And what do you want?" he snapped. "You have another case to follow in your room."

"Dr. Nettle, I have a narcotic discrepancy from the last case. A two-cc vial of fentanyl is missing."

"Didn't you give it to the patient?"

"No."

"Well, that messes things up, doesn't it? I better go talk to Jay. He's supervising today. I'll have to pull Jennie from breaks. She can start your case until we clear this up."

"Great," said the nursing staff scheduler. She leaned into Viktoria. "I'm kidding, but if you lost it, you could have recorded that you gave it, and we wouldn't be having this conversation or causing a case to be delayed."

The woman walked away, shaking her head.

Viktoria narrowed her eyes at how despicable it was to think or mention such a thing. Dr. Nettle had taken off, so she stood in front of the white board like a child in a principal's office.

The two anesthesiologists came scurrying down the hallway with their heads bent. "Dr. Thorsdottir," Jay Huff said, "I understand you've lost fentanyl! I'm calling the lab. Go procure a specimen cup from them and provide them with a urine sample. We're drug testing you."

Dr. Thorsdottir tried to handle her emotions as she marched into the lab on the top floor of the hospital. Being defensive over their request for a urinalysis would serve no purpose. It was very possible that someone in her situation could have injected the vial of fentanyl into their own bloodstream instead of the patient. After all, a minor percentage of people chose to practice anesthesia because of the availability of the most precious, pure, potent narcotics on the planet.

She spotted a woman with salt and pepper hair who gave her eye contact as if waiting on a ship to arrive. "I'm Evie," she said, reaching a thin hand to the overhead shelf and pulling down a plastic, sterile wrapped cup.

"How often do you hand these out?" Viktoria asked, outing the cup in her hand.

"To hospital employees? Not very often. However, we send down random drug screening requests at least once a month to the anesthesia department. I'm the director here. I run a tight ship as far as keeping tabs on people, in case they're abusing in this hospital, no matter what the department." The woman pointed to the back of the lab. "There's a rest room back there."

Dr. Thorsdottir nodded. With the sparsity of bathroom breaks, it was easy to produce a sample and Viktoria soon placed the container on the bench.

"Thanks, I think," said the woman.

Viktoria stopped right between Dr. Huff and Dr. Nettle when she returned. "I'm not having an unexplained narcotic mishap go on my record. Your CRNA, Jennie Shaw, gave me a break this morning. She was alone with my case and had access to all the drugs."

"That is, if you left the fentanyl there like you said you did," Jay said.

"Let her finish," Phillip said.

Viktoria sucked in a small breath between her teeth, calming her anger. "If you drug tested me, then it's your duty to drug test her as well."

"Jennie?!" Jay exclaimed. "She's as naive and American apple pie as they get. And I don't know about the drug culture where you come from."

"Do you ever curb your mouth or is it always spilling froth inaccuracies?"

Jay's forehead wrinkled up like a Shar-Pei, and he pranced on his sneakers. His colleague put his hand on him, thinking he may step forward and clout her.

"I tell you what, Jay," Dr. Nettle said, "she has a point. Since I'm running the schedule today, I'll be the unpopular one with the nurse anesthetists and I'll ask her to also provide a urine sample. Dr. Thorsdottir, go back and take over the case she started for you and send her out here. I hate to tell you; however, I don't think we'll have the manpower to give you a lunch break."

"I couldn't care less," she said. "Patients come first."

Viktoria weaved into her next case where country music was now the chosen genre. Dr. Parker was only beginning his case, a lumpectomy of a woman's breast.

"You made it back quick," Jennie said. "I heard they chose you to fulfill the department's minimum monthly quota for drug sampling. That'll make the rest of us happy. We won't be bothered."

"Not quite."

Jennie's eyes squinted. "What does that mean?"

Viktoria didn't want to question or confront Jennie about the missing vial. If the young woman had needed the vial that badly, more than likely she used it on herself and the testing wouldn't lie. "Report to Dr. Huff or Dr. Nettle after you give me report, and who did this patient's preop assessment?"

"Dr. Nettle, who was also here on induction. The patient's only in her thirties, and they found a suspicious mass on a mammogram which proved positive for cancer on biopsy. She wanted a lumpectomy and not a mastectomy. She has a clean bill of health other than that."

Viktoria nodded and noticed which anesthetics were turned on. "What did you check out of the drug cart for the case?"

"Two ccs of fentanyl and midazolam. I've given both."

"On induction when Dr. Nettle was here?"

"Gosh, do you want me to bring you up to speed by writing a book?"

"Go. The two docs are waiting on you."

Since Dr. Thorsdottir had acted ambiguous, Jennie's curiosity piqued as she turned the corner looking for Dr. Nettle. She found him in the anesthesia office which was close to the scheduling board. His eyes were widened like the rest of him as he plowed a knife down the middle of a hamburger.

"Lunch time?" she asked.

"It's about time. I didn't eat breakfast."

She doubted that. "The outlander anesthesiologist said you wanted to see me."

"Now, now. Interesting word choice for her. Yes, consider yourself the lucky winner of the drug screen lotto for this month and report upstairs."

"What? That doctor just went up there."

Phillip abandoned salting his French fries, and contorted his face. "How the hell? News and gossip travels through these walls faster than a nerve impulse."

"Seriously? How come you and Dr. Huff are making two people get screened this month?"

"Like you said, she's an outlander, so she doesn't count for our group."

She tried to think of an excuse not to go, but his expression turned serious.

"Okay, Dr. Nettle. I'm on my way." She swiped a fry from his plate and hustled away.

Jennie rode the elevator, fixated at the blinking yellow light as it passed each floor. With a ding, her ride stopped, and she crossed into the hallway and entered the lab.

The lab director frowned at her. "Two in one day," she said. "Hand-selected by your group. Good luck." She thrust the necessary cup in Jennie's hands and nodded towards the sign in the back for the bathroom.

Jennie walked slowly. She thought back over the three years she'd been working at Masonville General Hospital as a nurse anesthetist. Arriving straight out of CRNA school, this group was the only one she knew, and almost all her experience was attributed to this place. She'd hate for anything to go amiss.

Plus, the docs and the nurses were as familiar as a second family and, the following weekend, that would be truer than ever since she was marrying Casey. They started dating the last year of CRNA school and simultaneously sought jobs in the same places where anesthesia groups needed more than one anesthetist. They hit the jackpot when they both interviewed and nailed down two spots.

Jennie and Casey were die-hard nurse anesthetists and more political than the doctors in their group were aware of. The push for CRNAs to practice without physician supervision was dear to their hearts, and they contributed significantly to the CRNA organizations bent on making them as potent a caretaker in the field of anesthesia as doctors.

They'd learned all the tricks, such as introducing themselves to patients with words such as I'm so-and-so, and "I'll be your anesthesia provider today," or "I'm your anesthetist today," subtly leaving out the fact that they were the nurse and not the doctor.

Besides trying to work independently, the latest push by their head organization was a bill to call them officially "nurse anesthesiologists" instead of nurse anesthetists. Jennie and Casey tried to back the CRNA head organization financially as much as they could.

In essence, Jennie and Casey both thought that medical school and residency were great for those who did it, but they wanted to skirt by on nurse anesthetist school and advance as far as possible using only that education to reach the top most income, public perception, and professional independence. Solidly attracted to each other in their last year of CRNA school, their romance only grew until it tapered off into a solid partnership of love, friendship, similar ideals, and the push to propagate income on the side if and when they wanted.

Jennie pulled her pants down in the bathroom and peed in the cup. In the last three years, she had only done it twice. Thinking that she was due in the near future was the only way to consider the request half-way reasonable.

She returned to the bench where the director took the sample and said, "I like my job, but not when it comes to analyzing urine for drugs from OR workers."

CHAPTER 7

Happy that it was almost three o'clock, Viktoria finished her last case, and didn't need to turn it over to someone else.

Dr. Nettle's day was not over, however. He was tired of being on his feet and sat at the OR main desk glancing back and forth between the board and the case headed back to the OR. Dr. Thorsdottir stopped and put her hands on the counter. "You finished with me?"

"Yes, you can go. However, I called the lab a few minutes ago and the drug sampling results should be done soon. The director will be calling me back."

"I'll check back with you again. I'm going to go postop on my one patient from yesterday who stayed in the hospital. My diabetic foot ulcer patient whom I put in a central line is in house, but the cholecystectomy went home."

Phillip slid his glasses down and rubbed his eyes. "No. You don't need to do that. We send someone up every day to see and write postop notes on all the patients like we are required to do. The doc running the schedule sees that it gets done. Jennie saw some today and I fit in a few too."

"Most groups do take care of it. However, I always follow up with my own patients. I want to know how each and every patient of mine fared, if they experienced any anesthetic complications, and if they were satisfied."

"Suit yourself. But you won't get paid anything extra after three o'clock."

"Don't expect to."

Viktoria walked to the doctor's lounge and looked up the room number for Helen Grant on a computer. Her stomach growled from the lack of lunch, so she surveyed the counter. Under a covered tray, she found croissant sandwiches.

The door opened and in walked Jeffrey Appleton. "Dr. Thorsdottir!" His eyes beamed as he stood next to her. "I sneak in here although I'm not a doctor. The lounge is so close to my office, it calls me in. Plus, I'm more lenient about coming in here as the day comes to an end." His sleeves were rolled up and, although he wore a tie, it was loosened.

"Mr. Appleton, you indirectly pay for the edibles in here, all for the doctors' benefit. I don't think anyone will mind."

"Hopefully not. Can I pour you something?"

"Sure."

"An iced tea?"

"Anything here will help wash down this sandwich which tastes a bit ripe. However, I'm not complaining. Any food here will take care of the growling in my stomach."

He poured her tea from a machine dispenser and handed it to her. "The group is keeping you on your seven to three hours, aren't they?"

"Yes, no problem. I have a few loose ends to take care of and then I'm out of here."

"Is there a significant other who made this trip with you and is waiting for you?"

"No, for almost all my assignments, I travel solo." She peered at the cup, the dog coming to mind, and a trace of a smile crossed her lips.

He cocked his head. "Oh, then perhaps you're meeting someone while you're here."

Viktoria took a sip, without a response.

"Sorry. I don't mean to pry." His toned arm reached above them and brought down more cups from the cabinet; he poured himself a drink as well.

"You weren't prying. Actually, I befriended a dog yesterday. Do you happen to know where there's a pet store around here? I need supplies."

He gave her direct eye contact, and she returned it straight on. "The best pet store is a couple of blocks down from the vet's office, which is …"

Viktoria put her hand up. "I know where the vet's office is, so I'll find it."

"You're quite the explorer for such a short time."

"Sometimes." She pitched her napkin and cup. "I better get a move on. Nice talking to you."

Viktoria braced herself outside Helen Grant's room. No doubt, the woman would be complaining no matter how stellar everyone took care of her. She knocked and entered.

"Mrs. Grant, it's Dr. Thorsdottir, your anesthesiologist from yesterday. I'm here to check up on you and ask you how your anesthetic went."

The woman scowled and wiggled in the bed. "Somebody already kind-of asked me that today. Although they came and went like there was a fire burning in here."

"Well, there isn't, so feel free to tell me."

"I guess it went okay because I don't remember anything."

Suddenly, Mrs. Grant's expression changed because she considered that to be a funny remark.

"Perfect. And let me peek at the area where I inserted your central line."

Viktoria moved the woman's gown down a bit from her shoulder and observed through the sheer dressing. She nodded her approval. "The big IV looks fine. I hope you go home soon."

"Me too."

Viktoria wrote a postop note on her chart and went back to the OR. She went straight to the office where Dr. Nettle was seated eating popcorn while looking at the next day's schedule.

"Hey," he said, "Jay is the scheduler again tomorrow, but we're assigning you to supervise two rooms with nurse anesthetists tomorrow."

"No problem."

He continued dipping his hand into the bag while she waited.

"Did the lab call you yet?"

"Oh yeah. There was no incriminating result from your sample. No narcotics showed up, unless of course, you switched cups with someone else."

"Will your nurse anesthetist have the same result? And would you say something that derogatory to her?"

Phillip stopped chewing. "For your information, Jennie is clear, which is no surprise." He looked up at her. "We're back where we started. Where did your drug vial go?"

The front doors of the hospital slid open and Viktoria stepped outside to a gorgeous day. She inhaled deeply, purging herself of the muck and mire of the hours and OR behind her, and put her face towards the sun. The warmth felt marvelous while she considered the needed dose of

Vitamin D.

The pet store was closer to her now than going back to the hotel and returning, but she knew the right thing to do was to go release Buddy from the confines of the suite. His day with boredom had already been stretched out longer than she wanted. And who knows what kind of trouble he may have gotten into while she was gone?

On Hospital Road, she headed to the left and soon pulled into the Stay Long Hotel. When she grabbed her things from the car, she noticed the car from yesterday parked in front of the adjoining unit. She turned the key in the door and stepped in. At least light filtered in from the back windows and door and it was not dark and dreary. Swaying his tail in front of her was Buddy.

Viktoria immediately crouched down, dropped her things to the side, and encircled the dog in her arms. While he plastered her face with kisses, she saw the bandage on his back leg. Relief swept all over her. He had not torn it off. She returned his affection. How could he open his heart to her after being treated like dirt by another human?

Maybe the biggest lesson he learned, she thought, *was that humans come in only two varieties.* Those that are filled with distrust, cruelty, mockery and bullying towards others, and only live with their own inflated sense of worth. They play power games and to hell with every other living being except themselves.

The second type, in the minority, are the custodians of not only other living beings, but the planet as well. Not selfish, they are, in actuality, caretakers of any living or non-living thing that they are able to do something about.

Well, maybe the dog hadn't put *all* of that together, but he must have learned something. He can certainly trust her.

"You are charming and I'm happy to see you too." *Now comes the hard part,* she thought, standing up.

Careful about the limited clothes she had brought on the trip, she had put them all in the closet and in the drawers. They were safe, but the too many pillows which were stacked up by the headboard were all in new places. She held back laughing at their rearrangement, strewn about across the floor. One was even in the bathtub.

The smallest pillow of the lot was purely decorative. Now it was a lot more ornamental because two ridged corner seams were gone and some fluffy cotton interior littered the carpet. Viktoria bit her lip but again, had to smile over the puppy work. She scoured the rest of the room and found little evidence of further mischief. The few items previously in the kitchen wastebasket were dotted on the tile floor and a napkin was shredded to bits.

"All told, not too bad," Viktoria announced. In a stern tone, however, she held the pillow up to his face and said, "Bad dog."

She hurried to give the dog a tiny, interim walk, but grabbed the damaged pillow as she left the room. As she walked him close by, she was entirely grateful that he lasted in the room without any accidents. She then headed to the front office.

"Hi," she said as she walked in with Buddy.

A middle-aged man with a tidy mustache and a hotel shirt rose from a chair behind the counter. He put his glasses and newspaper on the counter while she read his name tag stating "Mason."

"I'm Viktoria, staying next door. I have a damaged pillow here from my room and want to make sure a replacement price is put down on my bill."

Buddy poked his nose around the corner and crept close, trying to greet Mason. The manager nodded and then patted the dog. "What did you do to the nice pillow?" He looked at Viktoria. "Not a big problem. At least not yet. Sure, I'll put it on your bill. Thanks for telling me."

"Appreciate that."

He placed both hands on the counter and frowned. "Your neighbor complained about your dog barking earlier today. I went outside to check, but I didn't hear a thing."

"Maybe he was being a watch dog and barked about someone coming or going in the parking lot."

"So true. I don't hold that against any dog, so there's no problem right now."

"Thanks. Let's go Buddy."

Viktoria went back to their room and changed into running clothes. The dog needed a run as much or more than she did. "Come on, Buddy, you're going to learn a new routine from your new owner."

Ben, Fred, and David had worked outside the whole summer so their skin was tanned, no different from if they'd hung out on some tropical beach for a few weeks. They preferred the outdoors, so the sunny day lured them back and forth from inside the third building of the Stay Long Hotel to the parking lot where Fred took cigarette breaks, they talked about women, and talked about getting paid.

"When are you going to give up that dirty habit?" David asked Fred as he stood against the doorway. He was the only one of the three that wore a baseball cap—always the same one; solid black, plain, and with a full brim which practically concealed who he was.

Fred laughed, mocking the question. "Don't you think that smoking is the least of my problems?" He pointed to the scar running down his cheek.

"He's not talking about your lack of good looks," Ben chimed in. "He's talking about your health." Although all three men were in their thirties, Ben had a few years on both of them and often made the business decisions.

"You both are off the deep end," Fred said. He sat on the top step and held out the cigarette. "Like this makes a difference."

Ben shook his head and walked to his pickup truck where he hoisted a new can of paint out from the cargo bed. As he reached, his blue jeans sagged below his skinny hips, revealing his butt crack. It was not his intent to be a flasher of that part of his body like the current trend, it was simply because he'd lost weight and couldn't be bothered to buy smaller pants. He sat back down next to Fred. "Only one more wall in there to do before starting the suite next to it.

"The man' better show up today," Ben added emphatically. Their employer was "the Man," whom they fondly and discreetly named since working for him for almost two and a half years. They could barely remember what his real name was.

David grabbed the handle of the can and set the paint just inside the door. "He'll show," he said, standing again in the doorway. "He said he'll be here, he'll be here. Money plus."

"I'm dying for my part," Fred said. "Like I'm overdue."

"It's a miracle you like something better than those cigarettes," Ben said.

"No comparison."

As if he couldn't stay still, Ben walked back to his truck and rummaged through a canvas bag. He came back with an open bag of mixed nuts, started munching, and tapped Fred on the arm. "Hey, isn't that the lady who came by yesterday carrying that dog?"

"One and the same," Fred responded.

Viktoria crossed into the lot for the third building and let Buddy pee on a tree in one of the landscaped grassy sections. She saw the three men outside the door and passed closer.

"Good day, gentlemen," she said and stopped. "I found the vet's office yesterday. It's that way, off of Hospital Road, in case you ever need to know." She nodded down the street.

"What happened to his leg?" David asked.

"Don't know, he needed stitches, but that was the least of his worries."

Fred finally tossed his cigarette butt but quivered his head like he couldn't wait for another puff.

Viktoria surmised each of them more closely and nicknamed them in her head: skinny, skinnier, and skinniest.

"You staying in one of the buildings?" Ben asked.

"Yes. I assume you three fixed it up already."

"Yup. One more after this one. We paint, renovate, and rejuvenate anywhere 'The Man" sends us."

"For a price," Fred added and laughed.

"Well, enjoy the rest of the sunshine." She tugged at Buddy and they headed towards the sidewalk and then down the road where she found him in the first place.

CHAPTER 8

Viktoria slipped in the door with Buddy. The dog went straight to the water bowl, and she unwrapped a rubber band off a bag on the counter and dug her hand in. She pulled out three sukkulaoihjupaour lakkris. Icelanders were superior at mixing liquorice and chocolate in multiple and tasty ways and these small, round balls were her favorite. She lugged bags of them with her wherever she went. These, in particular, had a white, crispy outer shell, followed inside by milk chocolate, followed by a sliver of black liquorice.

She let the first one melt in her mouth. The next one she indulged by chewing into it, and the third one she rolled around and made noise with her teeth, raising Buddy's curiosity. She knelt down and enticed the dog with the smell. "Kisses," she said, edging her cheek close to his face. After a few tries, the dog understood the trick and swiped her cheek with his tongue.

"Good boy, Buddy! I've taught you love on command." She put down his food and readied to go out again. They needed to go shopping.

Viktoria rolled one window down enough so that Buddy would enjoy the windy air on their way to the pet store. His pitch-black nose wiggled around, and she couldn't help but be joyful that she stumbled on him the day before. *By now, he'd probably be dead,* she thought. She shuddered thinking about that prospect—him all bound up, and absolutely in a state of fear at the terminal end of his very short existence. The imagery and recall was too horrible to visualize.

Of course, she was well schooled as a caretaker of animals because of her upbringing. In actuality, her caring for other living beings was what made medicine a natural choice for her. Her mother, father, and two brothers always kept dogs, but as much fun were their horses. Her animal love affair began with their Icelandic equine family.

She drove right past the hospital and reflected on her native country's breed of horse, different from the rest of the world. With sturdy builds and a heavy coat, the small, long-lived breed also had unique gaits which made them internationally popular. Her family had maintained a pasture and a barn with chestnut, black, and gray beauties and her oldest brother still owned many horses from the same line.

She did miss owning horses, and she often thought that not owning any was the downside to her lifestyle. *But better to leave her native country's animals where they are,* she thought, *where they are subjected to few diseases.* The law even significantly protected them by seeing to the purity of the breed and their isolation to prevent outside diseases. Horses from other nations were not allowed to be imported into the country and an Icelandic horse which leaves the island nation was not allowed to return.

Although her older brother mailed the chocolate liquorice candies to her that she enjoyed, he couldn't do anything about her love for the horses except send her pictures and videos. She frowned as she parked her Honda. Her heart yearned to go back to Iceland and visit, but she couldn't manage that happening in the near future.

Viktoria leashed Buddy who trotted by her side into the user-friendly pet store. A young man without a customer at his register beamed and exclaimed as he walked over. "Hey fella."

Buddy crouched to the floor and inched over, giving the man a submissive, friendly greeting.

"Point me to dog crates, toys, collars, and better leashes. Treats too."

The boy had a full face and smile wrinkles alongside his mouth. "All on that side of the store. Take a cart. Sounds like you'll need it."

It took Viktoria one hour, an hour she didn't mind at all. It gave Buddy the chance to socialize with other dogs and to become familiar with a public place. When she charged the contents of her shopping cart at the register, Buddy cost her another couple of hundred dollars.

The young man shook his head. "When people tell me they got their dog free, I laugh to myself. There's no such thing as a free dog."

"So true," she said. He helped her to the car and, together, they loaded it up. Buddy sat on the back seat and Viktoria felt pleased that she had stocked up. Back in the hotel she single-handedly assembled the crate and introduced him to it with a treat.

Like the dog, her energy was dissipating, but she needed to eat. Her subconscious favorite food surfaced to mind, and she got in her car. She didn't want to walk this end of town in the dark, so she drove over to the waffle restaurant. No matter what time of day, she could always eat breakfast. She debated where to sit; a booth or the counter. The answer was clear cut whenever she went into an establishment like this one. Did she want to look outside or watch the hustle of the employees behind the counter?

She chose a window booth and grabbed the menu behind the napkin holder.

"Can I get you anything to drink?" a waitress asked, a perky twenty-something year old with a bobbing-blonde ponytail.

"Sure. No coffee. Orange juice, but bring me water and an extra cup. And I'll order your number three." She pointed to the 'All Day Breakfasts' on the back of the laminated menu.

"Sure thing." She went off and returned quickly with water, o.j., and an extra cup on a tray. "Your food will be out shortly."

Viktoria poured half her orange juice in the empty cup and then filled the rest of the two juice cups with water. She was thirsty and started polishing off one of them as she gazed out to Hospital Road. Already familiar with the layout of the area, she knew the road to the right where she found Buddy was called Erie Trail.

Although dark, she noted the little activity out front by the street lights. A pickup truck was parked all alone by the street, and she wondered if it was one of the Stay Long Hotel workers. The window rolled all the way down on the dark burgundy truck and the man in the front seat flicked out a cigarette butt. He inched his head to the open space and his head reeled back like he inhaled a deep breath. She was confident the guy was the one she nicknamed "Skinnier."

"Straight off the frying pan," the waitress said and put down two plates.

"Appreciate that." Viktoria nodded her approval.

"Can I get you anything else?"

"You've got it covered," Viktoria said. The pony-tailed waitress left, and she tasted the scrambled eggs and bacon—piping hot the way she liked them. She took her time and then paused before starting the two pancakes on the next plate. With the truck still parked outside and the window half rolled up, the guy with the scar on his cheek now put his head flat on the head rest.

Viktoria spread maple syrup between the two pancakes. They tasted fluffy and light, and she polished off the other glass of half-diluted orange juice. She heard a ding on her phone and put it next to the plate.

"How was your day?" her husband texted. *"And what about the dog?"*

"Eating dinner now. Dog's fine."

"Let me guess. You're at a fine restaurant with white tablecloths."

"Yup. The maître de just sat me down to scrambled eggs a la mode."

"Sounds expensive."

He was kidding, of course, but she didn't want to go any further with the conversation. She was the main breadwinner in the family and had no tastes that ran up credit card bills. Her nice clothes were few and far between. He on the other hand …

"I'll leave a good tip. How about your day?"

"Plumber came today. Fixed the constant drip from the laundry room faucet."

"It's about time," she thought. *"That's good."*

"Also picked up an insurance client today."

"A successful day then."

"Guess so."

"Sweet dreams," she wrote.

"I'll be up for a while. Good night."

Viktoria polished off the two pancakes and thanked the waitress. She left a tip and paid at the register. Outside, she leaned against the back end of her Accord and scrutinized the pickup truck. The man in the truck turned his head in her direction. There was some semblance of recognition towards her, but he let his head rest again trying to fend off sleep.

Strange place to take a nap, she thought.

Fred, Ben, and David hung around the hotel later than normal and figured they'd paint the last wall in the unit that needed to be done. Waiting for the man to arrive to pay them was worth the wait, and they planned on docking the extra time today from tomorrow's hours. More than likely, each of them would enjoy the extra sleep in the morning a lot more.

Their boss arrived and paid them plenty. It was a short interlude and the three men were still in no hurry when he left. Although they needed to eat dinner, they each took a spot on the bare floor and hung around.

"I'm leaving," Fred finally said. He stood and leaned against the freshly painted wall, steadying his footing.

David peered up from under his baseball cap. He rubbed his eyes. "You dumb shit. You just ruined that wall."

Ben had assumed a stretched-out position on the nearby carpet. He had managed to pull up his trousers before going flat, but they rode up so high that he kept pulling at his crotch. "Fred, you run a paint brush over that tomorrow when you're saner."

David snickered softly. "Him? Saner or more sane?"

"I'll see you tomorrow," Fred said. "I swear I'm going to go eat something." He hoisted himself into his pickup truck but then had to figure out where he stashed his keys. First, he checked all over the cab, but finally found them deep in his pocket. He set the vehicle in motion, only to the nearby restaurant. Inside, he ate fried eggs and then ordered a bowl of chili.

The waitress with a pony tail grinned. "Now that's a new one," she remarked. "Eggs and chili."

Fred stayed hunched over at the front counter. He pulled out a hundred-dollar bill at the register. As he half-stumbled out, he leaned over and gave her a ten-dollar tip.

In the parking lot, he opened his front door. "Damn," he mumbled. On his seat back were paint smudges from having leaned against the hotel wall.

He was too tired to drive, so he enjoyed the thrill of hanging out in his truck. A half hour elapsed and when he poked his eyes open and to the side, he wondered if the lady out in the lot was the runner from the hotel.

He didn't care who was around and closed his eyes again.

Back at the hotel, Viktoria grabbed her bag but this time she decided to bring her handgun into the suite with her. She pulled it out from under the front seat, grasped the leather case, and locked the car door. The moon and the stars were dazzling, and she stood still taking in the view. In the direction of Lake Erie, it was even more magnificent where no ground lights dampened the twinkling in the sky.

She hated the fact that Long Island had changed in that regard. The night skies in Iceland had always been spectacular and had not changed one bit by the time she and her mother had left when she was thirteen.

And when they first settled on Long Island, the heavenly skies were nicely visible, but now twenty-six years later was a different story. For years, throngs of newcomers kept moving eastward from the denser city areas outside of New York City, and now the "island," was one big tie-up on the Long Island Expressway or the LIE as the locals called it, and the density of shopping areas, condominiums, retirement facilities, restaurants, and houses were heaped together with no separation like years before.

At night now on Long Island, there was so much light, that the clarity of the night sky was totally lost. She knew a single old man who had recently moved to a growing area in upstate New York to again see that night sky in the remaining years he had left.

She shared his sentiment that nature was not part of most people's everyday lives anymore. So, she gazed in silence a few more minutes and also made note that she heard not a peep from Buddy inside. She went inside, placed her gun on the counter, and slid open the closures of the crate. Buddy crawled out in front of her and exposed his belly for a rub.

"You are so sweet." She stroked his abdomen until he popped up.

She grabbed his leash to give him a short walk and the dog circled and jumped up. In his sheer excitement, he let out a puppy bark as she threw the slip lead over his head.

Before she opened the door, a pounding sounded on the wall from next door. She rolled her eyes and shook her head at the behavior of her next-door neighbor. *It doesn't take much to annoy him,* she thought, after they went out, and she let Buddy pee by the road.

Before she finally rooted herself into bed, she placed her handgun on the nightstand. She had a concealed carry permit and had purchased a gun because she traveled alone and stayed in strange locations. It was also one of her extra-curricular activities while away from home—going to gun ranges to practice shooting. She must finagle target practice into her Masonville schedule one of these days.

She smiled at Buddy after he jumped up on the bed and curled up against her. Running her hand through his fur, she realized how extraordinarily silky he was. Some white hair was a glistening silver and the official AKC coloring of "black with white markings" stood out, starkly delineated.

"My, my," she whispered, "you are a beautiful creature. And to think …" No, she reminded herself. She needed to stop thinking about his horrific ordeal because it made her so upset, it unhinged her soul.

She moved her hand to his head, and he nudged her back.

"And I named you correctly, Buddy."
She turned to her side. The left side. The side facing her Border Collie.

CHAPTER 9

Occasionally during the night, Viktoria felt the warm curled-up dog on the other side of the bedspread. For such an active breed and for being so young, he made a perfect bed buddy. She could get used to this, she thought, after the recent years of traveling alone as an anesthesiologist.

Now she recognized what she had been missing but, then again, Buddy had not been available until now. From her previous experience, she also knew this was only the beginning of their relationship. It takes time for a solid bonding to occur between a human and a dog, and she looked forward to every minute of it.

Viktoria drove down Hospital Road on the way to work and was comfortably on time. She pulled into the coffee establishment and went inside where a throng of morning coffee grabbers queued up placing orders. Her double-braided barista waved at her as the line shortened.

"Did you see Dr. Price?" Linda asked when Viktoria stepped up.

"I did. Thank you for the recommendation."

"How's the dog?"

"Surprisingly well after such an ordeal. He has stitches in his back leg, so they need to be removed in a few days."

Behind her, Viktoria heard a man sarcastically speak up to his girlfriend. "Is this place selling coffee or is it the ASPCA?"

"Do you know what you want?" Linda spoke softly.

"So early in the morning, I won't be ordering an iced coffee like the Venti mocha I ordered the other afternoon. I'll take the two-shot espresso Grande size. And make it an Americano house blend."

An exaggerated sigh sounded behind her as she glanced at items in the baskets on the counter and Linda rang up her drink. "And I'll take this banana too."

Viktoria paid and stepped to the "pick up orders" area. The couple soon waited on theirs as well, and she leaned in front of them and dropped a five-dollar bill into a glass jar labeled "Donations for the ASPCA."

"See," Viktoria said to them. "This place is partial to the ASPCA. Conversation about dogs is welcome here."

Linda handed Viktoria her drink. "Sounds like you're keeping the dog."

"I'm going to try my best. Thanks again."

Outside, clouds assembled in the sky after the clear night, and the first scattered raindrops fell on her windshield. Her easy drive to the hospital parking lot was accompanied by sipping on her Americano. As she gathered her things, she left the empty cup and slipped the banana into her purse. Bananas were available in the doctor's lounge, but she didn't mind the extra purchase she had made in the line that moved too slow for the guy behind her.

Viktoria silently made it into the changing room of the hospital OR. She slid off a cream-colored blouse, hung it in a locker, and slipped a scrub top over her head. Shoes banged around going in and out of the footlockers in the next aisle over as two women continued their conversation.

"Because of her, the anesthesiologists forced Jennie to give a urine sample to the lab yesterday."

"Locum tenens agencies hire the bottom of the barrel," the other woman said.

"More importantly, they send *us* the bottom of the barrel."

"Yeah. No different than the nurse they sent us a few months back. That one came from Mississippi. She said her husband sometimes went out to hunt quail for their dinner. Can you imagine that?"

"No. I can't, but I don't care about that so much as they must behave and do things differently down there. Remember how she talked to patients? So sweet I wanted to gag. Nobody around here is that gushy with patients."

"That's because we act professionally," the second woman responded. "However, don't knock everybody from down there. My all-time favorite musician came from there. Tupelo, Mississippi."

"Elvis Presley? No way. Michael Jackson is the historic best solo musician."

"You're not comparing apples to apples. Elvis had charisma and Jackson evoked electricity."

Viktoria pulled up scrub pants, pulled the strings, and tied a taut bow. She deliberated a call to action regarding the overheard locum tenens conversation, but decided against it. After already being verbally pro-active in the coffee place, she decided to be low-key. She grabbed the door handle and poked her head around to the women. First, she made note of their appearance: both wearing navy clogs, one wearing dangling layered earrings, and the other one with thick hair difficult to stash inside an OR bonnet.

"Good morning," she said to their surprised faces and made her departure.

At the front scheduling board, it was clear to Viktoria who was running the show in the anesthesia department. Jay Huff's narrow shoulders were hunched forward as he wrote an addition into a room written towards the bottom. She peeked from the side. He was scribbling in an obstetric cesarean section with Jessy Winter and followed by writing in the anesthesia personnel as "Dr. Thorsdottir."

Jay straightened himself. "There you are. You won't be supervising nurses yet because I need you upstairs on labor and delivery. Dr. Winter has a primagravida young woman needing a C-section. Baby's having late decelerations. He said as soon as possible, but you don't have to fly up the stairs. You're on your own. Nurses can steer you in the right direction up there for drugs etc."

Viktoria stifled a frown as she left. She thought the request unreasonable, like sending a blind person into the woods. She took two steps at a time in the staircase, and opened the heavy door to her first look at the obstetric floor.

"I'm Dr. Thorsdottir," she said at the obstetric desk where two nurses were scrambling about. "Where and which OR is the C-section going into? And did an anesthesiologist put in an epidural for the patient during the night?"

"No," a woman said. "And the patient only arrived an hour or two ago. No epidural. Room 3."

Viktoria hustled to check the equipment and machinery in Room 3. She checked the chart, dispensed drugs, and quickly talked to and learned about her patient, Wilma Lancet.

The woman gritted her teeth with a uterine contraction when Viktoria entered her room. She looked worn out for a thirty-year old and her dark bangs were matted.

"I'll be putting you to sleep," Viktoria said. Dr. Winter wants to get started. "When did you last eat or drink?"

"Yesterday at lunch. Since then, it's been one thing after another. This baby is going to be hungrier than me when it gets here." Another contraction seized her and Viktoria glanced at the fetal heart monitor. At the peak of Wilma's uterine contraction, the fetus showed a transient decrease in its heart rate, a result of hypoxia.

She hustled back to the OR and checked again that all was in order. Soon staff pushed the stretcher with Mrs. Lancet into the room and Jessy Winter followed them to the sink where he put on a bonnet and mask and began to scrub.

Some anesthesiologists did quite a bit of OB anesthesia, some did few cases, and some did none in their practice. Viktoria was not intimidated by the area of specialty and felt like she was proficient enough. She tilted the patient to her side for aorto-caval decompression, put the oxygen mask over the patient's face, and did a rapid sequence induction.

With the endotracheal tube placed correctly, they draped the sheets across the top of the bed by the patient's shoulders. Viktoria tweaked the anesthetic to the correct dosage … enough for the mother and yet not too much to decrease her blood pressure and have an effect on the baby.

The nurse quickly scrubbed Wilma's enlarged abdomen as Dr. Winter came in. His eyes appeared heavy. He stayed quiet, managing the uterus after his initial incision, and managed to bring a full-term baby out and suction out its tiny mouth.

The nurse declared the time of birth and Viktoria made a note of it as well. The robust baby cried and was whisked to the incubator. *A satisfactory, successful result,* Viktoria thought.

"Were you on call last night?" Viktoria asked Dr. Winter. She assumed so since he was available and there so early in the morning.

"No. I'm going over to the office, however, when I'm finished here."

The tech glanced at Viktoria and then paid attention to her instruments.

Dr. Winter's sutures had something to be desired as he closed the patient up. Viktoria walked to the end of the table and estimated blood loss to be heftier than the normal one thousand ccs for such an operation. She tended again to the head of the table and soon had Wilma Lancet's endotracheal tube out.

Wilma's first question was, "Where's my baby?"

In the OB recovery room, Dr. Winter wrote his note and addressed the nurse while Viktoria plugged her initial postop note into her iPad.

"In case you need me for the next few minutes," he said to her, "I'll be upstairs." He looked back at her as he left. "Thanks."

Viktoria patted Wilma on the arm. "By the way, congratulations."

She nodded at the recovery room nurse on her way out. "I thought he was going to the office."

The nurse twisted her mouth. "He's probably going to change his clothes. He wasn't on call last night, but he was here nevertheless."

Dr. Thorsdottir's curiosity piqued. He was like some loner obstetrician/gynecologist hanging around in the bowels of the hospital when there was life to be had outside of birthing babies.

"Why was he here?"

She leaned in and delivered a whisper. "He's going through a divorce which may or may not be final. Word is his wife threw him out of the house." She shrugged her shoulders and Viktoria responded with a flick of her head.

Viktoria took off for the main OR as she tried to wrap her head around Jessy Winter. That was a strange one she hadn't heard of, or seen before, in her assignments—a physician living in a hospital call room. Or stretching it further, he was like a homeless person. She couldn't fathom what he was going through.

Viktoria placed the paperwork for the case in the anesthesia record bin, a synopsis version of the full case recorded on her designated iPad app.

"How did the emergency C-section go?" Dr. Huff asked, stepping behind her into the anesthesia office.

"No problems. Baby came out fine."

"How did Dr. Winter fare?"

"He got the job done."

"Hmm. That's the best we can all say these days." He stood against the end of the counter and picked up Wilma Lancet's charge slip. After glancing at it, he placed the paper outside the box and rested his hand on top of it. "Go take a break," he said.

Viktoria peeked at her watch. "It's eleven. I'll skip a morning break if you let me simply take my lunch break."

"That's a deal. The hospital chef often puts hot Reuben sandwiches in the doctor's lounge on Wednesday. First come, first served. Don't say I didn't do you a favor."

"What?" She threw in a laugh. "Did you stay up all night to help prepare them?"

"No. I mean because I'm letting you go to lunch right now."

"I'll save my firstborn for you." She turned. It wasn't a wise idea to taunt the scheduler who could dump on you, but she didn't care. Her lunch break comes with the territory and the timing was also to his benefit.

Viktoria wished there were other, closer options for lunch, and she didn't want to waste minutes going to the cafeteria. All told, however, the close-by hot sandwiches sounded pretty good. The downside was, more than likely, she'd run into more negative personalities.

Dealing with negative health care workers in the current work environment, she sighed, was like trying to swipe Icelandic midges away from her face while she was tending to the care of horses. The flying, pesky insect was so representative of her country of origin, that they named a whole lake after them. And although they wouldn't bite or sting, they would swarm her face in droves. Like many of the folks in Masonville, and the majority of the people working in Masonville General Hospital, they were totally annoying.

She sauntered over to the doctor's lounge and opened the door. The smell of corned beef on rye wafted over to her nostrils, making her grateful for the early lunch break. Two doctors were sitting together at a table and Jessy Winter was making a lunch plate, already changed into clothes for the office.

Viktoria poured an iced tea first before approaching the hot food. "Grabbing food before seeing patients?"

"Yes, some things never change," Jessy said. Remember being in medical school? When you never knew when your next meal would be? So, you'd eat grub whenever the opportunity arose? Had we all consulted magic crystal balls to foresee our futures, we would have learned that when we became attending doctors, our lifestyles would not change."

"That's one reason why the choice of our specialties is so important."

"You really think that makes a difference? We get screwed no matter what we go into."

"I sense you are now referring to more than snatching food."

"I suppose so." Jessy leaned his head to the side of the sandwich platter and wiggled out the thickest packed rye bread he spotted. He placed it next to the potato chips piled on his plate and turned to her.

Jessy stood so much taller than her five-foot seven frame, but he seemed to shrink with disappointment.

"Dr. Winter, can I can lend you a listening ear?"

Viktoria avoided eye contact, selected a sandwich, and let him think it over. "I'm sitting over there," she added, pointing to the table farthest from the two other doctors.

Jessy poured a coffee and sluggishly pulled out the chair across from her.

"Obstetrics must often be demanding," she said. "I bet the most solitude and undisturbed meals come from being a radiologist, but that may be my own misconception. Certainly, they work hard and are experts in their field just like the rest of us."

Viktoria didn't expect Jessy to tell her his problems, but perhaps with a little rapport he'd open up. *Not everyone has people in their lives to confide in,* she thought. *But since she was a stranger, maybe she was just what he needed.*

"Do you have kids?" he asked.

"No. I don't have the pleasure or perhaps the disappointment. Do you?"

"A girl. She's in grammar school."

"How nice. Is she toppling the average height record like her dad?"

A shimmer of a smile crossed his lips, which warmed Viktoria's heart.

"Yeah. Her school is trying to sprout a girls' basketball team. My daughter signed up."

"Is she any good?"

"Don't know."

Viktoria leaned back and enticed more information with her eyes.

"I don't live at home with her anymore. My wife asked me to leave, she's filed for a divorce, but that's common knowledge around here even for you, the 'outlander.'"

"'Outlander?'"

"That's what your department is calling you."

"Why is that? Because I'm originally from Iceland?"

"I heard about that too. But it's not only because of your country of origin, it's also because you're from Longgg Island, and not from around here."

"AHH. And my gypsy, locum tenens lifestyle." She contracted her eyebrows. "Doesn't matter. I also don't possess the correct hair texture, the correct posture, the most tolerable accent, the best fingertips, the most alluring kneecaps, or the most precise width to my forehead."

"You forgot the fact that you wear your drawstring tie outside your scrubs. Almost all the women around here tuck it in."

"Stupid me." Viktoria smiled enough that Dr. Winter caught a flash of her white teeth.

CHAPTER 10

More anesthesia personnel were in the office than Dr. Thorsdottir had previously met. With a flurry of case turnovers, they congregated on the couch and chairs, eating take-out food and celebrating a birthday. A tall chocolate cake with decadent wafers decorated the middle of the table and slices of it dotted paper plates in peoples' hands. Dr. Huff kept his spot in the doorway with one eye on the scheduling board.

"Your hot sandwich recommendation was spot on," Viktoria said in passing.

"Glad you enjoyed it. Help yourself to cake. It's Susan's birthday, one of the CRNA's. You and she will be doing the triple A that's in the preop area. Came up from the ER. The abdominal aortic aneurysm has not ruptured yet and the patient is stable, but the vascular doc is not taking any chances and wants to do him right away."

"Dr. Parker?"

"Yes, that's right, you worked with him already."

Viktoria nodded and stepped over to slip a piece of cake on a plate.

"Just don't dilly-dally," Jay said.

"Who needs the calories anyway," Viktoria commented and aborted the plan. "Introduce me to Susan."

Dr. Huff pointed to the older woman sitting in the middle spot on the couch. "This is Susan Rust. You two will be working on the next case together."

"Happy birthday. Finish your cake, Susan, and I'll go see the patient and set up as much as I can." Viktoria turned and, in the preop area, met Mr. Sutherland, a sixty-nine-year old bald man with a sparse mustache. He wore a look of fear.

Along with lugging over the chart, Viktoria went out of her way to drag a plastic chair next to his stretcher and sat down. "I'm the anesthesiologist, Dr. Thorsdottir."

"Under better circumstances, I would say 'it's nice to meet you.'"

"Mr. Sutherland, you are in good hands. Dr. Parker will fix your troublesome blood vessel while you are under a general anesthetic and before you know it, you will wake up in the ICU. I usually keep my patients on the ventilator for a while after this procedure."

A fluid bag hung from the pole at the top of his stretcher, and she traced the tubing to his IV. Surprisingly enough, someone in the department had already placed a large bore catheter in his forearm as well as an A-line into his radial artery for continuous blood pressure monitoring.

"Do you have anyone with you today?" She leaned in closer giving him undivided attention.

"My wife is in the waiting room. She's more scared than I am."

"She must care a lot about you."

"Two more years, and we'll be married for fifty years."

"When you go home after your surgery, maybe you'll plan an anniversary cruise."

His taut scrunched-up face relaxed. "That's a damn smart idea."

"I see another anesthesiologist talked to you and left a preop note. Looks like your main medical history is high blood pressure and you smoke." Along with being a male and over sixty years old, Viktoria knew he carried the main risk factors to land him in his current situation.

"That's true. The surgeon said this aneurysm is in my aorta. Isn't that above the heart?"

"It heads that way from your heart but loops down behind your chest and abdominal contents and becomes the chief blood supply for a person's abdomen, pelvis, and legs. An area of it can enlarge or balloon out and it becomes more disconcerting depending on the size. In essence, it can rupture. Luckily, Mr. Sutherland, you came in before that happened."

"I'll get this over then. Will you be with me the whole time?"

"Perhaps not the entire case, but if not, another doc and a nurse will take over."

Viktoria explained more about the anesthesia and, at last, she gave him some sedation. Susan Rust appeared, greeted the patient, and they both went back to the OR before Mr. Sutherland's stretcher wheeled into the room.

Peering over the drapes, Viktoria was impressed by Dr. Tom Parker's skill with an abdominal aortic aneurysm. His assistant facing him from the other side of the table was his wife, an RN he had met along his career path. Before and after they married, she tied a noose around his neck that was so tight, the only other assistants that helped him were male. She made sure of it; she also worked in his office.

When the clamp came off Mr. Sutherland's aorta, the tension mounted up as the blood flow to the patient's lower extremity was reestablished. "How's he doing?" Tom asked.

"His blood pressure, and his urine output, is starting to stabilize. I thought he would need a dopamine infusion, but we're good right now."

Dr. Parker nodded, took a minute to stand still, and let that sink in. He glanced at Viktoria. "So, where have they put you up in this mediocre town?"

His wife's eyes glowered at her. Tom was oblivious as he continued to pause and Viktoria could swear steam rose out of the woman's head.

"The Stay Long Hotel. Just a joint up the way."

"Sorry," he said.

"It's not so bad," Susan chimed in. "They're renovating it."

"So true. I have everything I could possibly want."

Susan sat on the small circular stool. Viktoria thought she was a fine CRNA, probably close to retirement. She noticed the woman was slow to respond, but preferred her knowledgeable experience to new nurses fresh out of school.

Dr. Huff walked in and stood by the ventilator. "It's three o'clock, so I'm springing Susan to go home. Casey is one of the late nurses, so he's coming in to finish the case. You can go too, Dr. Thorsdottir, unless you simply want to finish this up."

The case was almost finished, yet they still had to transport the patient to the unit. She hated to leave the dog that long and of course, had an arrangement for three o'clock as her cut-off. Yet, switching off both caretakers made her uncomfortable. She also remembered Mr. Sutherland's being scared to death over his case.

"Heck," she said, "he has a big anniversary coming up. I can't desert him yet."

"That means you're staying?"

"Sure does. I'll go take a bathroom break if you stay for a few minutes and, also, Casey can come in and take report from Susan."

Tom Parker's wife patted her husband's right hand, attempting to refocus his attention on his sutures. His mouth was agape under his mask, impressed by the dedication Viktoria showed toward his patient.

Viktoria marched out of the bathroom, poured a half cup of iced tea in the doctor's lounge, and gulped it down in a hurry. All the while she thought about her case. Mr. Sutherland's postop pain management in the initial period in the ICU was her responsibility. He would be on the ventilator, but as he began to awaken from such a painful and important operation, she wanted him to be as comfortable as possible. What she gives him at the end of the case could go a lot further than the surgeon's standing orders for him later in the unit.

Plus, to tolerate the ventilator better, she would not reverse his muscle relaxant. The term 'muscle relaxant' was a misnomer in a way, because anesthetic muscle relaxants or neuromuscular blocking agents paralyze patients' skeletal muscles, making the surgical process easier for surgeons since patients won't move. In delicate surgeries, non-movement was essential.

Viktoria went straight to the drug dispensing machine. She typed in Mr. Sutherland's name and then selected a 2-cc ampule of 100 MCG of sufentanil. The vial contained the 'big gun' narcotic, almost ten times more potent than its parent drug, fentanyl, that they used all the time. Not only that, but the damn liquid was five-hundred times more potent than morphine!

When Viktoria was the anesthesiologist in charge of open-heart surgeries, she would check out the five cc vials. Having one's sternum sawed down the middle to crack a chest was one of the most horrendous tactics she watched in surgery and, obviously, one she never wanted a patient to feel at all. There was no bigger heavy hitter than sufentanil.

She cupped the vial in her hand, and in Room 5 she slunk between the machines, and stepped over the cords on the floor.

"Everything is under control," Jay said, "and Susan left."

"Thanks for the break," Viktoria said. She handed the sufentanil vial to Casey and she and Jay looked at the monitor. "Yes, his blood pressure has behaved and I'll make sure it stays that way."

Casey turned around to the anesthesia cart and slapped a sufentanil label on a 2-cc syringe.

Jay slipped out between both of them and made his departure. Viktoria drained the Foley catheter bag into a measuring container. "Another three hundred ccs," she said.

Casey logged the number into their iPad. He wiggled the sufentanil syringe in the air. "Want him to get this now?"

"Yes. Start titrating it slowly."

Casey nodded. "Potent selection for the end of the case. Wouldn't have thought …"

"The one thing that anesthesia is not, is a recipe from a cook book."

"What about cook books?" Tom asked.

"Nothing, Dr. Parker," she said. "Just making sure your patient's postop period is without pain and trouble free."

With his wife's help, Tom sutured up Mr. Sutherland's abdomen. The nurse and tech counted lap sponges and Viktoria and Casey added up fluids, and turned off the inhalation anesthetic agent.

With other personnel, they both transported Mr. Sutherland straight to the ICU, bypassing the recovery room. Satisfied with his vital signs and respiratory support, Viktoria finally changed and left for the day. She didn't mind the time she put in over three o'clock, but didn't want to make a habit of it.

After all, she thought, *she had one soulful puppy waiting on her*. She had taken him on as a responsibility and she was going to adhere to her commitment.

Viktoria waltzed into her hotel room, joyful to be free for the remainder of the day. Her OR hours had been full and stressful, and she longed to kick back and relax. Not left in the crate, Buddy popped off the bed and cowered at her feet.

"Uh, oh, what did you do? Besides hanging out on the bed?"

She rustled his belly full of long hair as he laid supine like he was dead.

"Let's go before you pee upside down." She leaned forward and picked up a small throw pillow in the corner. "You monkey. Not again."

Viktoria buckled him to his leash and went back outside, straight to the front office. The bell jingled as she went in. "Sit, Buddy."

Buddy did as he was told while Mason was fixing a one-cup brew on the side table.

"Hi, Mason. It's me again. Same pillow mischief to report, just a different day." She wiggled a second frayed pillow in the air and set it down on the counter.

Mason held his coffee up high while he bent down and patted Buddy on the head. "Must we make exceptions for him since his leg is bandaged up? Or because he's bored to death all day with nothing to do?"

"Maybe both," Viktoria responded. She wished like a kid blowing out a birthday cake that Mason would be tolerant of Buddy's actions.

He smacked his lips after a sip of coffee. "I'll put the cost of *another* pillow on your bill."

"That's fair. How about this? I'll bring the other two from the room up here for safe keeping. And, I'll buy Buddy his own. That'll make everyone happy."

"It's a deal."

Viktoria smiled. "Buddy and I thank you."

With canine in tow, Viktoria went back to the room. She chowed down a few Sukkulaoihjupaour lakkris and then lugged the last two pillows to the front desk.

By nightfall, Viktoria replaced four decorative pillows on the bed. Chances were that Buddy would have his way with them, but it was a small price to pay for the dog's entertainment. She went to a biscuit box on the counter and pulled out a handful.

With the handy treats, she worked on teaching Buddy some natural, almost innate, tricks for border collies. After he got the hang of spinning in front of her, circling her, and weaving between her legs, she taught him to roll over. He took to the challenges like a Chesapeake Bay Retriever retrieving a duck in water. She settled into bed and for a few more minutes, Buddy gnawed at a toy which was stuffed with a biscuit.

She grabbed her iPhone and snapped Buddy's picture. During the last several days, she had not sent Rick a photo of him, nor had her husband asked for one. The picture zipped off to his cell phone number with her statement, "Buddy Being Busy."

"Being busy" didn't last long because the dog extracted the milk bone from the rubber toy. He stretched, lapped up some water, and then jumped up on the bed. As he planted kisses on Viktoria's face, she clicked "photo" again. The picture was a keeper—a full head shot displaying his alert and loving eyes.

Her cell phone dinged back from Rick. *"Bet he needs attention after you working all day."*

She frowned. Although she never shut off her phone at night in case she needed to make an emergency call, she turned off her iPhone volume. No sense in texting him any more tonight. She knew he was high.

She placed the phone on the nightstand. Buddy curled alongside her, and she draped her arm over him. The last thing she thought before succumbing to a deep sleep was how soft the animal felt as her hand rested on his silky fur.

CHAPTER 11

The roads were wet from rain during the night as Viktoria drove along Hospital Road. She almost turned into the coffee shop, but decided instead to walk that way late in the day with Buddy.

At Masonville General, she first changed in the locker room. The piles of scrubs on the three racks of shelves were all mixed up, and she hunted for the labels in the tops and bottoms for mediums. They must have been the going size that morning, because they were damn near impossible to find.

An RN came in whom she recognized from the other day because she wore the same dangling layered earrings she wore on Tuesday. She popped open her locker, pulled out scrubs, and started to change.

So that's it, Viktoria thought, they hoard scrubs around here. "Excuse me, would you happen to have any medium-sized scrubs in your locker?"

The woman looked Viktoria over as if she didn't believe her size. She took her stash out and laid them on the bench. "Help yourself."

Viktoria grabbed a set, making sure they were medium. "Really appreciate this, otherwise I would have been tripping around in large all day."

"Don't mention it."

The door swung open and Dr. Parker's RN wife came strolling in. She smiled at the nurse and made an abrupt stop upon seeing Viktoria. "My husband did a great job with Mr. Sutherland yesterday, but you had to end the ordeal last night with an apparent pitifully unhappy patient and ICU nurses." She pranced straight into the bathroom and left the other nurse staring at Dr. Thorsdottir.

Viktoria gritted her teeth. She needed to change quickly and grab a cup of coffee before learning what the anesthesiologist-in-charge had in mind for her. Dr. Parker's wife acted way out of line, and certainly, Viktoria had no idea what she was talking about.

In the doctor's lounge, Viktoria weaved between three groups of physicians and their assistants. The coffee was piping hot and robust, and she filled a mug to the brim. Dr. Winter, who lacked a belt on his trousers, nodded to her from the end of the counter.

The only round, stocky person in there proved to be Phillip Nettle. He bobbed his head up from a bowl of cereal and glared at her. "Brace yourself. Tom Parker is going to chew you out. He better, because he used me to practice on."

Viktoria let some coffee slip down her esophagus and sighed before Dr. Parker marched right up to her. "Dr. Thorsdottir, Mr. Sutherland was extubated earlier and just gave me a mouthful on my a.m. rounds. The nurses hounded me all night about his high blood pressure and I relied on constant morphine doses to get him through the night. You suggested late yesterday that you would keep his postop pain under control with your anesthesia wizardry."

Dr. Nettle, although sitting down, looked from one to the other. He hated that an anesthesiologist was trashing the department's fine reputation.

"I wondered if there was some other issue going on," he continued, "but that wasn't the case at all. With horrid detail this morning, he described to me … what sounded like … he was paralyzed and in severe pain. In the unit last night, aware, and intubated. He did not make that up!"

Tom Parker whirled around and stormed out of the lounge. Dr. Nettle raised his eyebrows. "I told you," he said, putting put down his spoon. "See me after you go talk to Mr. Sutherland yourself."

Viktoria wrapped her mind around Tom Parker's every word. There was something amiss and the worst thing she should do is to act defensively. But, damn, she was a conscientious and skilled anesthesiologist and needed to get to the bottom of the problem. She always did her own postop visits on her patients and Mr. Sutherland maintained the foremost position on her list.

She washed her mug in the sink and Dr. Winter approached her. "It's always something, isn't it? If it makes you feel any better, our OB patient from yesterday is not complaining."

Viktoria nodded as Jessy leaned against the counter. She could swear he needed a shower as she reached overhead to put the mug away.

"Here, I'll take it." Jeffrey Appleton extended his hand and slipped it from her fingers.

"Good morning," Viktoria said. "Aren't you keeping early hours for the Director of Surgical Services?"

"Not at all." His amber eyes twinkled. "How are the two of you this fine day?"

"I've fared worse," Jessy said, "but Viktoria is ramping up demerits. Don't mind me saying, Viktoria, because news travels fast around here and there is nothing that Mr. Appleton doesn't eventually hear."

Jeffrey slid his rolled-up shirt sleeve a little further and poured coffee. "Viktoria," he said, trying not to linger his eyes on her, "sometimes this place gets a bit melodramatic. Don't worry, the law goes for medicine, too. You're innocent until proven guilty." He chuckled and gave her a warm smile.

"She's not being charged with a crime," Jessy said, "at least I don't think so."

Since the place was a verifiable rumor den, she decided not to add a word. Let all the men say what they will. "If you will excuse me, gentlemen, the person I need to speak to is one of my patients from yesterday."

Jeffrey raised his mug, acknowledging her departure. He focused instead on Jessy Winter, the doc about whom remarks were so rampant, they were spilling out of the OR.

The nurses' station in the ICU was quiet after shift change and Viktoria thumbed through each section of Mr. Sutherland's chart since yesterday. Since Dr. Parker had relied on Viktoria's promise to deliver excellent postop analgesia, he had not written standing orders for immediate pain relief. According to the nurses' notes, the patient did not move even while his blood pressure crept too high, and traces of his general anesthetic should have been gone, except for the residual pain management which she'd promised.

Dr. Parker, and naturally his wife, had received too many calls from the unit when they should have been sleeping.

She closed the chart and rose. Through the window, staff was unhooking Mr. Sutherland from all the monitors in preparation for his transfer to a regular floor. Medically, he was doing stellar, and was ecstatic about that. After all, abdominal aortic aneurysms were nothing to sneeze about.

Viktoria walked into the room where Mr. Sutherland patted down his mustache, eyeing himself in a hand-held mirror. An orderly placed wound-up EKG cables into the upper shelf and the nurse hep locked the patient's forearm IV.

Mr. Sutherland squinted. "It's you. The one I trusted." His expression changed and he became bleary-eyed. "I woke up from anesthesia late yesterday, but I couldn't move. Silently, I was screaming in pain. You did that to me."

The volume of his voice rose and the orderly turned his head quickly toward her. "You did that to me," he repeated. "After all that malarkey about my anniversary and taking excellent care of me, you failed at your job. And I was your guinea pig."

"Mr. Sutherland, I ..."

"My wife says I should sue you. She has a brother who's an attorney, you know. No, you're not aware of that, but you will be."

The nurse shrunk from the bed as much as possible and the orderly walked half backwards out the door.

"Mr. Sutherland, I gave ... "

"I don't want to talk to you. The wonderful people here need to continue their postsurgery plans for me and you need to leave me alone."

Viktoria gulped. Tension mounted in her chest, making it hard to breathe. She wadded up with emotion because he had such an awful, painful postop period, but she also felt like his dartboard.

She almost missed a step as she took the staircase back down to the OR. The more she fought thinking about the personal attack against her, the more she tried to conjure up what someone had said. The OB doc, Jessy Winter had said, "If it makes you feel any better, our OB patient from yesterday is not complaining."

She still needed to see Wilma Lancet sometime during the day after she had anesthetized the woman for her C-section entirely by herself—she had not supervised a CRNA, nor did anyone give her a break during the case. That fact struck her as being important. When she solely does her own cases at Masonville General Hospital, there do not seem to be any problems!

Jeffrey Appleton watched Viktoria leave the doctor's lounge. The medium-sized hospital's OR did not have a decent track record for the number of female surgeons or anesthesiologists now represented in most modern hospitals. He thought that was a shame because if many of them were like Viktoria, he would be happy to see a dozen of them.

Although he could not judge her anesthetic skills, Viktoria seemed more professional than most of the docs there. She spoke well, seemed empathetic, and had to be damn self-confident to jump into a new OR environment when she took on a new locum's position. He didn't think he could regularly work like that.

Jessy Winter still lingered over the breakfast fare. He stuck a fork in a hot pan, speared two sausages, and with two fingers, slid them on his plate. They stood a chance of rolling off to the floor since what was underneath them was already a mound.

Jeffrey pulled a chair out for him and the two men sat. "So, what was that all about regarding Dr. Thorsdottir?" he asked.

"Dr. Parker had his panties in a wad. Something about a case she did yesterday for him. She fell short with her promise regarding his patient's postop pain relief."

Jeffrey frowned with disappointment. "Not justifiable for an anesthesiologist, I suppose."

Jessy stopped listening. He made sure he downed the accessible, free breakfast before going to the office.

The cell phone hooked to Jeffrey's waist came alive with a loud ding, and he excused himself. He often had direct and spur-of-the-moment access to the President of the hospital, Cathy Banker, today was no exception. The fifty-year-old Ivy league schooled business woman wanted to see him. "Can you come up right away?" she texted.

Mr. Appleton backtracked and poured another coffee in a to-go cup. He took the elevator up to the top floor and thought back to Dr. Thorsdottir. Too bad she's married, he thought. All the good ones seem to always be taken.

He ambled through the hallway upstairs and peered into Mrs. Banker's outside room where a secretary smiled and simply waved him to the open door. He followed the natural light, where inside her office was one of the finest views of Masonville to be had. On a clear, bright morning like today, it was even possible to imagine the swells on Lake Erie.

Jeffrey went straight over to Cathy's desk where she finished a phone call, nodded at him, and took a seat. Maybe he imagined it, but he thought her usual optimistic smile waned, which was understandable. She had recently been diagnosed with breast cancer, but no one knew yet what she planned to do about it or what stage she had.

"Good morning, Cathy."

"Likewise. Glad I caught you available."

"Always for you," he said, putting his hot cup on the edge of her desk.

"We need to nip a problem in the bud. We can settle this ourselves. I'd rather not disturb the CEO with it, and in turn, bother the Board. I talked to our attorney already and what I propose seems legitimate enough to pull off and not be second guessed or sued over. Although, these days, you can never be too sure."

"You have my undivided attention."

"Of course, your opinion is important before I ask you to do the dirty work."

Not many people felt the same way about Cathy, but Jeffrey appreciated her candidness. "Shoot," he said.

"Last time we talked, we brushed over this topic. Now I hear about it whenever OR talk from downstairs weaves its way up here to my office. I also get an earful when I attend hospital staff meetings and business meetings.

"Dr. Jessy Winter is apparently an eyesore: unkempt, disheveled, and fragrant. At first, I heard he was living in our hospital, but after my own research, that gossip has been confirmed to be true. He has taken over one of our call rooms here and transformed it into his own private bedroom and living facility. So much so, that he thinks he is entitled to a wife or a girlfriend stupid enough to pick up after him. In this case, our housekeeping services."

"I have no reason to dispute what you're saying. I see evidence of his 24/7 presence here myself. You may be going somewhere with this, however, is there any unprofessional feedback about his work?"

"Nurses are beginning to grumble, as well as patients. Here's the thing. Under the circumstances, we can't wait for him to deliver a bad outcome. We cannot jeopardize patients because his private life is all screwed up and his professional actions are taking a toll. And to tell you the truth, I don't fully know what all his problems are, except that he's going through a divorce."

She tilted her head, enticing Jeffrey to comment.

He frowned and shook his head. "I suppose the wisest thing to do is to follow the attorney's advice. Make sure that we log records of any complaints. I can jot down what I know as well. What do you want to be done with him?"

"Take away his hospital privileges."

"Makes total sense, especially because that would require him to 'move out.' We'd probably feel the shortage as far as OB docs on call, but I suppose that's the obstetricians' problem. They are dedicated enough to fill in the gap."

"If push comes to shove, we can always allot the money to hire another one just like we did for the anesthesia department. How's that outlander physician working out anyway? I heard our closed-minded staff is giving her grief."

"I don't know how you do it. Find this shit out when the territory is right in my own back yard. Excuse my French."

Cathy shrugged.

"I personally like her."

"Hmm. Is that so?" She finally smiled. "So, getting back to Jessy Winter. You will be the bearer of bad news. By tomorrow, Friday, please tell him that his hospital privileges are being revoked by midnight."

Jeffrey gulped, without drinking any coffee.

CHAPTER 12

"Did you go to the ICU and appease that patient?" Dr. Nettle asked.

"There's no appeasing him," Viktoria said, waiting for him to write her name on the scheduling board, "but at least he's on his way out of the unit."

"He's a lucky man, then. People with triple A's have no idea that before their repair, they're walking time bombs."

"So true. Too bad the sufentanil I gave him had no effect. Can you imagine? 100 mcgs of the stuff?!"

Phillip's eyes grew larger. "Perhaps the vial came from China."

"Hmm. You bring up a plausible line of thinking. Although unlikely, bad drugs are a possibility."

"We don't routinely use sufentanil around here, you know."

"I understand that. I don't either. However, it is part of our pharmaceutical armamentarium and I dig into our box of tricks and use the best resources for the most appropriate situation."

"Now that you have that off your chest, I'm assigning you two rooms to supervise CRNAs. An anal fistula with Susan Rust and an exploratory lap with Tim Stuart. He used cursive on the white board, but stalled with the spelling of her name.

"d – o – t – t – i – r," she completed after he wrote "Thors."

He whipped his glasses off his nose, took another look to satisfy himself, and pointed to the preop area. "Your patients are waiting on you."

In the preop room, Viktoria pulled the curtain aside for the fistula patient. "Mr. Guthrie, I'm Dr. Thorsdottir, the anesthesiologist. Here to evaluate you."

The man glued his eyes on her and didn't let go. "I'm sorry. I already told everyone here that I only want people over sixteen years old taking care of me."

Viktoria's mouth froze in place. He had to be kidding. She unlocked her jaw. "I qualify, Mr. Guthrie. I am a whopping thirty-nine years old."

His eyebrows twitched. "You are yanking my chain. You look so young. Goes to show. I'm an ancient seventy-nine-year old, so everyone under forty looks like they're wearing a baby's face."

She let her amusement register on her face. "You just convinced me not to buy all those facial skin products. A baby's face is smooth as butter and doesn't need a thing."

"At least I did something right today before I go butt up in an operating room for all to see and make fun of."

"No one will make fun of you. That's a promise."

"I hope so, young woman. Otherwise, I'll turn over in my grave next year."

Viktoria shook her head at him and took his history. Lastly, she started his IV.

"Be aware," he said as she left, "only a thirty-nine-year old had permission from me to put in my IV."

She gave him a thumbs up, grateful for his humor after a bad start to the day.

With a concerted joint effort, the OR staff, Susan, and Viktoria flipped Mr. Guthrie prone making him "butt up," the position he dreaded. Making sure the endotracheal tube had not dislodged, Dr. Thorsdottir checked from below the table, especially making sure the tape was secure on the tube and his eyes. She re-listened to breath sounds over his back, making doubly sure that both lungs were equally ventilated.

Mrs. Rust made sure his IV was not kinked and padded his arms. When they finished his positioning, Viktoria recorded vital signs and Susan tweaked the anesthesia.

Susan huffed and puffed. "I'm getting too old for this."

"Are you okay? Turning a patient prone entails more physical exertion. Maybe it's too much for you."

"I'll be fine."

"In the eyes of our patient, your age is downgraded. He suggested significant aging doesn't begin until you turn forty."

"Hell, then I'm a good twenty years into it." She pushed the stray, graying hair over her ears into the OR bonnet.

"And I'm galloping up behind you. Be aware this morning that between my other duties, I will be happy to give you a break when I can."

"Appreciate that."

"I didn't notice Jennie Shaw or Casey Johnston's name on the board so far this morning. Are they the floaters today? Or are they absent from the caseload or working a late shift?"

"Oh, gosh, no. Their big day is on Saturday. They're taking off today and tomorrow. Although they hired help at home, they still have too many details to attend to, especially since the wedding and reception is at their house. No telling how elaborate their ceremony and party is going to be. I only hear rumors. If it means anything, even her dress was special ordered from New York City."

"I suppose you only get married once," Viktoria said, turning the dial on the vaporizer. "Hopefully, that is."

"You married?"

Viktoria nodded. "Are you?"

"Sure thing. He's still working too. Part-owner of a gift and card store. The business makes a little money, especially since there's a shortage of them in Masonville. Does a bit better during the summer from tourists spilling over from the lake."

"A blissful married and productive life if you ask me."

"Suppose so."

The nurse's prep was finished, and she hoped the forthcoming fistulotomy would be successful. As she walked around the table, the surgeon and Viktoria nodded at each other. The anal fistula looked painful, a nasty inflammatory tract running between the perianal skin and the anal canal. Mr. Guthrie would be one relieved patient to wake up after his procedure.

Jessy Winter rode over to his OB/GYN practice where he strutted to the back door. The entrance faced other complexes and a dumpster and kept the docs from fielding questions from patients in the front parking lot. Besides, Jessy loved anonymity outside of his profession. He was a loner, always had been, and the most he ever interacted with people was in his profession.

He had delivered a throng of babies over the years: healthy ones, sick ones, premature ones, late ones, ones with genetic defects hanging on for dear life, and sadly enough, dead ones. Over the course of his life, delivering well babies was the best thing he ever did which brought him joy. Bringing newborns into the world counted as a blessing. It was only too bad the specialty came with the high cost of malpractice insurance and the occasional poor result that a patient sued over. But he would still go into OB if he had to do it all over again.

GYN, on the other hand, was less rewarding, but nonetheless important. *He better start enjoying it more*, he thought, as he yanked open the door. Sooner or later, like a lot of docs, he would be forced out of the high cost of doing obstetrics, and fall back on only practicing gynecology. It may be sooner than he liked, too, if his final divorce findings go as bad as his attorney was thinking. Scaling down on the cost of doing obstetrics may end up being a necessity, so he can budget his income and expenses in a more favorable light.

He shared the practice with three other doctors, the newest one being a female. Patients loved her, and most new patients were trying to make it on her schedule. It was the going rage, women patients seeking out physicians of the same sex when it came to their private parts. He could understand it. No way would he go to a female urologist for prostate problems.

In the office, he peeked at the two women at the front desk. One of them came forward with his list of patients to be seen for the day. The chatter from the waiting room filtered his way, and he surmised that he and one of his partners were going to be hustling along all day. But he looked at the list anyway.

First patient was ready and waiting.

"Dr. Winter," his nurse said and then cleared her throat. "I'll get a clean white coat for you. Please don't think I'm being rude, but you may want to tuck in your shirt."

"Yes, Mary. Whatever you say. Point well taken."

She had watched the man deteriorate both mentally and physically in the past few months, and she worried about him, despite the fact that he was her least favorite doc in the practice. "Did you grab something to eat before coming in?"

"Sure. I stocked up over in the doctor's lounge."

She frowned, well aware that the rumors of him bunking over in the hospital were true regardless of whether he was on call. "I'll bring your lab coat into your office and grab you a cup of coffee. There's a phone message on your desk. Your lawyer couldn't reach you on your cell phone. Your first patient, Mrs. Brenner, can wait a few minutes."

"I'll pick up my own coffee on the way. Have to wash down what he says to me with something."

Jessy took the robust blend back to his office. All his degrees and significant framed medical accomplishments were hung on the wall or stacked against the wall. The ones on the floor were new to the office after he managed to snatch them from the marital house. *One of these days,* he thought, *he should put hammer to nail and squeeze them into some open wall space.*

He noted the paper on his desk stating his attorney, Toby Fisher, called a half hour ago. His sip of coffee went down smooth, and he tried to use it as a solacing gesture because the proceeding conversation may just be the end result of legal maneuvering for some time.

It would be much better to not call his lawyer on the office line in case someone accidentally picked up. After touching his cell phone screen, it came alive, and he speed dialed.

"Dr. Winter, you're officially divorced, so at least that's over with. I will email you the documents, the final findings of the court."

Jessy rolled the saliva around in his mouth. Except for the official date, getting divorced was no big news. His wife had initiated the proceedings and had been a bull to expedite things through her attorney. What he really wanted to hear were the details and, no doubt, his lawyer was too much of a coward to tell him over the phone.

"Patients are stacked up, so why don't you give me the highlights?"

"Dr. Winter, you're out of the house, so it won't come as a surprise that your wife keeps the house."

Jessy cringed. "That was not what I wanted and you know it. I left because she was going to cry mental anguish, physical abuse, or something or the other if I stayed, and we lived under the same roof. Besides, I bought that house lock, stock, and barrel."

Toby Fisher let what he said go right over his head. Empathy was not part of his job. If he had any, it would only serve to slow down his clients' cases. "I hear you, Jessy. The judge had the final say. You and I did our best to present your case."

"I'm already strapped financially. It's going to be difficult to get a half-way decent place. I just can't swing it right now, especially after paying all these GD legal bills. Maybe I can find some low-cost rental unit because my daughter is going to need a place to stay."

Now it was Toby Fischer's turn to cringe. He kept it short and launched ahead. "She'll be staying with her mom. You can see her every other weekend and one night a week, but no stay-overs because of your living situation."

Jessy thought he'd stroke. The highlight of his whole life was his daughter. The anger welled up in him so suddenly that he felt like throwing the phone across the room. Punching a wall would be better.

Toby expected the doctor to tear into him. He plunged forward with more awful findings, so he would not get bombarded by his client's rage in installments. Now came the alimony part.

"Your wife mostly ran around doing part-time, low-paying social work and dabbling in philanthropic causes. Besides child support for your daughter, the judge ordered you to pay her alimony for a long time."

Dr. Winter's heart pounded so hard, now he thought a heart attack would follow a stroke. "That's insane. What about me?"

He squeezed his eyes tight as Mary walked in. He opened them to find her standing in front of his desk, so he spun around to face the back wall.

"This is deplorable! I guess if we want to take a stab at changing it, I would need to appeal."

"That's correct."

"More money down the drain. For what? Other liberal judges will just uphold what the lower court ruled while I stay a homeless victim of the whole process."

Dr. Winter was correct of course, Toby realized, but no sense in siding with him not to appeal. An appeal would put more money in his pocket, but he left Jessy's comments alone.

"I gotta go. My nurse is here and patients are waiting on me. Thanks for trying to work this out to my benefit. The writing was on the wall. I have M.D. behind my name and my wife's been living a tidy, expensive existence which is now going to be even better. So, in the end, thanks for nothing, Rick. I have mostly myself to blame."

"Like you said, Dr. Winter. You better get going. You have patients to see."

Dr. Winter pressed off the call. *Sure,* he thought, *I better hustle through*

*my office hours. Anybody having something to do with my divorce has their
open hand stretched out.*

Mary uncomfortably stepped from one foot to the other. She should
have left right away when Dr. Winter was divulging personal divorce
findings, but it was too late. Her poor boss. In her estimation, she gathered
that his bad times were not yet over.

"Much better," Viktoria said. She stood to the side of Mr. Guthrie's OR
table glancing at the surgeon's repair of his fistula. "He's going to be
happy with you, once he can sit down properly again."

"Hopefully my ears won't be ringing and pain medication will help him
out."

Viktoria nodded and went up to Susan Rust. "I only now found time to
give you a break. Go get yourself a nice hot coffee and a donut."

"But Dr. Thorsdottir, we're almost finished."

"That's okay, Susan. Take your full break. We'll turn him back supine
while you're away, which will make it easier on you."

The woman cocked her head, wondering if that was Viktoria's intent
to start with. "Whatever you say."

"How many narcotics has he had?"

"Two ccs of fentanyl."

"Sounds fine. And his vitals seem to like it."

Susan straightened the syringes on top of the cart for a moment then
walked around the cart and was out the door.

Viktoria began preparing for the end of the case as the surgeon dressed
Mr. Guthrie's hind end. With the surgical part over, someone stood at the
top and bottom and both sides of the table, so they could turn the patient
supine. Soon she had his eyes untaped, his endotracheal tube out, and all
the monitors unhooked. Viktoria waved off Susan when she came back in,
and said, "You can take over again by giving report in the recovery room."

Susan liked that idea and headed over ahead of the stretcher. En route,
she passed Dr. Nettle and Dr. Huff. "Were you happy with your
attending?" Dr. Huff asked.

"As much as can be."

"Patient do okay?" Phillip asked.

"Jeez. I'm only a senior citizen with busloads of experience and despite the cold shoulder Dr. Thorsdottir gets around here, I'd have her do my anesthesia in a jiffy."

The two MDs looked at each other. Susan realized she wasn't needed anymore and continued on her way.

"Let's ask her," Jay Huff said. "If she goes for it, I'll be ecstatic."

CHAPTER 13

Mr. Guthrie's eyelids slid open in the recovery room, and he succeeded in giving half smiles to the surrounding faces. "I'm alive," he said. "I will live to sit again."

"Congratulations," Dr. Thorsdottir said. "Your surgery is behind you."

"Ha, ha," he chuckled. "That was funnier than mine."

"I aim to please and you did absolutely fine." Viktoria glanced again at his vital signs while Susan gave the nurse a report. She spun around and hustled through the automatic door to come face-to-face with Jay Huff and Phillip Nettle.

"Dr. Thorsdottir," Jay said, "Do you have a minute? How about we find out what the chef put out for lunch today?"

"Sure thing. I planned on something over there whenever I can."

They sauntered over and Jay opened the door. Inside, Viktoria started to recognize a few faces. Most of the chatter was work related; especially docs talking about their morning consults to one another.

Jay snatched an empty table and placed his coat on a chair. Viktoria ladled a small bowl of chili and a half sandwich and went to the table.

Dr. Huff brought back drinks for both of them and settled across from her. "Schedule's not too bad today. We may all be able to leave by the time the night call doc comes in. Not you. You're out of here at three no matter what."

"Officially, but like I've mentioned, sometimes I have inpatients from the day before whom I prefer to check on myself."

"Oh yes, I forgot about that. That's commendable of you."

They both bit into their sandwiches and Viktoria added a sugar packet to the tea. Jay leaned forward and flinched his narrow shoulders together.

"We were wondering," he said, "if you wouldn't mind doing something different tomorrow. Come in at 7 p.m. instead of 7 a.m. and be the anesthesiologist on call? There is a back-up doc on call in case you get in over your head."

"Get in over my head?"

"Well, you know what I mean."

"No, I don't know what you mean, which is why I asked."

"For instance, what if you couldn't find something or had trouble with a surgeon?"

"Are you patronizing me? Dealing with surgeons is what anesthesiologists do on a regular basis."

"I'm sorry. I didn't mean to suggest you can't handle yourself."

Viktoria thought about his actual request and Buddy sprung to mind. Although she would need to take a nap tomorrow to manage making it through the night call, she would be able to spend time doing something fun with him. Dog bonding!

She shrugged off his other remarks. "If I do this night call, I would expect to be reimbursed the extra four hours."

"Not a problem. I will instruct Jeffrey Appleton about the extra hours and pay to go to the locum's agency for you. In addition, I'll try to get you time and a half."

"Now we're talking." Viktoria sipped the tea and raised her eyebrows. "So, what's in it for the group if I'm the one pulling call?"

Jay accentuated his wrinkled forehead. "Now, I'm scheduled for tomorrow night. However, if I have a bad night, it'll trash my alertness for the CRNAs wedding and reception on Saturday. Should be fun to watch those two get hitched, plus, we're in need of an awesome party around here. I want to make sure I go and that I'm not walking around like a sleep-deprived zombie."

"Okay, then, sign me up." She could see Buddy's tail wagging a mile a minute.

When he finished lunch, Dr. Huff brought over two pieces of chocolate cake dolloped with whipped cream. "Thanks, and this is in anticipation of Saturday's wedding cake. Help yourself."

It did appear like he was practicing for the CRNAs' bash.

"Time is quarter to three, but you're finished," Dr. Nettle said. He held a see-through plastic cup and, as far as Viktoria could make out, it looked like a milkshake. "You can't staff another case with only fifteen minutes to go."

"Makes sense. I'll go postop on Wilma Lancet from yesterday."

"I'll start telling the CRNAs not to round on your post op patients.

They'll like that, it will save them some work."

"That will go over big. Where on earth did you procure that anyway?"

"My caramel frappe? One of the three-to-eleven OR nurses just brought it in for me. When I arrange for her to pick something up, I treat her as well."

Viktoria wiggled her head. "This OR is teaching me more about what to buy in a coffee shop than my continuing medical education audio disc teaches me about anesthesia."

"Hey, listen, have a good night and day tomorrow. I heard you took Jay up on his offer, so just be here tomorrow at 7 p.m."

"Can do."

Viktoria sprang up the staircase to the OB floor where she found Wilma Lancet in the first room by the nurse's station. Comfortable in bed, the thirty-year old strained to keep her eyes open.

"Mrs. Lancet, it's Dr. Thorsdottir. I've come to see how you're doing after your C-section."

She pushed off the pillow and sat up. "You just missed my baby. I'm breastfeeding, you know. One of the most beautiful, natural things I've ever done, but I wish I wasn't so tired."

"You had surgery yesterday and, before that, you were trying to thrust your baby out. You're entitled to be tired."

"Not only that, the nurses woke me up routinely during the night. Hospitals are the last places in the world to fall asleep."

"So true. How about your anesthetic experience? Any problems that you're aware of?"

Wilma shook her head. "I don't remember counting backwards from ten."

"I didn't ask you to. There wouldn't have been enough time for you to count back to nine."

Wilma gave Viktoria a thumbs up. "Thanks, Dr. Thorsdottir."

"You're welcome. Good luck with your baby and enjoy your breastfeeding."

Viktoria left to write a note in her chart. It was the exception rather than the rule for patients to thank her for their anesthesia, so she felt pleased. She took a seat but noticed Jessy Winter in the cubbyhole desk behind her.

"Dr. Winter, I thought you'd be in the office all day."

Dr. Winter swiveled his chair and widened his forlorn eyes. "I had a cancellation, so I'm making my p.m. rounds, and then heading back." He rested his elbows on his lap, his hands forward and clasped. His upper body sagged lower with the weight of apparent despair.

She scrutinized his body; he seemed a lot shorter than his six-foot three frame. "Your patient, Mrs. Lancet, is a happy camper after her C-section yesterday."

"Newborn babies do that to OB patients," he said with no enthusiasm.

"I'm off-duty now. Is there anything I can do for you?"

"Nobody can do anything for me."

Viktoria leaned forward. "Don't assume that, Dr. Winter, because it's not true."

He bolted upright. "My divorce decree is all sealed up tight as a wad. The only positive outcome is that I'm rid of someone who wants nothing to do with me—although she doesn't want to be rid of my money."

"Money means nothing. Your happiness is what's important. I suspect that a greater percentage of people who are poor are happy compared to the rich."

"If the money comes in because you're working like a dog and then exits to someone else who isn't, then that means almost zero happiness."

"In such a situation, you must create your own happiness from the bottom up. For instance, start an immense love affair with the time you spend with your daughter, or a puppy, or the beauty of Mother Earth."

Jessy rubbed his hands together. "Viktoria, that sounds perfect in theory, but it doesn't work that way."

"It can, if you allow it to."

Jessy frowned and slowly rose. "Whatever you say, but I better swing back to the office. I'll see you around."

"Please holler. My ears are open for listening."

From the open door of the driver's seat, Viktoria swung her legs to the ground. She could hear an argument going on inside next door as she pushed the car door closed behind her. She walked around to retrieve her things on the passenger's seat, including her gun from the glove compartment. A thud sounded at the man's front door, making her uncomfortable that the fight had escalated into things being thrown.

From her unit, Buddy responded with a bark, so she scampered to open the door. She no sooner put her purse down in the room and matched his greeting with a full hug, when someone struck something against the partitioning wall in response to the bark. The verbal fighting began anew between the man she'd met before and a woman.

Viktoria scoured the room while intermittently picking up words from the sideshow next door. She found one of the store-bought pillows shoved under the bed, but it was not frayed.

"Not bad, Buddy. Good boy!"

She changed quietly, slipped on running shoes, and packed a water bottle and a cloth travel bowl in her small backpack. She popped a Sukkulaoihjupaour lakkris in her mouth and a few in her pocket. When she reached for the dog's leash and fastened it to his collar, his excitement ramped up.

Viktoria cracked the door open as the door next door opened and a young woman burst out to the wooden landing. "Get yourself someone else to sleep with, you prick!"

The woman took a second look at the step down before she set her short heels on it and beeped her key fob to open her car. She threw her gaze at Viktoria and eyed the sky like the man inside was a piece of work. Her sporty sedan took off.

"And keep the trap on that mutt shut." The man stood, shoeless, at the doorway. He leaned his upper body toward Buddy like a blow to his head was imminent.

Viktoria tugged Buddy closer to her. Damn, she hated situations like this. When you must decide whether to cross the line for standing up for yourself, or caving into a bully because you're afraid of the consequences for yourself or a loved one. In this case, her new dog.

"My poor dog didn't know how to respond. He must have been afraid someone was going to get hurt next door when he heard some thumping on the wall."

With a stupefied expression, he narrowed his eyes and retreated back into his suite.

She sighed with relief as she coaxed Buddy forward. He was overdue for his walk, and had been detained, so he lifted his leg on her front tire. The yellow stream pinged on the hubcap and ran down the rubber to make a puddle on the ground.

"Great. You created a call signal for every dog who passes my car before the next rainfall to pee over that scent you just left." She shook her head. Talking to her dog outside while alone was not a wise practice.

Viktoria and Buddy circled the areas by the trees and looped back to the front office. She dinged the little bell on the front counter and Mason peered around the corner of the tiny back office.

"Miss Vikky," he said.

"How are you today, Mason?"

"Finished my newspaper, so I'm a wealth of knowledge about what's going on. In the United States, anyway."

"What about at the Stay Long Hotel in Masonville?"

"Funny you should ask. Your neighbor lodged a complaint again about your dog."

"Then match his with a grievance of my own. His argument this afternoon with a woman in his room went on to throwing things at the walls."

"I'll make a note. Say, how'd your pillows fare?"

"Not too shabby." Viktoria pointed at Buddy. "He accidentally pushed the one he was engaged with under the bed, which saved it from the pillow monster."

Mason stepped out to the counter and reached underneath. He leaned over the top. "Here you go, fella." He opened his hand to a mini milk bone and Buddy swiped it into his mouth.

"You've made a friend for life," Viktoria said. She tipped her forehead with her hand and egged the dog outside. "Let's go, Buddy."

Viktoria proceeded briskly down Hospital Road, this time in the direction of the coffee shop. She fastened Buddy to an outside table and went in.

Linda faced the espresso machine where steam piped into the air and a hot drink fell into a cup.

"I can tell those braids anywhere," Viktoria said.

Linda swirled around and smiled. "How's the dog?"

"Stitches still bandaged. He seems to be a happy camper."

"I should say. Better than what fate had in store for him before you found him. Maybe I'll see you and him when you go back to have his stitches removed."

"He's outside now."

Linda strained her neck. "He's a beauty."

"Someday you'll be taking care of dogs just like him."

"I can't wait."

"Just remember, enjoy the journey along the way, which is more important than the end result."

"I'll take that to heart. What'll you have?"

"A small dark roast today." She chuckled and added, "I want the caffeine to rev me up to continue my run. Going to turn and head in the other direction for my 'breakfast' dinner."

Linda rang up her coffee and poured from the nearby dispenser. "The vet's office took care of another sad dog case this week after yours."

Viktoria rubbed her chin.

The barista leaned forward with Viktoria's drink. "A driver brought in a young, mixed German Shepherd hit by a car. He found it by the side of the road. I call any of those a hit-and-run. Dr. Price treated his dehydration and injuries, but he's waiting to see how much function the dog will have with his hind legs."

"What's wrong with people? That sounds awful and that's a bad record for this town. Poor thing. Is the man going to keep him?"

"He says no. We're hitting social media hard for someone to adopt him."

"Good luck."

Viktoria stepped outside and crouched down to Buddy. The dog focused on her with undivided attention and suddenly swiped her cheek three times in a row. She almost spilled her coffee.

"Let me drink this, Buddy." She sat at the wrought-iron table and enjoyed the view and the dog. The area was more upbeat and vivacious than down the other end by the waffle joint. There was a medium-sized chain clothing store across the road as well as a nearby movie theater. An ice cream store was close to the coffee shop. Two girls stopped and petted Buddy until Viktoria had to excuse herself with the dog. They went back out to the sidewalk and began their jog the other way.

CHAPTER 14

A light sweat gathered on Viktoria's forehead by the time she slowed her pace. She fumbled for her keys in front of her suite as Buddy swayed his body with eagerness, coaxing her to continue their run.

"Don't you want to eat?"

When she swung the door open, the dog ran ahead. "Well, you must understand what 'eat' means."

She measured out his kibbles and made sure to reinforce the meaning of 'wait' while she placed the bowl on the floor. True to his style, he inhaled the food with a few gulps.

Now it was her turn to grab dinner. "You mind the house," she said, rinsing the bowl. "It's my turn to eat, but you can chill here."

Buddy lapped up water and then followed her to the door. He planted himself flat on the carpet as if understanding he wasn't invited.

She slipped out without any more reassurances to the dog. He was catching on to their routines. She was also amazed that he left the wrapped bandage alone around his lower leg, sparing him from wearing a nasty cone device around his neck.

Outside, she contemplated whether to drive or to walk to the waffle place. She leaned against the railing watching a woman and a burly teenager unpack suitcases from their car, after pulling up to the last rental.

She stepped down to her car and peered over to the other buildings where one of the worker's pickup trucks was now parked in front of building two. Digging in her pocket, she grabbed another milk chocolate liquorice to suck on, and strutted over. One thing she had learned while staying in strange places, was to be aware of her surroundings. That included keeping tabs on people or workers who spent time regularly in the facility and grounds. Plus, what if she ever needed help from them?

The baseball capped man, who Viktoria recognized as "Skinny," went to his truck and pulled three long boards out from the bed. "Hey, lady," he said while laying eyes on her.

"Working hard, I see. You guys now working on this building?"

"Yup, just starting." He tapped the wood resting on his shoulder. "Baseboards and walls need painting. By the way, I'm David."

"Viktoria, a temporary resident."

"So, we've noticed."

The "skinnier" man came out, only to toss his cigarette butt. He walked over to help by grabbing more boards from David's truck and tossed his head in Viktoria's direction. "I could'a sworn I saw you at the restaurant down the street two nights ago."

"Likewise. Any particular suggestions about what to eat there?"

"You won't find no Greek yogurt, avocados, or spinach salads there. Just a middle-class skilled workers' menu to fill bellies when there's a stomach hole to be filled." He grinned as he took a step. "However, they make a BLT on Texas toast. Now that's pretty tasty. Problem with me is that I'm either hungry or I'm not. I'll eat two of them in a row but other times I can't even go in there. I skip meals."

When she saw him sleeping in his truck the other night, she thought, *maybe he'd had one of his sporadic eating binges, his sugar spiked, and then it fell like a rock.*

"Peek in and see how bad this place looks before we refurbish it," David said.

Viktoria scanned the room. The ceiling wore a stain from a water leak, the discolored sofa needed to be replaced, and the corner of the counter bulged inward with a dent like it'd been rammed with a wheelchair. "It's shabby, but not as terrible as some places."

"Our boss, the 'Man,' pinches pennies," Skinnier said. "He knows the breaking point before he starts losing business, and then he puts us on the new job to salvage a place. It's like he's saving up to pay us at the same time. "By the way, I'm Fred."

"Viktoria." Her eyes settled to the left, the bedroom area. The third, skinniest man was inclined on the bed, not lying down, but not sitting up against the wall either. The lumped-up horde of pillows boosted him to forty-five degrees and his eyes were shut. One arm draped across his abdomen and the other one was extended and gauze stuck out from a wide bandage.

"He cut himself on some sharp metal," David said. "We told him to get off his feet, and he's damn well fallen asleep."

"Working in these places, make sure you're all up-to-date with your tetanus boosters."

"We'll ask him when he wakes up," Fred said. "Are you a nurse?"

"Doctor."

Fred's eyebrows popped up. "If I get sick, I'm coming to you."

Viktoria let it go. They didn't need to know anymore about her.

"Say, where's that dog of yours?" David asked. Holding the wood the whole time, he finally placed the pile on the floor.

"Taking it easy. Well, I better run."

"See you eating pancakes," Fred winked.

Viktoria went outside and decided on taking her car. She hit the key fob and grasped her key chain tighter. Besides having a gun, she always carried a small can of mace on her key chain. She went in and out of establishments and held her can of mace in plain sight. Everyone was 'blind' to her obvious, out-in-the open "weapon."

At the door, Fred lit up another cigarette as he watched Viktoria leave. "She didn't think this place was too bad," he said over his shoulder.

David lined a baseboard against the nearby wall to measure it. He would need to cut it down to size. Behind the wall, a scratching, scurrying sound went by. "If she knew about the mice and rats behind the walls and running amok around here, she'd think differently."

"Yeah, but she's in the best building. Thank goodness, especially since she's a doctor and all."

"She should be staying in that ritzy hotel for tourists closer to the lake."

"But that would be an unnecessary long drive. Hey, I wonder if she's married."

"Dream on. I think it's time to make Ben get off his ass and help out around here."

"Leave him alone. It was his turn."

Friday morning, Jeffrey Appleton meandered over to the OR to grab the day's OR schedule. Sometimes he would go over for the heck of it. The pulse of activity at that time of day was intoxicating to him and, having worked in an OR as a nurse before, he understood the push to move cases along on time and the efficiency needed to prevent delays.

He nodded at the secretary at the desk. Although he grabbed a sheet, he peered over at the case board. Two OB/GYN doctors had morning cases and one of them was Jessy Winter.

The Director of Surgical Services sneaked back to his office to think through his plan of action. Only once before had he needed to revoke a physician's hospital privileges.

Jeffrey held the paper and studied it at his desk. Dr. Winter should be done with both cases by noon, he figured. Maybe he could catch him in the doctor's lounge where he'd be eating lunch, and ask him back to his office. Cathy Banker, the CEO, made it clear that the OB/GYN doc needed to receive his walking papers today, so Jeffrey could deliver the blow over his last hospital croissant sandwich.

He dreaded his assignment. At his core, Jeffrey was a softy, with a heart of gold. As his career had progressed, he had toughened up his exterior to appear more dogmatic and stricter than he really was. Overseeing the hospital operations and staff he was in charge of, was no easy feat, but it came with the territory.

Jeffrey just wished that no matter what Dr. Winter's personal problems were, he hadn't taken up residence in the hospital's call room, putting them in an awkward position. He unclenched the schedule and leaned back. Friday's were the busiest day of the week for him, tidying up all business for the week, and especially making sure too many things weren't going to hang over his head for Monday morning.

He rolled up his sleeves for the day, took a big sigh, and put Jessy Winter out of his mind until lunchtime.

Bleary-eyed, Jeffrey stepped out of the Patient Financial Services Director's office at twelve-thirty. For two hours, they had analyzed last month's patient payer mix, and the result showed a non-desirable financial outcome for the hospital. He wished someone would wave a magic wand and let health care costs benefit both patients and caregivers at the same time.

He deviated into the OR and looked at the scheduling board. Lucky for him, Jessy Winter's morning cases were erased. The doctor may still have office hours the rest of the day, he figured, but that had nothing to do with the hospital. In actuality, he grimaced, his group would be in a quandary once their colleague was stripped of Masonville General Hospital's privileges. How could he possibly work in the group's practice when he couldn't do cases in the hospital?

Jeffrey headed to the doctor's lounge as he rehearsed the careful dialogue he needed to spill on Dr. Winter. He opened the door and spotted Jessy at his own table. He was eating, making Jeffrey's plan to lure him to his office more difficult. The lounge would have to do, so he stepped over to the counter to check the coffee pot.

Satisfied with the freshness of the coffee, Jeffrey poured a cup. He also scouted around for the interim female anesthesiologist. It would be nice to mix doling out bad news with a more satisfying, short interaction, he thought, but no such luck. He had not seen her all day.

Jeffrey strolled over to Jessy Winter. "Mind if I sit down?"

Jessy speared a piece of cantaloupe from a small plate of mixed fruit and glumly nodded.

"Are your OR cases done for the day?" Jeffrey asked.

"Elective ones, yeah."

The OB/GYN doc slouched over his plate, making butterflies twirl in Jeffrey's stomach. He wanted to deliver the blow in a soft, gentle manner, and a bit of social chitchat beforehand would be beneficial.

Jessy swallowed and twisted his mouth. "I just thought of something. My status changed yesterday. I guess I better go change my personal physician staff information on record with the hospital. Like there isn't a 'Mrs.' anymore."

Horrors, Jeffrey thought. The man's divorce decree came through. However, Dr. Winter opened up the door for him to tell him *his* bad news. He held off raising his cup to his lips.

"Actually, no update on your part is necessary, Dr. Winter. Masonville General Hospital has decided to revoke your staff privileges."

The lines around Jessy's eyes twitched. "Did you say 'revoke,' like 'take away?'"

"Yes sir."

"You are kidding? Right?"

"No."

"How can you do that? Hospitals are capable of pulling crap on physicians, so I've heard, but how can you do that *to me*?"

"I'm sorry, Dr. Winter. This comes straight from the president of the hospital and the Board of Directors. They'll be sending you a letter with more detail. There have been complaints about you living in the hospital and your personal upheaval … which spills into your work and interactions with patients and staff. They have documentation."

Jeffrey held his coffee cup tightly. "Holy shit," he mumbled. "When is this supposed to happen?"

"Technically, this is your last day on staff."

Jessy reeled back so his body was flat against the wooden chair. He inhaled deeply and blew it out. "Just like that?"

"I'm sorry."

Dr. Winter pried his back off the chair and leaned in. "Your demand may be difficult. I am the OB/GYN doctor on call tonight. Officially, I go off call at 7 a.m. tomorrow morning. I don't see how my colleagues would be able to juggle around the present arrangement."

Jeffrey was in a position of authority and knew he needed to make a judgement call and a decision. "I understand the implications. Yes, then, fulfill your on-call duties through to the morning. We'll date and time your revocation of staff privileges to reflect tomorrow at 7 a.m. I will inform the hospital administration."

Jessy eyed the fruit plate and slowly pushed it to the center of the table.

Jeffrey waited for a response, and when none was forthcoming, he stood slowly. "Good luck, Dr. Winter. Thank you, especially for all the babies you delivered while here the last few years."

"Yeah, right," Dr. Winter said under his breath.

The clouds overhead moved swiftly, low and elongated like they were imitating the contrails many miles higher up. Viktoria took in a deep breath while Buddy lifted his leg on the curb. Luck was shining down on her since the weather was pleasant, and she was free until night call.

With Buddy at her side, they trotted to the coffee place where she claimed an outside wrought iron table. She tethered him to a chair and went inside. Linda was not working, but she made an amicable purchase from a young male with a bulky studded earring and a decorative neck tattoo.

Viktoria brought out a large cappuccino. Although gone but a few minutes, Buddy greeted her with his heart and his body. His back end swayed, his tail swished back and forth, and his paws danced on the cement. She sat, grabbed the dog's snout in her hands, and kissed and nestled him.

She thought back over the last few days since she arrived in Masonville. As always, hospital dynamics were a challenge, but her cases and patients had done well and that was what counted the most. With one week over, there were only three more left and, by then, she would know where and what her next position would be.

As she looked down at Buddy, she realized he was the highlight of her week and her position there. She had taken his bandage off earlier in the morning to check his stitches and, pleased with his healing, she rewrapped his leg with new gauze. Each day she was growing fonder of her four-legged pet. She already couldn't imagine going anywhere without him.

She sipped the hot beverage and then pulled out her cell phone. Communication between her and her husband had waned over the last two days, so she went to text messages and began typing.

"Did you finish the client's roof repair insurance claim the other day?"

With no indication that he was actively texting her back, she re-read another text which she had not yet answered from Regina at the locum tenens agency.

"Hope you're well settled in by now at Masonville. It always amazes me how fast you accommodate yourself to a new place. I'm looking ahead for you, so let me know if you have any geographic preferences for next month. A group in Florida needs somebody, but it's all pediatric anesthesia."

Viktoria thought it over. Pennsylvania had been a long drive and Florida would be further. Plus, she frowned at the idea of putting Buddy through that long of a drive. Now she had to consider him as well.

"Regina, can you imagine? Me being a little less flexible? While here this week, I took in a stray, abused dog. We'll count Florida out for now. That would be a burdensome drive for me and a puppy."

Unlike her husband, her phone dinged with a quick response.

"That's big news. He sounds restrictive, but I'm glad for you."

Viktoria stooped over. Buddy was lying flat with his ears alert and his eyes glistening. She snapped a picture and sent it off.

"Precious! Does the dog have a name?"

"He's a he and his name is Buddy."

"All right then. Welcome him to the locum tenens lifestyle. He'll be

going places!"

"Thanks. Keep me posted. Make sure all my future accommodations are pet friendly!"

Viktoria slowly finished her drink while the number of customers picked up going in and out of the door. Buddy accumulated pats on the head from strangers and gazes from drivers heading through the drive-through line. She was about to take off when a text came through from Rick.

"Finished the claim work yesterday, the client found a roofer, and work will start next week. Not like you to text from work."

"I'm pulling a call tonight, so I have 'off' during the day. Will take a nap this afternoon."

"Heck of a way to spend a Friday night."

"Wouldn't be doing anything special anyway, but now I'll be earning time and a half."

"That's worth it."

She frowned. *More money to subsidize his lifestyle,* she thought.

"Depends on how busy it'll be. Or how hospitable the night staff is compared to the day staff."

"Good luck then. I won't disturb you. How's the dog?"

"Peachy. Talk to you tomorrow."

She slid her phone into her pocket, pitched her empty cup, and jogged back to the hotel where she relaxed with her favorite companion.

CHAPTER 15

Viktoria seldom worked night calls while on assignments. Usually it was under special circumstances, like working the whole job on nights, having off during the day, and being extra-well compensated. This one-night call on Friday was an exception, but it was going to work out fine since she was going right into Saturday and Sunday when she could catch back up on her sleep if she needed to.

The trick was planning her day and, luckily, Buddy cooperated like a charm. She took her nap, fed him dinner, and walked him an extra couple of blocks.

"Good night, Buddy," she said at the door. "You mind the room. I'm trusting you out of the crate, so you can have your way on the bed. Keep my spot warm for tomorrow."

Buddy sat and cocked his head to the left. She could not resist his sweet face, so she stooped down and kissed him. As she turned on the engine, she was glad to see the next-door man's car missing.

She was due in the OR in another half hour, so had plenty of time to zip through the drive through and order a grande cold drink which automatically came with two shots of espresso.

Linda reached out the window and placed it in her hand. "Kind of late for that espresso fix, isn't it?" she asked and laughed.

"Not since I'm going to work all night. It's just what the doctor ordered."

"Literally!"

Viktoria raised the cup. "Thanks."

Down the road, the hospital parking lot was less jammed than during the day, so she parked close to the entrance and grabbed her overnight bag. She sipped the iced mocha in the elevator, stepped out, and headed to the changing room. Since most of the OR staff presently working started at 3 p.m., the locker room was empty. She was off to a pleasant start since there was no other female present to give her the cold shoulder or talk unpleasantries to others about the "outlander."

She found the correct size scrubs in a meager pile and changed, intermittently stirring and sipping the treat. Over the course of the evening, she planned to pick over whatever real food the docs had left in the lounge during the day, especially in the refrigerator. That and a baggie of Sukkulaoihjupaour lakkris in her scrub jacket pocket should satisfy her appetite and sweet tooth.

Viktoria showed up at the OR main desk five minutes early.

"Doctor Viktoria!" Dr. Huff exclaimed. "Right on time." He flinched his narrow shoulders like a bird ready to take flight to go home.

"Always," she said, sucking through the straw and eyeing the board. "What can you tell me?"

"You're coming on to a typical evening around here. The last elective case is on the table, a teenager receiving a skin graft to close the wound of a prior fasciotomy. The kid is totally healthy except for a rare type of epilepsy for which he's on no medication and, of course, what happened to him due to an original sports injury."

"Arm or leg?"

"Arm."

"Who's in there?"

"A nurse anesthetist named Bobby Wright. He's on call. His back up is Susan Rust, whom you worked with yesterday. She's finishing up preop rounds upstairs for the two elective cases on for the morning."

"Nothing else to follow? Susan Rust can leave when she's finished?"

"As of right now, yes."

Viktoria nodded. "Enjoy the wedding tomorrow. See you next week."

"Thanks. Don't forget, I'm your back-up doctor in case all hell breaks loose, but I don't expect to hear from you. Also, the doc relieving you at 7 a.m. is Everett Benson."

He glanced at the circular wall clock and announced, "I'm out of here." She thought she heard the last from him as he swiveled around. "And by the way, the squatter obstetrician got canned from the hospital today. He's 'out the door,' but he *is* on call tonight. I'm only telling you in case the two of you cross paths tonight."

Dr. Huff showed no interest in elaborating and kept walking. Viktoria squinted her eyes. *Truly,* she thought, *what a shame.* Hadn't poor Jessy Winter had enough?

Viktoria rubbed her hands and interlocked her fingers together as if in prayer. She hoped she would run into the OB doctor because she had promised to lend him support if he needed it. She slipped her empty cup in the trash can, donned an OR bonnet and paper shoes, and went straight back to the OR. It was time to get on with her overnight duties.

"Bobby Wright," the CRNA said when she stepped into the surgery case and straight into his work space. He stood attentive, backing off on his anesthesia, as the surgeon finished his work.

"We haven't worked together this week. I'm Doctor Viktoria. Dr. Huff mentioned that our patient has a rare epilepsy."

"Correct. Jay had to look it up—idiopathic photosensitive occipital epilepsy."

"Never heard of it."

"Dr. Huff was clueless too. He went straight to a medical textbook."

"There doesn't seem to be many medical books in the anesthesia office."

"Only a handful. He went to his private office where he keeps old-fashioned bookcases with medical information."

"I would also like to read about it. Do you think he would mind if I checked his resources?"

"I doubt it. His office is in the opposite direction of Jeffrey Appleton's, past the doctor's lounge. Last door on the right. In the meantime, there are no problems here."

Bobby smiled under his mask. "Maybe we'll have a quiet night."

"A Friday night without trauma surgeries is rare, but perhaps at Masonville General Hospital."

"Dr. Viktoria, the big trauma stuff goes up the road towards the lake. And if not, the ER docs ambulance patients to the hospital up there."

"Thanks for letting me know."

She stopped and introduced herself to the surgeon. The lanky patient's arm was a scary sight to behold but on the way to healing. "Poor guy," she said. "No high school sports for him for a while."

"Next season he'll be good as new," the surgeon said.

Viktoria first went to the anesthesia office and scoured the bulk of the books which qualified as anesthesia related and not in-depth material on medical diseases, especially rare ones. Susan Rust popped in and, with a big breath, sat on the couch.

"Good evening," Viktoria said. "How are you today?"

"Better than I deserve at my age."

"Well, if you're finished seeing those two elective cases for tomorrow morning, you can go home and rest your ankles, knees, and hips, and everything in between."

"Appreciate that."

"Anything important to know about those two cases?"

"No Ma'am."

"Marvelous. You are free to go home. Perhaps your husband is finished in his store and you two can go out to eat—if you've caught your breath by then."

"Thank you. Sounds like a fine idea, if I have the stamina left."

"To eat, why not?" She reached in her pocket and handed Susan a chocolate liquorice.

"A white malted milk ball?"

"Not at all."

Susan put it in her mouth. "On that note, I'm leaving. I'll figure out what I'm eating on the way out."

"Suck on it," Viktoria said.

"Oh, I plan on it."

"It's an Icelandic treat," Viktoria said as she also exited the office. She went straight out to the hallway and quietly padded down the corridor to the end. A name sign next to the door said "Jay Huff, M.D." She frowned at the closed door, wondering if it was locked.

With a twist to the doorknob, she discovered Jay's office was open. She went in, flicked on the light, and left the door ajar. The room was half the size of Jeffrey Appleton's, but messier. There were a lot of books, more than she would have guessed. Probably every book he had accumulated since medical school, which suited her just fine.

Viktoria stepped behind the cluttered desk and ran her eyes over the top at anesthesia journals, pain journals, cords for electronic devices, and three framed pictures. Other pictures graced the only open side wall. Lots of them. Many were photos of Dr. Huff with other anesthesiologists, most likely at conferences and meetings. She got the impression he was politically active in the field.

She pulled her eyes away from the extraneous items and scanned the spines of the texts in the first bookcase. To her surprise, the stash of books had a method to their madness. Major specialties like OB/GYN were all together, whether anesthesia related or not. Especially since the group practice did OB anesthesia, she liked that.

Quickly, she figured out the medical specialties in the next bookcase. *The patient's subject matter of a rare epilepsy should be written up in internal medicine and/or neurology*, she thought. She came to Harrison's two volume set of the Principles of Internal Medicine right behind Jay's chair where a paper tray sidled next to it. It was the same type of tray holding the anesthesia records in the anesthesia office, the records of cases done and then submitted to Jeffrey Appleton so the hospital could submit them to insurance companies for reimbursement to them.

She locked her hand around the seven-pound Harrison's first volume and jimmied it forward, but it jostled the tray next to it and the pamphlets lying on top fell to the floor. They were only anesthesia related information for patients, and she grabbed them from the carpet and started to put them back.

But as she stood straight, she realized their absence revealed the true contents underneath, fitting squarely into the plastic tray. Like from the anesthesia office, the paperwork she saw were also anesthesia charge slips and time records of cases done.

She grabbed the stack and slumped into Jay's chair. The paperwork qualified as originals, not copies. She thumbed through them and one fact stuck out. The cases appeared to be from the last week or two and all of them had a designated "E" which meant they all qualified as emergencies. If it had anything to do with it, that meant they never showed up on the official day's surgery schedules that Jeffrey Appleton would see. And since these were originals, that meant he wasn't getting them either.

Which meant he also was not getting reimbursed for them!

Which meant that, although the anesthesiologists got paid a salary by the hospital, maybe they were double-dipping and also getting reimbursed for cases over and above what they were submitting to the hospital and for cases the hospital didn't know about.

Viktoria stared at the pile on her lap for a full five minutes. The idea that the department might be embezzling money disgusted her, and she sat motionless thinking it over. Then she realized it was not so much the department that was crooked, but Jay Huff, the President of the group. *No wonder he walked around with a furrowed brow all the time,* she thought. He could be worrying about getting caught!

She yanked her iPhone out of her pocket, opened up "notes," and entered a few abbreviated case descriptions, the date and time, and other succinct information from the pile on her lap. *Was her train of thought flawed?* she thought. The possibility of pulling something like this off, because of case load checks and balances of OR information sent to Jeffrey Appleton, was probably slim. Then she snapped a picture of one of the charge slips.

Finally, she took a deep breath, and slipped the paperwork back into Jay Huff's plastic tray. She covered it up with the pamphlets and reorganized her thinking. Her purpose had been to research "Idiopathic Photosensitive Occipital Epilepsy."

With a heavy heart at how despicable some, or most, human beings can be, she lugged the heavy medical book to her lap and dove into the index.

When Viktoria arrived in the recovery room, Bobby Wright was perched on the long nurse's counter talking with the second nurse on duty. The other RN scrambled from one side of the stretcher to the other, adjusting the bed sheet and pulse oximeter of the young male patient all finished with his surgery. The patient dozed and no signs of pain flashed across his expression.

As Dr. Thorsdottir gripped the railing, she read her patient's vital signs, watched his chest rise with a normal respiratory rate, and nodded her approval to the nurse.

She turned and leaned over the counter. "Nice job, Bobby. Many of the patients whom I've seen arrive in this recovery room are not as comfortable as yours."

"Funny you say that. I notice that myself." He smiled, flashing bright white teeth, a harsh contrast between the hint of a mustache and beard growing in black as his hair. He raised his arm and patted himself behind his own shoulder.

"Bobby's a proficient nurse anesthetist," the RN added. "If I need surgery, I'm requesting him. Better yet, I'd request who I *don't* want."

"I hear you," Bobby said. "So, are you going to the wedding tomorrow?"

"Of course! Wouldn't miss it for the world."

"Then I'll see you, unless for some reason Dr. Thorsdottir here calls me back for most of the night, and we have cases to do. I do need to get my masculine beauty sleep before duding up for a wedding." He turned to Viktoria. "Do you need me anymore?"

Viktoria was stuck on the previous conversation and Bobby needed to tap her arm.

"Sorry, Bobby. Sure, thank you. You're free to go. Just check at the front desk to make sure there are no cases in the ER that may be coming our way."

Bobby waved and strutted away. Viktoria went straight to the anesthesia office and took a seat. Their case had qualified as an after-hours emergency, and she wanted to trace the anesthesia charge ticket. In a few minutes, the nurse anesthetist walked in and put the sheet straight into the reimbursement records in their plastic tray.

"Bye again," he said.

"Have a wonderful time tomorrow. I will do my best to not call you back in."

Viktoria absentmindedly brewed over the practice while she popped chocolates in her mouth. It did seem strange. Some nurse anesthetists in the group did not keep their patients' pain under control like others. Patients arriving in the recovery room immediately needed the standing pain orders to be implemented and others were satisfied and content, and they reported a low pain score when asked. Of course, many factors come into play with patient's surgeries and background, but if she dived deeper, kept tabs, and figured it out, she bet that the two CRNAs getting married tomorrow fell short as adequate pain providers.

After Viktoria's young patient was discharged from the recovery room, she felt comfortable enough to forage in the doctor's lounge for something substantial enough to call dinner. The room was empty and quiet except for the minimal drone of the television which was tuned to the weather channel. "After a possible shower or two overnight, tomorrow should bring sunny skies and temperatures in the sixties," the meteorologist reported for the local area.

Viktoria stepped up to the counter to find it bare except for a bowl of fruit and a basket of crackers and cheese. She opened the compact refrigerator below and luckily found a plastic tray with left over sandwiches, a tray of picked-over fruit, and a variety of drinks. The ham and cheese sandwiches looked the most appealing and, to her delight, she uncovered a small cheesecake as well.

She placed her assorted dinner on one of the tables. After eating, she realized, she needed to go upstairs and pick out a call room. She hoped the hospital catered to doctors' needs while they stayed on call in-house and not at home, and that the rooms were comfortable and stocked with a few essentials.

Viktoria felt grateful and relaxed while chomping on the croissant sandwich and even intermittently closed her eyes and thought about Buddy. He was such a find. *He was meant to come into my life*, she thought.

In the next moment, the wooden door to the lounge whooshed open, an RN barged in, and Viktoria startled. She jerked her head up as the RN surveyed the room and stopped short. "Have you seen Dr. Winter?" she asked with a hurried speech.

"Not at all."

"He's the obstetrician on call tonight. I can't find him anywhere, and he's not answering his pages." She turned and began fleeing out the door.

"Can I help you with anything?" Viktoria called after her.

"Only if you can deliver a baby!"

CHAPTER 16

Viktoria pushed back and jumped up. The nurse had disappeared, but there was no way she could finish her dinner sandwich after being told Dr. Winter was not responding to the nurses' calls and a delivery on the obstetrics floor was imminent.

She dodged into the hallway. "I don't know your name, but I'm right behind you."

"I'm Linda," the RN shouted over her shoulder. "Who are you?"

"Dr. Thorsdottir." She hurried her steps behind the short woman in tight scrubs and loose hair flying down her back. "With anesthesia."

They both bounded up the stairwell and flung the door open on the obstetrics ward. "Any luck?" Linda shouted towards the desk.

"Nope. Still can't reach Dr. Winter," someone yelled back.

Linda's eyes snapped open wider as she nailed her focus on Viktoria.

"I'll do my best," Viktoria said, "but it's been years since I delivered a baby. What can you tell me?"

"Gravida 2, Para 1. She's at full-term and I believe she suffered no complications during the last nine months. Her 'significant' other is in the room with her, or at least that's my guess who he is. These days, the guys sometimes aren't significant at all."

Linda moved towards a closed door and grabbed the handle.

"Fetal heart rate monitoring been normal?" Viktoria asked.

"Yes, no fetal distress."

Viktoria allowed herself a sigh of relief. The situation could be a lot worse.

The two women flung into the patient's delivery room. Viktoria allowed her eyes to take an instantaneous snapshot of the scene before her as she bounded to the patient's bed set up in the lithotomy position. The patient's legs were spread apart and the fetus's head was crowning. The woman's face contorted as her teeth gritted down so hard, Viktoria thought that, any second, she would hear her back molars crack.

Alongside the bed, a thirties-looking man stood wearing a frightened expression. He took a step back towards the window. "Finally, someone who knows what they're doing!"

Viktoria ignored his remark. She was no obstetrician. Without time to gown up, she reached towards the tray table to grab a pair of gloves from the cardboard box. But she didn't make it. The grimace on the woman's face ramped up as she pushed with all her might. A slippery, moist male infant slithered out into Viktoria's forearms.

Two thoughts imploded in Viktoria's brain. The baby was alive and kicking, and full of vitality. And secondly, thank God he hadn't been a breech presentation!

Mother, father, and baby weren't the only ones who needed to simmer down their heart rates. Viktoria gulped a big breath of air and let it out with relief. She shot a glance at the male whom she assumed was the dad. "Want to cut the cord?"

The man slowly came out of his frightened state and nodded with assurance that he was up to it. Linda handed Viktoria the tools she needed from a delivery tray and soon put the infant in the bassinet to dry him off and swaddle him in a blanket. Doctor and nurse decided on an Apgar score of eight and nine, a healthy index of the newborn's status.

The commotion in the room settled into a peaceful state as Viktoria prepared to leave. She needed to write a note in the chart exactly what happened as best she could. She certainly couldn't write it as good as an obstetrician, but decided to be very thorough. It would be better if the real obstetrician and pediatrician came and checked on mother and baby.

Viktoria penned the delivery information needed and then called the pediatrician on call, explaining the situation. "I can't take much credit for bringing this baby into the world. Mom pretty much did it all."

"Nevertheless," he said, "your presence and know-how was invaluable." Close by in the pediatric NICU, he promised to zoom over to evaluate the infant.

Viktoria scanned the hallway where Dr. Winter still did not appear. Since he was the obstetrician on call for the night, she didn't want to be delivering any more babies at Masonville General Hospital. *Time to track down Jessy Winter,* she thought.

Jessy Winter's office and case load on Friday was a tad lighter than usual. But today that did not translate into something positive. It gave him a little more leg room to dive deeper into the abyss of his mind and concentrate on the horrid situations that had taken over his life.

After holding back anger most of the morning and early afternoon, by 4 p.m. his troubles demarcated themselves into segregated punishments in his brain. For one hour straight, his brain rattled with thoughts of his divorce. Sure, he knew, the "results" had been pending before this week, but he'd been in denial about just how bad the outcome could be.

Although he and his wife had been married for nineteen years, they had gone through their ups and downs and had waxed and waned with their arguments and differences. Before their daughter Lucy had been born, they had tried for several years to conceive. The fertility expert claimed there was nothing wrong with either of them and if they would quit trying so hard, nature would take its course.

Sure enough, their baby girl was conceived, and nine months later he spilled over with joy to see his own baby be born. And how she'd grown! Overnight, she'd jumped from the crib to a spot on the girls' soccer team in grammar school. Lucy became the joy of his life.

But now? He would be lucky to get little, ridiculous "visits" with her. It would surely qualify as less time than her soccer coach spends with her, whoever that might be. After all, how would he know her coaches when he would be working like a dog paying *all* the bills?

His little girl was being torn away from him and that was as good as tearing out his own heart.

This deep thinking rumbled these thoughts around like marbles in a satin pouch. How could he tolerate this through her years in grammar school, through her high school, and through whatever she would negatively think of him during college and as an adult?

He exhausted himself with the divorce thoughts and the knowledge that he would be a slave to working and paying the bills without so much as a respite from the oppressiveness of it all. As it was, he had been living in the hospital to make ends meet and to allow his wife and daughter to have their home.

Which brought him to 5 p.m., at which time he avoided the doctor's lounge and isolated himself in a corner of the cafeteria. He scarcely bit into a slice of meatloaf. When he finally left it uneaten, he took the elevator up to his call room.

Jessy pushed open the door and frowned at the mess. Apparently, the housekeeping service had cut him off, which made sense. Jeffrey Appleton may have handed down the message to him of his hospital privileges being revoked, but to be crispy clear about it, he'd been "fired."

Yes, fired from the hospital. This was the second humongous problem for him, which tied in severely to the first. *Picking up and procuring someplace else to live could be done,* he thought, *even if it meant getting a cheap option at the Stay Long Hotel place where the outlander anesthesiologist stayed.*

But what for? He could not work at Masonville General Hospital and no other hospital in the vicinity, or anywhere else, would be trusting enough of him to allow him on their staff. He was in deep shit.

And wait until his colleagues learned all this. He'd be segregated to only see patients on their return visit *after* they delivered their babies. But that was thinking positively. By next week, he would be as good as canned from his office practice. All those years of studying biology and chemistry in college with the intent of being accepted to medical school, four hard years of medical school, and four grueling years of residency. For what? For nothing.

Jessy stood like a mummy staring in the room. Finally, he cleared a spot off the bed and sat down. Only to stare at the floor.

He leaned forward and buried his head in his hands. There was no escape. Trying to resolve these problems was impossible. They were set in stone and could not be undone. Thinking about them highlighted the hopelessness and helplessness of his situation. He was doomed.

For the last two days, his cloud of despair had ramped up so much that he wanted nothing to do with living the continuance of this imperiled fate. He wanted to be dead right now, so how would that change when the morning came? When the morning hours rolled around, he'd be technically ousted from being an MD in the hospital where he had delivered umpteen infants by vaginal and Cesarean sections, tied women's tubes, did D&Cs, and performed a multitude of other procedures. And tomorrow he didn't even have what he considered "visitation" with his own daughter.

No, life would not go on like normal. That is, life would not go on for him. Period. At least being a physician gave him choices, options in how to go about killing himself. He could immediately march down to the pharmacy store, fill a prescription, and pop a handful of drugs which would send him off from Mother Earth in a deep, nonarousable sleep. But, hell, he felt too lazy and too impatient to do that.

On his computer the night before, he had googled people well-known to have committed suicide via hanging, and learned a lot about the atrocity of the gallows and that the first known account of execution by hanging was in Homer's Odyssey. Which, of course, he had never read.

As far as he could tell, the method started to be used in medieval times for capital punishment, but he suspected humans were doing it a lot further back than that. Humans were nasty, so they must have been tying nooses around peoples' necks for criminal *and* trivial reasons. If, in more modern days, they were doing it because of the color of people's skin, then any reason must have sufficed.

He wanted to go out dramatically. Let the medical system, which only caters to the patients and not the doctors; the damn ex-wife; and the lawyers and the judges, think about what they made him do.

It was, however, mind boggling to think that his preferred method of hanging meant he needed to make a choice between three basic methods. Before last night, he knew nothing of such a morbid subject. Now he knew about the three basic types of hanging oneself: the short, standard, or long method.

For once, Jessy wished he was not six-foot three. Being so tall could be too much of a hindrance for him to commit suicide via the "long" drop, or a lengthy drop which is long. Apparently, it was the most humane way to hang because irreversible spine damage and death occurred instantaneously. That is, if the person did not end up decapitated first. Besides the difficulty of his long frame, he didn't want to be left in two pieces.

Another type of hanging was called the "short" drop and that made little sense to even call it a hanging. If the drop was barely a foot long, body weight and gravity would do most of the heavy lifting for suffocation and a person could have the life squeezed out of them for up to a half hour. "No thank you, Mr. Hangman," Jessy quipped quietly into his hands.

That left Jessy only one option. If the execution of the method went without a hitch, so to speak, then the "standard" drop was for him. With a perfect attempt, the base of his neck should snap clean as a whistle, he should go unconscious, and die.

He took a deep sigh and wiped a tear away from one eye. He stood and removed his white doctor's coat. The jacket, symbolic of everything he had worked for, he cast to the side.

Jessy's hands yanked the coverlet off the bed, and he heaped it on the floor. Next, he yanked the top sheet away from the fitted sheet and twisted it lengthwise into a rope-like spiral.

He intently focused. No way would he change his mind. With the weight of his body, he pushed the twin bed out of the way, and then dragged the wooden chair out from the desk. Up above, a ceiling fan circled on low. It was the hospital's way of saving on what little air conditioning was needed in the call rooms in the warmer months.

Jessy was no engineer or builder. All he could hope for was that the damn fan mounted on the ceiling would hold his weight … for the "standard" drop.

He pitched the sheet up, but needed to stand on the chair to grab the other end and tie a knot around the downrod. Happy with the result, he cinched it as tight as possible.

Jessy continued to stay in the same spot. One more wave of thinking fluttered over him. What would it be like … what he was getting ready to do? He couldn't answer that question and anyone else who'd succeeded in hanging themselves would be too dead or too mentally incapacitated to answer that question as well.

He tied the other end of the sheet tightly around his neck. Now he needed to be super fast. No turning back and no looking forward into an empty life. He kicked a leg behind him.

The wooden chair banged on the floor.

The vision of his white lab coat concentrated on his retina as he struggled and thrashed after the drop.

CHAPTER 17

Viktoria leaned into the OB nurses' station and questioned the two women at the desk. What exactly had they done to reach Dr. Winter?

"Texted and called his cell phone," one of them responded. "Which is what he prefers. Thank goodness you stepped up to the task of delivering that baby."

Viktoria grabbed the landline phone and dialed the operator. "Please overhead page Dr. Winter to the obstetric ward." She replaced the phone and all three women exchanged glances as the announcement came over the public address system.

Ten minutes later, he still didn't show, and with no call from him to the desk, Viktoria grimaced. "I'll go scout out the call rooms. I need to go up there anyway to claim one for tonight, for myself."

"Dr. Thorsdottir," one of them said, "he's a squatter in room number seven. We all remember that because the number on the door is not bringing him any luck at all."

"I see. Well, perhaps he's dead to the world taking a deep nap."

"More power to him, but that doesn't excuse him from taking care of his patients."

Viktoria nodded. She stopped in the anesthesia office first to grab her overnight bag and then jumped on the elevator. Upstairs, she padded to the left and stopped at room three. When she popped her head inside, it appeared to be an unused room, so she set her bag on the coverlet.

Viktoria found a key on the desktop and slipped it into her jacket. She locked the room door, stepped over to lucky room seven, and rapped on the outside. With no answer after a few more knocks, she leaned closer and spoke louder.

"Dr. Winter? Dr. Thorsdottir here. They really need you on the obstetrics ward. We delivered a baby."

She glanced up and down the hallway. Hopefully, no other doctors were nearby whom she may be disturbing. "Dr. Winter, are you in there?"

With no response, the only explanation she could think of was that the obstetrician had left the hospital. But not taking his calls and ignoring them was downright inexcusable.

Although she figured the door would be locked, she took a chance at trying the door knob. It opened with a turn.

"Dr. Winter?" she asked, inching her head in. At least the room had dim artificial light, so she figured he must be there or had been there recently.

She opened the door wider. He wasn't inside and, looking straight towards the bed, it took a second to process that the bed had been moved. That's when her eyes rolled upwards and caught legs dangling in the air and the rest of the doctor's torso strung from the ceiling fan.

Viktoria let out a cry. His hung body was too gruesome to witness for one second. Her heartbeat sped with terror. She raced over and grasped the doctor's lower limbs to try and provide some slack.

With difficulty, she whipped out her cell phone and, with one hand, speed dialed down to the ER.

It seemed like an eternity. As Viktoria waited through the few minutes it took for personnel to arrive from the emergency room, it felt like she was embedded in a horror movie. She clutched a dead man on a rope. He was unlike any type of deceased person she had ever come in contact with, including medical school cadavers.

The door crashed all the way open and three individuals rushed straight for her. Her load lessened and one of the men used the same chair Jessy Winter had just used as a prop. The knot loosened and Jessy fell into the other man and woman's arms.

Viktoria qualified as an expert at airway skills and advanced cardiac life support, but the three individuals were over the obstetrician in a flash.

"No, don't," one of them said to his partner who leaned forward as if contemplating chest compressions. He palpated no carotid pulse, and peeking under Jessy's scrubs, his feet were blue, and his face waxed over in shades of purple.

"He's been here, like this," continued the ER physician, "up to a half hour already."

"Nurses have been trying to find him at least that long," Viktoria said. "I just did one of his deliveries."

"We should call the cops," the man said. "Need to cover all the basics."

"I better try to get a hold of one of his colleagues in his practice to cover the rest of his call," Viktoria said.

"Cops may want a statement from you. How you found him." He shook his head. "I heard some rumors about Dr. Winter's state of affairs only today. This went too far. It's a crying shame when people take their own life, and more so when it's someone who's made a career of helping others."

"I talked to him yesterday. He was really down." She sighed and her eyes moistened. "I feel terrible. I should have read between the lines and realized how deep his despondency went."

"You're not a psychiatrist," the other female doctor said.

"But still, we all know the warning signs …"

"You better get the operator to get a hold of one of his partners, otherwise all three of us will need to step up and deliver babies tonight."

Viktoria went back and forth to her own call room. She broke the bad news to one of Jessy's partners and was assured the call night would be covered.

A robust police officer soon asked her questions and, although most of them were easy to answer, she hated to describe the grisly scene she encountered and how she found Dr. Winter. She told him her concern about his depressed state due to being kicked out of living in the hospital and his own home.

"A marriage and a career all blown away in one week," Viktoria said.

The officer didn't flinch, much like he'd heard the same scenario before. "I'll tell the ex-wife when we get done here." He glanced down at the dead body. "Nothing smacks of foul play, unless we want to include the doctor committing his own suicide. But an autopsy will tell us for sure, as well as the security camera mounted in the hallway. That is, if anyone else lurked around at the time."

"You finished with me?"

"You bet."

With a few steps, Viktoria entered her own call room. She slipped under the covers soon and her thoughts concentrated on her discussion with Jessy Winter the day before. When they had talked about his situation, she told him to seek happiness in other ways, such as spending time with his daughter, or a puppy, or nature.

"It doesn't work that way," he had retorted. And then, even though he said "I'll see you around," he didn't mean it.

She admonished herself. She should have done more than say "My ears are open for listening."

As mental exhaustion set in, Viktoria somehow fell asleep. To her surprise, the rest of the night made an abrupt turn and treated her kindly. Not one call came through for her to do an emergency surgical case in the OR.

By habit, Viktoria woke at 5 a.m. She couldn't help that because waking before sunrise went along with the specialty she had chosen. Even retired anesthesiologists that she knew continued to wake at that time. The typical anesthesia doctor started work at 7 a.m. or before because OR cases started at 8 a.m. and patients needed to be seen and ready by then.

In addition, if a major surgery was booked first, invasive monitoring needed to be started. Anesthesia procedures needed to be done expertly and like clockwork to assure they would start on time. For a hospital, every single minute of OR time was worth hundreds of dollars and, if a room was empty, that cost them.

She brushed her teeth and rubbed her face with liquid soap. After letting down her hair, she ran a brush through it, and piled it back up on her head. Finding Jessy Winter hung from the fan still bothered her, she doubted the creepiness of it would leave her memory for some time.

Dr. Thorsdottir left the call room towing her bag and totally ignored room seven. In the doctor's lounge, she brewed a robust blend, and brought a hot cup into the anesthesia office.

On her thirteen-inch computer, she researched the medical literature. For the last few years, the subject had grown out of the dormant state it had previously assumed, and become more mainstream with both physicians and for those following such data. The general public had less interest in the sub-category of "physicians" taking their own life.

Any joy she felt from her lucky night of not doing cases was soon blown away by the bleak statistics. She was aware for some time that doctors had the highest suicide rate of any profession, including the military. One physician succeeded in "doing it" in the United States every single day, and they outnumbered the general population by two to one.

But further statistics were worse than she thought; worse than those she remembered reading about two or three years ago. Female physicians, although their mortality rate was the same as male physicians, attempted suicide at far greater rates than men. Up to 250% the rate of men.

She shuddered and read that the most common underlying condition was depression. Like the general public, if depression remained untreated or under treated, the consequences could be devastating.

Psychiatrists and mental health experts were worth their weight in gold, she thought, because early diagnosis and treatment of depression was critical. Regrettably, she should have reached out much more to Jessy Winter when he voiced his predicament to her. Now it was too late.

Viktoria sipped steadily until the only coffee remaining at the bottom of the cup were a few grinds which had escaped the glass pot. With only ten minutes left to her "shift," a young anesthesiologist walked in wearing scrubs and his white doctor's jacket.

"Hello there," he said. "You must be the one and only Viktoria Thorsdottir."

"I am. And you are Everett Benson?"

"At your service to spring you loose for the big wedding today."

"Not exactly. I'm temporary help and I never succeed at making it onto local invitation lists."

"You're working in the department, aren't you?"

"Sure, but ..."

"The entire anesthesia department is invited and practically every doctor, nurse, or tech who has anything to do with the OR is invited, and the list spills over into other departments too. Nah. You should go. Food will be plenty and there will be folks who can't make it. Fill their shoes." His chest rose with a deep breath. "Like Dr. Winter. He's obviously not going to be there. The news of what happened last night practically hit me in the parking lot. How awful."

"I should say. I found him."

"Oh my God." Everett stared at her and gritted his teeth. "Then you really need to go. Best to deviate your thoughts today. Did you sleep?"

"After midnight. Thank goodness."

"I heard he was going through a rough time, but nothing justified his suicide."

"But physicians are the worst. They have personal problems just like everybody else, and if you lump in their time constraints due to their job, their responsibility, and the need to constantly fulfill their educational requirements, that makes for a heavy burden."

The young doctor's eyes narrowed. "You're right, I'm sure. Someone I knew committed suicide in medical school. Can you imagine? As my dad used to say, he had barely mounted the horse yet."

Viktoria closed her eyes for a moment. "That's sad."

"But listen, I speak for Jennie and Casey. Our two romantic CRNAs would be happy if you showed up. I'll tell them I twisted your arm. Plus, you're in a strange town. What else can you spend your Saturday doing?"

Viktoria tilted her head. "I befriended a dog."

"Here." He grabbed a notepad, wrote down their address from his phone's contact list, and put it straight into her hand. "Dog or not, you still have to eat. Now there's no excuse. Wedding's at four and the reception follows."

"I'll think about it."

"That's good enough."

A second cup of coffee was on Viktoria's radar, but she didn't have the heart to keep Buddy waiting any longer than necessary. She passed right by the coffee shop and ended up pulling into the Stay Long Hotel. A dark sedan and an old-fashioned station wagon were newly parked in front of her building. She sprang out of her Honda Accord and went straight to her door.

Buddy gave her the biggest greeting yet when she opened the door. As if chasing his tail, he spun around, and then jumped to her waist several times.

"Whoa, Buddy! No jumping. Let's get you outside immediately."

Viktoria leashed him and they went for a short walk. As Buddy peed on a tree, she scanned the sky. So far, it looked to be the perfect day for a wedding. With blue skies and a cool breeze, Jennie's outdoor planning was close to paying off.

Remembering her own wedding, Viktoria kicked a pebble. The ceremony and the reception were both indoors. *Maybe that was what set them off on the wrong foot*, she thought. They didn't tie the knot outside in the great outdoors or fly off in a jumbo jet to the Hawaiian Islands. No, she figured, that was not it at all. Had she known then what she knew now, the wedding would have never materialized.

Viktoria guided Buddy over to the front office and stepped in to find Mason at the counter.

"Good morning," she said. "You're not hiding in the room behind the wall."

"I guess not. Everything going okay for you?"

"Peachy. I see you have new weekend guests."

"Sure do, but it'll start slowing down as the cooler weather begins, much to the detriment of the hotel. We're just lucky that he's putting money into the place and updating the accommodations."

"So, I've noticed. Buddy and I have met the workers; Ben, David, and the smoker."

"Fred. Good old Fred. Don't get downwind of his smoke."

"I try not to, but I don't see them or their trucks this morning."

"They're off for the weekend, at least from here." He sat down on a stool and pointed to the one-cup coffee machine. "Going to help yourself?"

"No. I'm going to change out of these scrubs and head to the coffee shop with Buddy."

"Any more pillow mischief from him?"

"I was gone last night and just discovered that he was a good boy by himself. I trusted him and he delivered."

Mason stepped to the end. He and Buddy closed the gap and Mason scratched his belly. The supine dog remained in the same spot, egging either of them to continue rubbing him.

Viktoria shook her head while Mason straightened up and smoothed his mustache with his fingers.

"Any complaints last night from my next-door neighbor?" Viktoria asked.

"Except for check ins, I was told it was a quiet night." He picked up the television remote and turned down the volume. "So, any sight-seeing plans for the weekend?"

"No. Only dog time with Buddy."

"Enjoy, but try to get around town. Your pup will be welcome most places."

She turned towards the door. "Actually, I may go to a wedding this afternoon."

"Wow. Not bad for your first week here. Enjoy."

"Thanks," she said, noting he wore no band on his wedding ring finger. "The only thing better than attending a wedding is if it's not your own."

"Sounds reasonable to me," he quipped.

CHAPTER 18

Viktoria stood in line at the coffee shop. Since it was her first Saturday in Masonville, now she knew what to expect. Locals, serious about the start to their weekend, treated themselves to robust morning coffee. Conversation buzzed around her and the baristas tended to the drive-through line as well as the customers inside.

Linda waved a hello from her post where she conjured up orders and delivered them to the pick-up counter.

"What'll you have?" asked a young man wearing a baseball cap featuring the store's logo.

"Hot and frothy, I'll take a grande vanilla cappuccino."

"Coming right up," he said pleasantly. He wrote her name on the cup as she handed him a fifty-dollar bill.

"You don't work in a coffee shop, I can tell. I'll have to rob a bank to give you change." He smiled as he counted out her change.

"Thanks for the change and your happy attitude." For sure, she appreciated his good-nature. After all, twelve hours ago she had held up a dead doctor.

Linda peered over as she measured out a capful of vanilla syrup. "Is Buddy outside?"

Viktoria pointed out the window. "He sure is, and he's on very good behavior today."

"Strays saved from the street are the best. Are his stitches out yet?"

"No. Sometime this next week." She reached for the cup Linda handed over and added, "Your double braids are exquisite today."

"They last a few days, you know, but like a fresh loaf of bread, I whipped them up this morning. You should try it sometime."

"I'm overdue. Thanks. Today may be the perfect opportunity." She followed a couple out the door and slid in the chair beside Buddy. With his leash tied to the black fence and his eyes focused on Viktoria, heads turned to acknowledge him.

Viktoria first enjoyed the cappuccino, the beautiful weather, and the smiles which appeared on peoples' faces as they peered at Buddy. When she finished, she opened up messages on her iPhone. Nothing from her husband.

"What's the weather like on Long Island today?" she texted. Mid-morning on a Saturday, she figured, she stood a fifty-fifty chance of hearing back from him by noon.

She threw her cup away and untied Buddy. The dog's eyes beamed at her, and she snapped a picture. He gave her a nudge, and they walked briskly back to her unit. But before she figured out what to wear for the wedding, she played an exhausting game of ball with her border collie. She finally needed to stop because his energy was inexhaustible.

Viktoria settled on a quick nap and woke up wondering about what to wear. She hoped she wasn't going to make a mistake by going because during the whole last week, not many people had made her feel welcome. However, Dr. Benson did seem adamant that her presence would be absolutely fine. Plus, if there was a big crowd, her presence would not make a dent.

She poked her head in the closet at the smooth, wrinkle free, and nice clothes she'd hung up, much better than anything she'd thrown in the drawers. Seldom did she wear dresses because the opportunity rarely existed, but she took one out and held it to her chest. The short sleeved blue dress, with a zipper in the back, came with a cropped darker jacket which put a dressy spin on it. The perfect choice, she decided.

For a full half hour before feeding Buddy an early dinner, Viktoria showered, applied light make up, and fixed her hair. It had been some time since she attempted one, but her fingers nailed the task and soon a beautiful single braid graced the back of her head. She threw on casual clothes, gave Buddy his Purina, and walked him. Inside again, she slipped on her outfit and a pair of low heels. She said good bye to her dog, grabbed a leather fancy bag, and typed the couple's address in her GPS.

Viktoria's GPS steered her west and then a tad north, which brought her closer to Lake Erie. She drove on a well-maintained, less-travelled road, but heading further away from the hospital surprised her. Instead of living in the immediate urban area of Masonville and closer to the hospital, the two CRNAs had chosen a longer commute.

A few more miles out, the greenery became denser, and a few gated communities showed up, barely set back from the road. Then the generic, yet handsome, subdivisions disappeared, replaced by single estates where homes were barely visible from the road.

Viktoria had no idea that a mecca of wealth was embedded in the region, but it made sense. From Masonville to the lake, there were at least two hospitals, tourism remained significant during the summer, and there had to be other industries she was not aware of. Besides that, she'd heard gossip of political and Hollywood types owning second homes in the region. And as far as she could tell from her vantage point, some upscale builders and architects had made their mark with custom built estate mansions.

For sure, she was leaving the neighborhood of the Stay Long Hotel, the coffee shop, and the hospital in the dust. The hype she heard all week about the two CRNAs throwing a huge wedding party began to more and more pique her curiosity. Was this going to resemble a Long Island Estate party given by the super-rich and famous?

After a right hand turn off the main road, she faced a road with a sign that stated "No Outlet." Her GPS warned her that her destination was imminent. The grass on either side was manicured perfectly and pruned trees dotted the landscape. Another quarter of a mile, the road became cluttered with parked cars on either side.

"Destination is ahead on the right," her car's voice blurted out.

Viktoria swung behind a car on the right and shut off her engine. It was no bother to walk the distance to the house. The change of pace from the small area she'd been trolling in for a week would prove to be refreshing.

Her senses heightened as she breathed deeply and took in the increased breeze which wafted down from Lake Erie. She loved the effect that bodies of water had on her mood—*most likely because she grew up on an island continent.*

She zig zagged between parked cars as the house came into view. It stood not quite at the end of the road, but then she realized that the whole road must be privately owned by the couple, or at least one of them, since up until now they were not even married.

The house dazzled with stonework all around the lower half. The windows were larger than most homes, or at least the ones she was accustomed to, and the dark green roof had multiple pitch lines. The landscaping out front was simple yet elegant but, most certainly, Jennie Shaw and Casey Johnston did not do the weeding, pruning, and mowing of their own property.

One of them must have inherited family money, or won a lottery, she thought. CRNAs do make a healthy living, but not enough for this. She gave them credit for working at their profession full time because maybe they really didn't need to.

Viktoria checked her wrist watch. She had been in no hurry and it was already after four-thirty. The wedding ceremony could be well over. By the looks of it, a glut of people covered the grounds, and her presence would not mean a thing.

She walked up the drive and, on the front porch, three people held drinks while they talked. Noticing Viktoria's hesitancy, one of the men nodded toward the entryway. "You can go straight through or around the back. The newlyweds are having pictures taken somewhere around here."

"Thanks," she said and set foot in the foyer. To the right, a wooden carved statue of a horse and a rider stood as high as her waistline and to the left, a mahogany table held a marble statue of three breaching dolphins. She peeled her eyes away and scanned the rest of the area. Although she couldn't afford a fraction of what she saw, much of it seemed too lavish for her liking.

A woman wearing a tight bun nodded. She wore a black skirt and blouse with a crisp white apron. "Welcome to the Johnston's wedding," she said, holding a tray of champagne. "Are you a friend of the bride or groom or both?"

"I am a temporary doctor with the anesthesia group, so I'm working with them both."

"Welcome. The champagne is my useful prop. They assigned me to be the easy-going front door monitor." She nodded to the tray. "Help yourself."

"No thanks. I'm not a fan of sparkling wine."

"There are hors d'oeuvres in the kitchen and dining room, so help yourself. Just be sure to leave room for a fantastic meal starting in about an hour."

"Thanks, I'll heed your advice." She ignored the two rooms off to the side and went straight back to the elongated kitchen. With two granite counter tops, there was too much hot and cold finger food to sample. Familiar faces dotted the room with couples wearing fancy clothing. Straight out through the large windows, a deep and wide wood deck also housed groups of people, from teenagers to the elderly.

Viktoria sidled along the counter top near the sink and found glasses filled with iced tea or lemonade. She grabbed an iced tea, slinked between two couples, and speared a stuffed mushroom.

"Dr. Thorsdottir. Nice to see you, especially out of OR clothes." From her side, Jeffrey Appleton put his hand on her sleeve. "Sometimes it's difficult to recognize someone out of scrubs, but you do justice to both. It is much better, however, seeing you without a shower cap."

"A shower cap?"

"Outside the realm of the hospital, that's what I call OR bonnets." He was all smiles.

"I like that. I won't tell anybody ... you being the Director of Surgical Services and all."

"Appreciate that." His charismatic brown eyes locked onto her, but his smile faded. "It's been a terrible morning. The phone calls were endless."

"Dr. Winter?"

"Exactly." His voice lowered. "I heard. You were covering anesthesia services." He tilted his head away from the counter. "Mind if we talk?"

"Let's." She took a napkin and a bacon wrapped meatball and followed him to the window where now she could see the expansive area out back. Overhead canopies were set up, as well as tables with covered food, and tables and chairs. All the tabletops were covered with white linen and flower vases with fluffy red bows.

Jeffrey leaned forward, "We both ended up directly or indirectly involved with Jessy Winter's death. How are you feeling today?"

"After finding him hanging last night, my emotional stability is not out of the woods yet. Especially because he confided in me two days ago."

Jeffrey let out a long sigh. "I'm sorry. Really, I am. You were in the wrong place at the wrong time."

"Someone needed to find him." She grimaced and finally put the hors d'oeuvre in her mouth. They stood in silence while she swallowed. "What about you?"

"I was the one who broke the news to him that his hospital privileges were revoked. I feel greatly responsible. We should have talked to him about the problem of his squatting in a call room instead of just giving him an ultimatum. They appointed me to be the bearer of bad news, straight from the CEO, Cathy Banker, and the board." He smoothed his fingers over his eyebrows. "But, of course, the politics and blame game has started. She made me the middle man, but now she's asking me how sensitive I was when I told him to be gone by this morning."

"Hmm. A physician committing suicide in the hospital where he worked doesn't look good for the hospital."

"You bet. Can you imagine the front page of tomorrow's regional newspaper? I'm afraid to find out. The story probably made headlines today: *'Longtime regional obstetrician, Dr. Jessy Winter, commits suicide by hanging at Masonville General Hospital, the very place where he brought life into this world.'*"

"I won't look if you don't," she said, offering a slight smile and a bit of relief.

Jeffrey nodded. "I'm glad you were invited to the wedding."

"Ha. I was kind-of invited."

"That counts. Plus, after last night, this party will be a relief for you." Briefly, he glanced down at the rest of her. "You do your outfit justice."

"Likewise." Viktoria took a sip and tried not to give him a return glance. Were their comments as boldly flirtatious as she thought they were? His coat and tie fit him like a glove and his damn eyes and light smile were charismatic. She felt an attraction she tried to shake away.

The glass door to the yard opened and two of her anesthesia cohorts came streaming in. "Viktoria, just the person we want to see!" Jay Huff held a glass of wine and wiggled his way next to her. "What the hell happened last night?"

Phillip Nettle squirmed in as well. "This is the worst thing that ever happened since I've worked here."

Jeffrey darted her a glance and stepped back. "Catch you later," he said softly over Dr. Huff and stole out the door.

"The bottom line is that he slipped between the cracks," Viktoria said.

Barbara Ebel

"He didn't receive the help needed from anyone in the health care system to prevent such a tragedy."

"Viktoria, he mostly kept to himself," Jay said.

"But, precisely, all the more reason for another doctor to have reached out to him."

"You do have a point," Phillip said. "In the last week, I wondered if the other OB/GYNs in his group were paying any attention, or ignoring his circumstances."

Viktoria swirled the ice around in her glass and frowned. It was exhausting to remember what happened. "Maybe they were weary of the talk about him, like his behavior sleeping in the hospital. Anyway, to change the subject, how was the ceremony?"

"I give them credit," Jay said. "It was short, sweet, and elegant. You know, they've been living together for six months, so this is the icing on the cake, an excuse for a show-off party, and for Jennie to play bride and doll up in a white tulle wedding dress. She looks fabulous."

Viktoria raised her eyebrows and glanced outside. "They must have help to arrange for all of this. And this place is crazy. I had no idea nurse anesthetists make a fortune up here. The hospital pays their salary as well?"

"Yes, and their salary is competitive. But, like many CRNAs, they make more money than primary care doctors. So, they don't come cheap."

"But still …"

"Casey is no sloucher," Phillip said. "He's also a slum landlord, mostly for properties southwest of Masonville. Have you seen that area of town?"

"No. I go from the hotel to the hospital and this is my first full weekend here."

Jay laughed. "Southwest of town is the complete opposite of the streets around here."

"I imagine no section of Masonville can compare to this. This house is like the multi-million-dollar homes on eastern Long Island that producers put in movies."

CHAPTER 19

The back yard started to fill up with the people filtering out from the house. The photographers had finished taking pictures of the wedding party and the female announcer readied to have the newlyweds prance in from the back trellised walkway and have the band start up the music for their first dance as Mr. and Mrs.

Viktoria, Jay, and Phillip had skimped on sampling the food, so they decided to graze.

"If I've seen one 'first' dance, I've seen them all," Dr. Huff said and laughed at his own comment.

"It's true this house may be a clone of those Long Island mega-houses," Dr. Nettle said, "and Casey works extra being a low-income housing landlord, but he told me once that Jennie comes from a wealthy family. Maybe that has something to do with it."

Jay placed mini-spoonfuls of caviar on round crackers until the gold rim around the plate was blotted out. "That's strange. Jennie told me one day that she helped to pay off her parents tiny home outside of Pittsburgh."

"You probably got that wrong, like you sometimes screw up the schedule."

"I beg your pardon. No way. Actually, I recently kidded her about this house and implied that she and Casey were modern Bonnie and Clyde's. She shrugged off my comment and hinted that money flowed to Casey right through from his grandfather's estate."

"Hmm. Neither one of them knows which one of them is rich. That's a new one."

"I wish I had mysterious income problems in my marriage," Viktoria said.

"What does your husband do?" Jay asked.

"Hell if I know." She sighed and shook her head. "Sorry. He puts together an occasional art auction on line, in other words, he links buyers with sellers. On a more regular, yet rare occasion, he sells insurance."

"Sounds cushy," Phillip said. "I guess not being married to a woman in the kitchen works out fine for some guys. I'm not being mean; it's beginning to be a serious problem for some women. Bet some professional women curse the woman's movement from years back."

"From a female's point of view, the income and work disparity can work either way in marriages anymore. It's tough to find some kind of balance and compromise. And when there are kids involved, it must be that much more difficult."

The band started and a female singer with a remarkable voice began, "You raise me up, so I can stand on mountains…" Casey and Jennie approached each other and started to slow dance.

"I'm impressed," Viktoria said, "with this Cinderella wedding."

Viktoria blended into a line along one long table with hot stainless food units set up one after the other. The choices ran from shrimp scampi to braised beef and seared Brussel sprouts to glazed carrots. Knowing she faced only the hot buffet selections, she kept her portions to a minimum, and wanted to tackle the other tables afterwards.

A few couples who knew what they were doing danced on the portable dance floor and the newlyweds and their wedding party were positioned at a main table. Viktoria felt comfortable because she had fallen into line with mostly anesthesia providers and workers from the hospital. With their plates full, they began grabbing places to sit at two empty tables.

She pulled out the end chair while Susan Rust scooted the seat in next to her.

"May I?" Jeffrey Appleton appeared and pointed to the seat across from her.

"Be my guest. I haven't seen you in such a long time," she kidded him.

"I was talking with family members over there, but the conversation has turned to memories of Jennie as a kid. Best to stay out of that."

Viktoria patted the table-top. "You don't need an excuse to sit with us."

Jeffrey pulled in his chair and unfolded the linen napkin and silverware. He pulled out an envelope from his inside pocket and held it. "The table is piling high over there with gifts and envelopes. Better go make a spot for this."

Viktoria grimaced. "That's the problem with a spur of the moment wedding invitation. I'm not prepared with a gift. I'll need to do something about that."

Jeffrey opened the unsealed envelope and pulled out a pen. "I have the solution. Let me add your name to this card. There's a check in here which will suffice from all three of us."

"Three of us?"

"Cathy Banker, our CEO, likes to add a personal touch to hospital employees whenever she can. She added to my monetary gift, and we both signed the card. Add your name, please."

Viktoria leaned in over her untouched plate. "Are you sure?"

He tilted his head. "If you don't sign your name, I will."

She nodded and reached for his pen as he slid the card open and placed it beside her plate. She signed her signature and gave him back his pen.

"Thorsdottir. It is an unusual name."

"Patients sometimes get tongue-tied."

"Does your fathers family's surname have a meaning?"

Viktoria sat up tall. "Thorsdottir is not a family name in the traditional sense. Us Icelanders hand down names differently than all the other Scandinavian countries."

Susan Rust cocked her head. "I'm listening in, eavesdropping."

"No problem," Viktoria said. "The more the merrier."

"Pray tell us." Jeffrey slipped the wedding card back in the envelope.

"For short, the name indicates that I am the daughter of my father's patronym."

Jeffrey and Susan stole a glance.

"You lost us." He threw his hands up in front of him.

"My father's name is Thor Engillsson. My last name is not Engillsson like my father's. It is Thorsdottir. It incorporates Thor, which is my father's given name, and the suffix '-dottir' which means daughter. So, literally, I am the daughter of Thor. My brother's name is Alexander, he is the son of Thor, and his surname is Thorsson. He's Alexander Thorsson.

"That sounds too complicated." Susan flinched. "In addition to all that last name mumbo jumbo, the name Thor comes from mythology. So, you're the daughter of a god. On that note, I'm going to go grab some wine. Save my spot."

Viktoria nodded and Jeffrey leaned in. "The explanation of your name is fascinating. There is nothing boring about you, is there?"

"No one is boring, unless they live on a sofa." She sampled a shrimp and nodded her approval.

"Maybe I'm aware of too many full couches in Masonville." He winked and tapped the envelope. "I'll add this to the pile."

"By the way, thanks a lot for adding me."

"My pleasure." He rose and scurried off to the envelopes and gifts piled on the table beside the one with the ceremonial white wedding cake.

After the champagne, wine flowed freely the rest of the late afternoon, which allowed everyone's urge to hit the dance floor much easier. The area jammed up with couples while the newlyweds visited tables hoping to socialize with folks they had not spoken to.

Casey wrapped his arm around Jennie's waist and guided her to the end of the table with the anesthesia providers. "Thanks for coming everyone," he said. "Dr. Thorsdottir, I'm glad you joined in with our festivities today."

"Dr. Benson was kind enough to extend an invitation. I hope you don't mind. Your wedding has turned my boring day into a festive one and you both make a marvelous couple."

"Thank you," Jennie beamed.

"This is quite a place you have here," Jeffrey said. "The rumors I've heard about this 'estate' are true."

"Rumors? An 'estate' may be an exaggeration. A big spread is more like it."

Jeffrey shook his head. "How about a mansion in the middle of Masonville?"

"Call it what you like," Jennie said unabashed. "It didn't come cheap. We don't scrimp when it comes to money."

Viktoria guessed that Jennie had more to drink than Casey or her ability to hold it lagged in comparison.

"Here's to inheriting family money," Dr. Huff said, sitting next to Jeffrey. He held up his wine and sipped.

"I wish," Jennie said. She slightly bent over and laughed.

"Come on, honey." Casey coaxed her by the waist and headed to the next table.

The band switched gears and began a slow song. The dinner plates were already cleared off the table and Jeffrey leaned across a cup of coffee. "Before we all get lost in a thick piece of wedding cake and can't move anymore, would you like to dance?"

She twisted her mouth and he squinted his eyes. "You won't let a little thing like being married stop you, will you?"

"No. I'm a klutz on the dance floor."

"I doubt that very much. Come on." He shoved his chair back.

Susan Rust poked her elbow Viktoria's way. "If you don't go with this handsome man, then I'm going in your place."

"Maybe we can both take turns." Viktoria stood and he let her walk ahead first. She stopped where the grass and temporary floor met, their hands fell on each other appropriately, and they fell into a rhythmic motion together.

Viktoria felt her pulse bound in her wrist. She could not remember when she last danced with a man. Not 'just' a man, but a handsome one, one in whom she needed to occasionally avoid eye contact because she was afraid she'd lock onto his gaze for too long. "I hate to mix business with pleasure, but may I ask you a business question or two?"

"As long as we don't skip the 'pleasure' part." He set a comfortable pace and they flowed together nicely.

"That won't happen."

"Oh?"

Viktoria gulped, wondering if he was thinking of more pleasure than from dancing. She stole a glance and, sure enough, a mischievous smile crossed his face.

"I am married, you know."

"Yes. I'm sorry about that. You are forthright, aren't you?"

"Iceland and New York have had a lot to do with who I am. Icelanders don't like to beat around the bush and New Yorkers can be rude."

"I haven't seen a rude side to you, yet we lack bumping into each other as much as I'd like."

"I can be rude and forthright, but I don't always recognize when I'm rude."

"I'll holler if I notice. So, what's your business question?"

"Obviously the hospital pays the locum tenens agency who, in turn, pays me. But as far as I know, the anesthesia department at your hospital is not a private self-sustaining group. The hospital also pays anesthesiologists and CRNAs their salary which means that the hospital directly bills insurance companies for anesthesia cases, and they receive reimbursement for same."

"Correct." He motioned for them to swivel into a turn.

"On a finer note, how does the paperwork flow from surgeries completed to the hospital people doing the billing?"

"Nothing complicated there. Someone from interdepartmental mail makes rounds twice a day to all the in and outboxes everywhere in the hospital. For instance, when he or she arrives at the anesthesia office, they stuff the charge slips from the plastic tray into an interdepartmental envelope. They scribble 'billing' office on it, and it makes its way there during their rounds." He stopped, wondering if she wanted to hear more, and she nodded.

"And it's dumped into an inbox in the business office."

"It seems like a stupid question but, besides the charge slips, how does the billing office know what cases were done?"

"They receive a copy of the printed OR schedule every day, which is another 'loose' record of OR hospital time, supplies, and anesthesia. Different groups of employees file and keep track of these areas' charges separately."

"But what about all emergencies and after-hour cases which are not printed on the morning's schedule?"

"Nurses tend to handwrite them in, but not always. The billing office mostly relies on the actual billing slips. Believe me, the hospital recovers every penny they can from those eleventh-hour cases."

"What about anesthesia cases?"

"The interdepartmental mail carrier grabs the charge slips from the anesthesia office inbox twice a day, like I mentioned, so those emergency cases' paperwork are heading to the billing department just like the scheduled cases."

"Have you ever considered that to count as a loophole in the system?"

He paused and wrinkled his brow. "What makes you ask that?"

"Mr. Appleton, you answered a question with a question."

"Please, call me Jeffrey, or Jeff if you'd like."

The band finished playing the slow song, and they came to a stop. The music revved up with a faster tune.

"Are you up for another dance? We are doing so well."

"Perhaps not," she said, pointing towards the table. "I am thinking about going back to the hotel. I don't want to be a negligent pet owner and leave my dog endlessly cooped in a room."

He nodded with a frown, and they slid between tables back to their seats. Viktoria snatched her purse off the white linen.

"You're not leaving yet" Susan Rust asked.

"I am," Viktoria responded. "This has been lovely, but I must go walk and spend some time with my dog."

"You're going to miss the best part," Jay Huff said, "the wedding cake and the throwing of the garter. I heard that Jennie is wearing a garter on both legs, so the question is whether she'll throw out the left one or the right one?"

Viktoria squinted her eyes. "I can't remember my own wedding let alone anyone else's. I still should head out."

"Well, we're glad you joined the department outside OR time. Now you know what we all look like with a couple of drinks in us."

"Yes, we're *all* glad you came," Jeffrey added.

"Thanks." She turned to Jeffrey. "And thank you for the dance."

"My pleasure. See you in the hospital."

She turned around and was close to the front entrance when she felt a tap on her shoulder.

"I never asked you." It was Jeffrey, with his brown eyes locking her in. "Did you find the pet store I told you about?"

"Yes, no problem."

"It's a decent one. I buy most of my dog supplies there."

"Oh? You have a dog?"

"Yes, I'm single, but not totally single. I have a female Golden retriever. Her name is Mattie."

"How sweet. Too bad you can't bring her to work."

"Wouldn't that be nice. Why? Would you like to meet her?"

"Ha. Maybe some day." She took a step. "I better go."

He stepped along with her. "You never told me."

"Told you what?"

"What did you name your dog? The stray you rescued?"

"Buddy."

"A befitting name." He smiled, strolled back in, and watched the newlyweds cut into the wedding cake.

CHAPTER 20

Viktoria dashed into the room to surprise Buddy. She caught him staring out the back-sliding glass door. Two squirrels darted after each other and the dog wanted nothing more than to join them.

"You slacker! I could be a burglar stealing into the room and all you care about are two bushy tailed rodents. They're simply arguing over who's going to squirrel away an acorn."

Almost apologetically, he leaned against her legs, and she rustled his coat. Her heart melted. She changed into leisure clothes first, unwrapped his bandage, and evaluated his stitches. He cooperated and, satisfied with the progress of his leg, she bandaged him back up.

She checked her phone for new text messages, but nothing showed up. Rick had not contacted her since she inquired about the Long Island weather that morning, nor had he enlightened her about anything else.

She and Buddy walked as far as the overpass where she had rescued him almost a week ago, and she shivered to remember the sight. They turned and, back at the hotel, she heard a text ding from her iPhone.

Rick Richter wandered one block down from the Long Island Sound where a few upscale sailboats came in to call it a day. The walk occupied his time long enough, but now he wanted to satisfy his craving. He ducked into a local favorite restaurant, ignored the tables, and positioned himself at the bar.

A waitress with a generous number of freckles on her cheeks came straight over. "What'll it be, Rick?"

"A beer and ..." He paused to think. In essence, he had already eaten a light dinner and now he wanted to satisfy an uncontrollable craving to snack. "Spinach artichoke dip with those blasted pita chips."

"You got it."

He set his cell phone on the counter. It seemed like Viktoria had texted him at some point during the day, but he couldn't be certain if he texted her back. He pressed the green icon and up popped the message. *"What's the weather like on Long Island today?"*

Oops, he thought and answered her. *"Not bad, although I've been busy. Washed and vacuumed my car."*

He left it at that. It was a little white lie, of course. He didn't like fibbing to his wife, but there was no harm in that silly, small message, so what difference did it make?

The waitress placed Rick's beer on a napkin in front of him. "Thanks, Sally," he said.

The appetizer plate soon arrived and Rick dove in. He scooped the tasty dip on chip after chip. Second to the "high" of smoking pot, it was the best kick he derived from his marijuana addiction. Most long-time addicts he knew eventually lost their munchy attacks, but not him.

And he was a dedicated stoner. Faithful to the core. Now thirty-nine, he'd started at age thirty, two years before he and Viktoria had tied the knot. The habit started like a slow-growing cancer, or like when one medical procedure leads to another and then another. So, a few joints in the beginning was no big deal, especially because of the learning curve it took to smoke correctly and transport the stuff to his brain. It took a lot of exposure to marijuana for him to be hooked, and the enjoyment also ramped up with the process. Even learning how to roll the damn flower into a joint made his creative juices flow.

Sally leaned against the back-cash register, scanned her customers, and settled on Rick. "You eat like a race horse when you want to. Want to order a twelve-ounce steak?"

Flashing his sparkling smile, Rick laughed. He stuck a pita chip between his fingers. "No way. That's not as much fun as throwing these in the back of my throat. Plus, I ate dinner already."

"Don't know how you eat so much and maintain a normal weight."

"Blame it on the local beer. The brew passes right through me with anything else I slide down with it."

She rolled her eyes and stepped forward. "I wish I had that problem. Let me fill that mug up again."

"Only half-way," he said.

Rick savored the flavor of artichokes as he ignored the television screen over the bar. He checked his phone, but there was no return text from his wife. Since it was taking him all day to respond to her, he didn't blame her for not answering him. His thoughts turned to Viktoria.

They started dating eight months before being married seven years ago. Eight blissful months of in-depth conversations, lovemaking, and courting. Even then, she didn't smile a lot, but the beam she threw at him when he first approached her, he hadn't forgotten. Down the block along the shoreline, where he had just walked before entering the restaurant, was where he had first met her...

He was into his second year of smoking weed, less than what he used now, and as he finished off a joint and leaned against the pier railing, he noticed an attractive female hoisting a kayak off the top of her vehicle. Spellbound by her athleticism, she performed each maneuver with the car, the water craft, oars, life jacket, and personal paraphernalia like a trained Olympian. When she got everything lined up, she reparked her car, and then began lugging the equipment down to the short beach.

She carried the little stuff first and made a little pile on the sand. As she pulled down her baseball cap tighter on her head, she took a deep breath, and snappily walked back to the kayak. Even though she obviously didn't need any help, her fortitude was commendable, and he couldn't resist going over to her anymore.

Rick went straight to the opposite side of the kayak as Viktoria. "Please, I'm going that way," he said, pointing towards the beach and the water. "Let me grab this side and walk it down with you."

It was the perfect dialogue to feed her. He always believed that if he had offered to "help" her, she probably would have said no. Once a women's libber, always a women's libber.

It was a partially cloudy day. A cloud rolled by, and she no longer needed to squint at the man who'd approached her. "Thanks."

They both clasped a black handle and went silently to the beach, which resembled more of an idea of a beach than anything like Jones Beach on the Atlantic side.

They set the kayak down, and they made the first longer eye contact. His brain scrambled to think of something to say before she went about her dedicated pursuit to tackle the Long Island Sound.

"Do I guess correctly?" he asked. "You're going out alone? Pitching into this choppy water by yourself?"

"Always do. However, I keep to the shoreline and the marina. The weather around here can change in a flash."

"I'm a Long Islander, so that is a fact. The wind can change direction, too. You could end up in Connecticut!"

A gust of wind blew past them and she frowned. "If I don't capsize before then."

He nodded. "I'll refrain from commenting then, like a knight in shining armor. You are obviously knowledgeable and capable of what you get yourself into. Hope you have fun out there."

She leaned over her pile and tugged on her orange life jacket and snapped the buckle. "I'm Viktoria. Thanks again."

"Any time. And I'm Rick."

He backed away and watched her from his previous perch at the railing. Wearing water shoes, she waded in a short distance. Too quickly, it became too deep. She scrambled into the one-seater and immediately used the oar to push away. He stared her way for a mere five minutes and then continued on the walk he had begun before.

Before an hour was up, he headed back to his car. The bright, small kayak was on its way in, the short waves pushing it along, albeit erratically. Viktoria struggled skillfully with the oar, stroking whichever side was needed to keep the water craft headed inland. When the nose hit the sand, it kept inching backwards as she kept trying to place her foot down.

Rick could not help himself from rushing down to the water's edge. If she didn't want or need his help, she could tell him so. "Do you mind?" Without waiting for a response, he put his hand on the handle at the front of the kayak. His sneaker was already wet, so he hoped it was not for naught.

"Under the circumstances, not at all."

With an adept tug, he yanked the kayak along for a good two feet. Viktoria held up her hand, placed both feet down, and walked forward with the kayak between her legs. They both pulled it forwards until it was completely on sand. She looked squarely at his face.

"Were you watching me the whole time? Afraid Connecticut would gain a Long Islander tonight?"

"No, truly, I'm not stalking you. I happened to notice you on your return just now."

"However, is that the correct terminology? Can you stalk someone who is on the water?"

"Good question. How about I help you strap this baby up on your car, and we go get a beer, a bite to eat, or both, and we'll figure it out. My treat, of course."

A slight smile crept over her lips as she considered his offer.

"Really," he added, "you must be famished after all that hard work."

"Work? No way. That was pure exhilaration. Sure, I'd love to grab a bite, but only if we each pay Dutch treat."

"You're on."

Rick stepped off the bar stool, dropped a bill on the counter for Sally, and left, satisfied after the beer, pita chips, and dip. He walked around the block for his car and stopped in front of the very restaurant he and Viktoria ate at the day they met. With big, bold gold lettering which said "Captain's by the Water," and four seasonal black tables out front, nothing had changed.

As Viktoria sat sideways from her vehicle that late afternoon eight years ago, she had changed into dry shoes as Rick waited. They left her car with the kayak on top and walked with no particular place in mind. When they came to "Captain's," they shared a glance and nodded.

Viktoria studied the menu taped to the window longer than Rick. "I'm aiming to eat dinner, so don't mind my pickiness."

"No problem. Anything grab you?"

"Hands down. Crab cakes."

Rick opened the door, they marched in, and stole a bench by the window. They skipped a menu from the waiter and asked for the same two dinner selections and drinks.

"So, what do you do when you're not kayaking?" Rick asked.

"Put people to sleep."

He had no idea what she meant. If she meant it to be a joke, he didn't find it funny. "You are not the least bit boring. I don't see how anyone can fall asleep around you."

"No, no, not literally in *that* sense. I am the provider of anesthesia. The anesthesia puts patients to sleep."

He scrunched his brow. "Don't doctors do that?"

"Some types of nurses do too, but I'm a doctor. I'm not that long out of residency and now I practice on my own."

"Damn. That was a long haul, wasn't it? Longer and more challenging than the solo kayak haul you just did."

"Sure was. In so many ways, I'm finally reaping the rewards. What do you do?"

His head spun. The woman across from him was probably brighter than anyone he ever gone out with before, if he could call their dinner "going out."

"I have a bachelor's degree in physical education. I am the only personal trainer in the YMCA's huge gym a couple of miles from here, but I also run the gym and athletic programs there."

"Sounds like fun. I'm not a member there, but I understand its state of the art."

"You should come by sometime. If you like what you see, become a member. I also know a damn good trainer for when you're not knocking people out."

A waitress set down two iced teas from a tray and another one came forward and set down their dinner plates.

"Can I get you anything else?" the second waitress inquired while taking a step back.

"I'm good," Viktoria said.

"Makes two of us," Rick said.

Rick snapped out of his thoughts from eight years ago, and stepped aside. A couple breezed past him on the sidewalk and went inside "Captain's by the Water." As he turned away from the restaurant, he marveled at how harmonious that Saturday had progressed, the day he and Viktoria first met. It was as if his being at the marina, her kayaking expedition, and their walk and dinner had been pre-programmed ahead of time. *Sometimes fate takes over,* he thought, *and destiny takes hold.*

Rick pressed his key fob and jumped into his car, ready to go home. The sunset and the choppy waves from the sound seemed to stir the breeze up the narrow streets, and he quickly slammed his door. He heard a ding on his phone. Looking down, Viktoria barged into his evening again.

"I'll let you wash and wax my Honda as well," she answered to his reference about washing his car. *"When I get home, that is."*

"It'll be another long drive for you when you leave Pennsylvania, so no problem. What did you do today?"

"Went to a wedding. Not bad for being out of town."

"How'd it stack up to ours?"

"No comparison. This one was lavish and extravagant."

"It's the couple that matters. Bet we outshone them in every way."

"Perhaps, but they did make a handsome couple."

"Who were they anyway?"

"Two CRNAs in the group."

"Hmm. Do they show each other favoritism on the job? Like extra breaks?"

"Good point. There may be a trace of that kind of behavior."

"How's the dog?"

"Buddy's fine. A true friend."

"How can an animal who can't even talk be a true friend?"

Viktoria frowned. She could hear his voice say that in a nasty tone. The tone which would ramp up with more sarcasm and more volume, like a continuous escalating hill, with the more weed that would get into his system.

Rick looked up and observed a stationary car, the driver waiting for his parking spot.

"Better go," he wrote, *"someone's waiting for my spot."*

"Where are you?"

"By the water. Walked around a bit."

"Bye," she signed off, knowing his car had not been washed, and hers wouldn't be when she got home in three more weeks.

CHAPTER 21

After texting with Rick, Viktoria pulled her legs up Indian style on the bed and Buddy joined her. She ran her fingers through the long, silky hair on his chest as he lay sprawled supine anticipating every stroke. He was like therapy for her, allowing her to chill and shake off the still overtly memorable experience of finding a fellow physician hung from a ceiling fan twenty-four hours ago.

She pushed her cell phone to the edge of the bed. Hopefully, she was done with Rick for the night. At least when she was away from home, she succeeded in thinking about him less often. Of course, he wasn't in her face, which made it a lot easier. Sometimes she couldn't believe how far the relationship had deteriorated.

Eight years ago when she met him, he was just what she needed. She had fended off any relationships during med school and residency, always staying aloof to the opposite sex, always aware that a relationship during training could divert her undivided attention and cause her training to suffer.

When she began practicing independently and met the sporty man during a kayak excursion on the North Shore of Long Island, she was open-minded to dating. Had the timing been different, she would have never ended up with him.

"I wonder how nice husband Rick is going to be with you," Viktoria said aloud to Buddy. "If he treats you the same as me, he'll be passive and sweet one minute, and blow at you the next. Of course, he was not always like that. I'll have to watch your situation with him closely."

From upside down, Buddy's eyes opened half-mast, but he shut them again when she quieted. She remembered one of the turning points in the marriage as far as his job was concerned. True to what he told her, he made the perfect personal trainer and handled the business aspect of the gym and sports' programs at the Y like an expert.

One day he came home and announced that they hired another person with a physical education background and he was the one to show the guy the ropes of the job. The Y wanted to expand and someone else needed to know as much as Rick.

"He's not going to take your job, is he?" she had joked.

Rick had always been easy going and non-irritable but, that year, his personality began changing by the week. "Why the fuck would you say something like that to me?" he barked at her. "I don't tell you that other anesthesiologists are a threat to you."

She let his nastiness go unanswered. Little did she know, that the "new guy" did just that. Over a few months' time, Rick lost the tasks of putting together the summer soccer programs; then the swimming teams, events, and hiring of coaches, and then the scheduling of gym programs like yoga and exercise classes.

One day, with only personal training clients left on his daily itinerary, he rolled his eyes at a woman customer, and told her not to "waddle over to the treadmill like a fat penguin."

Later, as that woman complained secretly to the director, Rick simultaneously told a teenage client "you're as feminine as a fruit loop and you'll never grow muscles like a guy."

The young man was so hurt, he weaseled out of the rest of his hour with Rick and went to talk to the director to ask about a substitute trainer. As he overheard the "waddling" woman inside the man's office complaining about Rick, he asked to join them. The teenager walked inside, closed the door behind him, and the director heard their complaints in full.

The man in charge now had more ammunition to fire Rick. After all, one of the Y's most important employee assets had taken a spiraling tumble over the last year as far as work ethic, punctual and skillful performance of duties, and civility to customers and families. He had no idea why the man's personality had changed, and he didn't care to find out. Now Rick's rudeness and deplorable social skills had gone too far. The fine reputation of the organization on Long Island was at stake.

At five o'clock sharp, the director found Rick stacking dumbbells on the rack. "I'd like a word with you," he said, pointing towards his office.

Rick grimaced. *What now,* he wondered. As a personal fitness trainer, no one could usurp him. He followed the man, not worrying about a thing.

The director swung the door closed himself and sighed. "I'm giving you two weeks' pay, which is what I'm required to do. I'm letting you go. Grab your things from your locker now on the way home because you are officially fired from your job. Don't report back tomorrow."

Rick stood dumbfounded. A few times during the day, he had sneaked outside and smoked a joint. He grappled with the buzz inside his brain as he made sense of his boss's remarks.

"You're giving me the ax?!"

"Unequivocally."

For the time being, Rick was too preoccupied with his own delusions of grandeur to think about his "career" disintegrating or what effect it would have on his marriage. How could the organization no longer be honored to employ and use his superior skills in the gym?

Instead of blowing up, Rick thought it too preposterous to argue about. Clearly, the Y would regret their decision and come crawling back to him.

But they didn't.

Viktoria held her tongue at home for six months while Rick made the weakest pursuits to find a similar job. Although she tried to cut *herself* some slack, the anger she felt towards her own stupidity grew. Every time she mumbled to herself that she was the stupidest smart person she knew of, she reminded herself that Rick excellently camouflaged his reefer use when they had met, dated, and married. He never lied to her that he didn't use it because he never told her that smoking pot was a part of his life. And he had her fooled for quite a long time.

Because his marijuana usage ramped up behind her back during his six months of total unemployment, his mood swings became more troublesome. They leveled off when he finally "switched" careers. Since physical education interviews were few and far between, and went badly, he found work as an insurance salesman, and somehow put together an online art auction program.

Meanwhile, for her, Rick became more unbearable to live with. After speaking to a truthful divorce attorney, she learned the bad news. Since she was either the only or the main breadwinner, she'd be paying him plenty in alimony if they split. And since he was an addict, chances were he would be plenty thirsty to have a chunk of her paycheck paid to him, all to support his dope habit.

For the time being, and also a few years ago, Viktoria put thoughts of a divorce on the back burner. She had decided to get away from him on a regular basis. She gave notice to leave the anesthesia group she had practiced with, and signed up to be a locum tenens doctor. A doc on the road.

The term "sky blue" was totally descriptive of the view above as Viktoria set out from her hotel suite Sunday morning with Buddy at her heels. Although plenty of cars dotted the parking areas, the grounds were quiet and none of the weekday workers were around. Buddy spied one of the squirrels darting to the back and yanked too exuberantly on his leash. She harshly scolded him and, as they headed to the coffee shop, the dog trotted nicely at her side, nudging at her knee to make amends.

None of her favorite baristas were at the shop, and she walked the dog back to the hotel with a refill coffee in hand. She opened the door to the front office and stepped in with Buddy.

"You must live here," she said to Mason, who had the Sunday newspaper spread open on the counter.

"Just about. How are you today?"

"Not bad for an out-of-towner. It's awfully quiet around here. Don't even see the car out there for my complaining next-door neighbor."

"Lucky for both of us, he checked out this morning. Said your dog made a ruckus yesterday while you were gone, and disturbed the hell out of him. He wanted a fifty percent reduction in his bill for staying here."

"I am so sorry," she said grimacing at the dog. "Do you want me to compensate you?"

He smiled and fiddled with his mustache. "I wish everyone was considerate and dutiful like you. He got no discount from me. That was his ploy all along—complain about your dog, who gave him no trouble at all, and come in here and cry wolf. I was here when you pulled out yesterday and not a peep of a bark sounded from your room while you were away."

Mason dug his hand into a container under the counter, slipped around, and presented the Border Collie with a biscuit. When Buddy finished gobbling up the strewn pieces he'd broken off, Viktoria squatted and hugged him. She looked up at Mason. "People really are despicable, aren't they?"

"Always have been, and always will be." He extended his hand and courteously helped her up. "I tell you what you can do, next time you visit Masonville, be sure to book here again. You are the kind of customer that makes my job easy. My boss likes decent folks staying here too. He has other real estate properties, and he has to deal with a lot of skulduggery."

"He owns other hotels like this?"

"No way. They go downhill from here. This is his Taj Mahal."

Viktoria passed Jeffrey Appleton's office on Monday morning as he stood near the door hanging up his sports coat. The somber look on his face disappeared when he spotted her.

"Good morning," he said. "I hoped to see you this morning."

"Aren't you here extra early? I thought business people don't keep the same hours as anesthesiologists."

As if letting go of a burden, Jeffrey let out a big sigh. He pointed to the newspaper sitting on a circular table and shook his head. "I saw it coming. The bad press for the hospital with Dr. Winter killing himself on Friday night. It was in Sunday's paper, and they went ahead and did another mini-story today. Cathy Banker wants to see me in five minutes and the entire board is meeting after that. People like them get up at eight a.m. and are lucky to be functional for any meeting by nine a.m. I am still an early bird from my days of working in the OR.

"Which means," he added, "that they are taking the matter very seriously. The CEO is no fool. I bet she's got a team of professional media people already hired to put out the fire. In a way, she's a middle man like me, and she better beef up the public's perception of Masonville General Hospital or patients are going to be headed up to the Lake Erie area for their hospitalizations. After all, a pregnant woman comes here to deliver her baby after nine months, only to find out that her doctor is swinging from the ceiling in a room on the premises. The articles downplayed his divorce problems and focused more on his role in a physician's practice and as a staff obstetrician and gynecologist at this hospital."

"Jeffrey, this will blow over in a few months, if not in a few weeks. While the adults are trying to slant the story away from the real issues, the person who's going to suffer the most is his daughter."

He looked down at his shoes. "She's in grammar school. Poor girl. This may sound cruel, but the greedy ex-wife has lost her cash cow."

"No, not cruel. Who is going to see to his remains?"

"I heard the ex-wife is stepping up to take care of things. After all, he's the father of her daughter."

Jeffrey opened his eyes wide, smiled, and stepped to his desk. "I didn't forget." He picked up a paper plate with a cellophane-wrapped piece of Saturday's wedding cake and handed it to her.

"How sweet," she said, taking a serious look. "Thank you." The top of the cake was iced with thick butter cream frosting and between the vanilla layers was a raspberry filling.

"Believe me, it tastes as good as it looks."

"I better go store this in the refrigerator in the doctor's lounge. I'll enjoy it later. Thanks again."

She rounded the corner into the hallway, but he suddenly remembered one more thing and followed her. "Viktoria, we started talking on Saturday about another issue. You said something about a 'loophole,' but we never finished the discussion."

"So true. Unfortunately, I better hurry. I don't know yet what cases I'm doing this morning."

"I have a better idea. How about meeting for coffee or a casual dinner after work today? I am anxious to hear what you have to say."

"Perfect. It may be better to tell you away from here anyway."

"Okay, we'll correlate later."

Viktoria slipped away and slid her cake into the refrigerator in the doctor's lounge. Although she thought Jeffrey Appleton was handsome, smart, and considerate, the appointment with him would be strictly business.

CHAPTER 22

Viktoria changed into scrubs while the nurses for the beginning and end of the shift had so much to talk about, the chatter never ceased. Not everyone had attended the CRNAs wedding and not everyone had been around Friday night for the discovery of Dr. Winter's suicide. The nurses and employees in the "know" for either event prided themselves with gossiping about the details.

As she slipped on her clogs, someone mentioned her name. "Dr. Thorsdottir over there found the body. I'm glad it wasn't me. The hospital doesn't pay me enough to discover dead doctors."

Viktoria grimaced. "What happened is a real shame for everyone," she said. "May he rest in peace." The discussion quieted down and the woman respected Viktoria's comment.

Dr. Thorsdottir pushed open the locker room door and hurried to the front schedule on the wall. Dr. Nettle held a hinge of his glasses with two fingers, and with the other hand, rubbed a lens with a cloth.

"Looks like a mighty busy Monday morning," she said.

"No kidding. I can't decide what to do with you. Want to do your own cases or supervise?"

She wondered why all of a sudden she had a say in the matter. Maybe because it was her second week? "If I supervise, I may be of more use to you since the schedule is jammed full."

He hooked his glasses behind his ears and nodded. "That's what I was thinking. Cover rooms three and four to start. I'm putting Casey Johnston and Bobby Wright in those rooms."

"Casey Johnston? Really? He's here and not off on a honeymoon?"

Phillip swiped the air like he was swatting a bug. "Are you kidding? Casey and Jennie live together and take well-deserved, expensive trips when their vacation time comes up. Their wedding was their big bang for the time being. If I know him, he's going to bask in the glory of having everyone talk about the Hollywood drama wedding they pulled off."

"Even so, there must be days' worth of cleaning up to do."

"You don't understand them. They'd rather work in anesthesia for their substantial CRNA salaries and pay the catering clean-up services to do that. They are a smart business couple."

Viktoria grabbed a printed schedule and parted the curtain in the preop holding area for her OR Room 3 patient. Ashley Turner was a sixty-six-year-old woman for a portacath insertion. Her patient shivered under a sheet while a nurse hustled in past her and began covering the patient with a warm blanket.

"I'm Dr. Thorsdottir, the anesthesiologist." She pulled the white blanket up on her side. "Now your teeth won't chatter!"

"Much appreciated," Mrs. Turner said. "I haven't had anything to eat or drink since last night, and yes, I am starving. Look at this shriveled up skinny body. It's you anesthesiologists that won't let me eat. I'm a frequent flier because there's always something wrong with me and surgeons are frequently taking a stab at me."

"Oh no, that's no fun. Well, getting your cancer port in will help a lot so the chemotherapy can be given without your being stuck for blood and IVs all the time."

"That's what I was told."

"Which side is he doing today and which side is your breast cancer?"

"Breast problem is the left and port's going in on the right."

"And can you tell me your other medical problems?" She clutched the pen out of her lab coat.

"Arthritis, a bad knee, a new hip, neck pain, glaucoma, high blood pressure, and breast cancer. And my doctor diagnosed me last year with irresistible bowels."

Viktoria's pen slipped from her fingers. She never heard that one before and the humor of it was endearing. "I hope your doctor meant irritable bowel syndrome."

"Oh, yes, I guess that's it."

Viktoria gathered the rest of the information she needed. "This should not take too long. We'll give you a general anesthetic through a mask and you should do fine. A nurse anesthetist will be in the room with you the whole time and I will be in and out."

"Thanks, doc."

After explaining more to Ashley, she parted the drapes and found Casey approaching. "Morning, newlywed. Congrats again and I appreciated being an accepted guest. It was fun."

"It was. Jennie is psyched. Everyone seemed to have a great time, and she loved being the bride."

"You two make a beautiful couple."

"So, what's the story with our patient and I'll go get some drugs checked out."

"Breast cancer for a portacath. Appropriately, NPO, and we'll watch her for hypertension. Port will be on the right. For you Monday morning comic relief, she has a new GI problem called 'irresistible bowels.' And I was thinking a general anesthetic with an LMA."

"Sounds like a plan. Yes, an interesting GI problem," he said with a smile.

Casey introduced himself to his patient and Viktoria went to see the orthopedic patient, Kenny Abrams, who proved to be a relatively healthy sixty-eight-year-old with arthritis and stomach ulcers. He was well versed with his surgeon's explanation of an anterior hip surgery approach.

It was time to get her second Monday morning rolling at Masonville General Hospital. The second week of doing locum tenens in a new place was usually a more settled atmosphere, but nothing quite usual had been the norm yet for the urban OR. For a second, her mind jumped to later in the day. It would be fun to meet Jeffrey Appleton outside work again, both for the work-related topic they needed to discuss, and the enjoyable social interaction they seemed to have.

Ashley Turner's eyes closed after the propofol went into her IV and circulated through her bloodstream and into her brain. Viktoria handed Casey the supraglottic airway device, the LMA or laryngeal mask airway, and he inserted it into his patient's hypopharynx, covering the supraglottic structures and allowing the isolation of her trachea. Viktoria cranked on the sevoflurane inhalational anesthetic and the nursing staff prepped Ashley's right chest wall for the surgeon.

"Your wedding was magnificent," Viktoria said. "Was Jennie the main planner?"

"She was, and if she was not sure about something, she left the decisive vote for me. Like prime rib versus roast beef, stuff like that."

"You seem to be a very compatible couple. That's rare. It was probably about time you two got married."

"Sure thing." He taped Mrs. Turner's eyes closed and readjusted her beeping pulse oximeter.

"Someone told me that you're a low-income housing landlord too. That must take a lot of time."

"I have hired help, fine workers for me, and they end up with spin-off secondary businesses."

"How's that?"

"For example, when folks get evicted or leave without notice, and don't pay any past due rent, the guys clear out the furniture and stuff that's been left behind. They can either keep it themselves or put it in the second-hand thrift store that they started. It's only for limited hours. This all helps me because the loot they get is part of my deal to pay them. I shouldn't tell you all this," he said lowering his voice, "because it's all off the books. I don't pay them much of a 'salary' but, as you can appreciate, I pay them by other means."

"I won't give you my opinion about your methods. Must be profitable for you."

"Sure. There are a variety of buildings and rental options outside of town, but not all of my places are in the south."

Viktoria nodded as the surgeon came in, gowned and gloved, and asked for a scalpel. He gazed at Dr. Thorsdottir for her okay to proceed. "She's ready for you, sir."

Casey turned around and grabbed his syringe of fentanyl, which was drawn up as two ccs. He pulled off the cap, approached the stopcock, and made a motion to push the narcotic.

Viktoria put her hand out quickly and stopped him. She hadn't even planned to, but the syringe ended in her hand. "Maybe Mrs. Turner didn't tell you, but she requested no narcotics as she thought a Lortab postsurgery would suffice her better. This isn't a significantly painful procedure, and she gets terribly nauseated with narcotics. I told her we would try our best." She glanced back at Ashley's vital signs and there appeared to be no signs of increased pain. She put her hand out, Casey handed her the cap, and she plugged it over the syringe.

"But I checked it out for her."

"No problem. We'll waste it." She turned around, and with her back to Casey, she pretended to unscrew the needle and dump the two cc's in the sharp's container as well as the entire syringe. The full fentanyl syringe she slipped straight into her scrub jacket pocket. Her heart pattered rapidly against her chest. She had never done anything devious like that before in anesthesia.

"Oh," Casey said. "I'll note down the wastage in the medical record. Good thing I didn't check her out a five-cc vial instead of the two ccs." He bit his lip and frowned. "Such a waste," he mumbled.

"Yes, well, a five-cc vial would have been overkill."

"Dr. Thorsdottir, I believe you have made innuendos to me before like that. I wonder if you give your patients the amount of narcotics they need, versus what you think looks better on your medical record, or something like that."

"How about giving patients what they require versus what the anesthetist wants to give them? Or give the patient what the anesthetist is not actually giving them when they should be?"

"What the hell is that supposed to mean?"

Viktoria shrugged and studied his narrowed eyes. "Things are going along smoothly here, so I must step out and start my case next door with Bobby Wright." She peered at the surgical site where the surgeon had made a clear, straight two-inch incision along the patient's chest, and then headed for the door.

"Good morning." Viktoria squeezed to the head of the bed in the next room where the CRNA was waiting for her. Kenny Abrams smiled from under the oxygen mask Bobby held over his face. "I'm ready for this new hip," he said. "Put me under, doc."

"We'll take good care of you," Viktoria said as she scanned the monitors and Bobby began pushing the propofol. Soon the sixty-eight-year old was intubated, positioned, and ready for his hip prep and draping.

"I cannot believe all the goings-on over the weekend around here," Bobby said.

"Yes, that was some wedding."

"Not so much that, but your finding Dr. Winter upstairs. I tell you, Dr. Thorsdottir, there were people who despised and talked negatively about his recent lifestyle hanging around in the hospital, but he was going through a lot and somebody should have spotted his deep despair and gotten him to therapy or something."

"You're spot on, Bobby. He had a serious work-home conflict and that catalyst for physician burnout is often overlooked because of the other major reasons—tremendous workloads, inefficiencies in the health care system, and lack of autonomy. He talked to me a little bit, and I wish I had been more proactive in getting him help."

"During your first week here, did he open up to you?"

"Yes, somewhat."

"He must have spotted your openness to listen. Around here, I think there's a lot of negative talk and derogatory action towards people undergoing difficult times."

"That's too bad, Bobby. So, if you need to justifiably complain about something, my office is open."

"Ha, ha. Where is it?"

"At least for fifteen minutes today, it's going to be in the doctor's lounge. I have a piece of Saturday's wedding cake in there that someone was kind enough to bring me. See? Someone cared enough to think about me to do that."

"You're lucky. Locals like other locals around here and don't adapt to newcomers very well." He checked the nurse prepping Mr. Abrams hip, who was talking shop with the surgeon.

Viktoria nodded. "That's not an impression I failed to notice last week."

"Perhaps you're going to beat the normal record of hostility to newcomers which can last for months around here."

"I'll be gone, Bobby, so I don't plan to find out."

Since the patient's case for a portacath insertion would not take that long, Viktoria swung by the preop holding area to see her next patient and then poured herself a cup of coffee in the lounge. She swung open the refrigerator door, brought out a creamer, and eyed the wedding cake. Too early to eat, she thought, but it was tempting her.

She poured a vanilla creamer in the dark brew and debated to sit down as Everett Benson waltzed in.

"So, did you go to the wedding?" he asked.

"Yes, thank you for encouraging me. It gave this out-of-towner something to do."

"Awesome. You deserved an outing after what you went through Friday night."

"And how was your call on Saturday?"

"Not so bad." Everett grabbed a small orange juice bottle from the refrigerator, plucked a pastry off a tray, and motioned to a table. He was wide-shouldered with long arms and started chugging down his juice in several gulps.

Viktoria sat and crossed her legs. "Everett, every once in a while, I consider permanent placement, so I often compare the salaries of anesthesiologists in different areas. Do you mind if I ask what the docs in this group make?"

"No, not at all. We don't do big cases here, as you are aware. No hearts and no transplants or significant trauma, and our call schedule and hours are not terrible. You may be aware that the hospital pays our salaries, and we're all the same at two hundred thousand a year. Except for our President, of course, Jay Huff. He makes two-twenty. That is because he goes to a lot more meetings to represent the group and has more business with the hospital to attend to. In essence, you could say he puts in work after hours. Me, I hate a lot of boring business meetings."

"You're the youngest in the group. Seems to me that in the beginning of our crazy careers, after finally becoming a doctor, we must get used to being an independent practitioner, and also catch up on extracurricular activities that we put off during med school and residency. The desire to be politically and business minded often comes later. Enjoy these years after working so hard to achieve them."

"So true. Right now, the extra twenty thousand dollars a year that Jay Huff makes isn't the least bit attractive to me."

Viktoria smiled. Everett had his head in the right place. Maybe the president of his group was a lot greedier than being satisfied with the extra stipend the hospital afforded him. She stuck her hand in her pocket. There was something else she needed to attend to.

CHAPTER 23

An 80s song collection piped through the room as Evie walked down the middle of the laboratory aisle towards Viktoria. "You again?" she commented. "Is the department wanting another urinalysis drug screening, even though you and Jennie Shaw came up crystal clear last week?"

"No, not quite. Would you mind running the contents of a syringe through the mass spectrometer?"

The woman adjusted her white collar as she watched Viktoria take a syringe from her pocket—the fentanyl syringe she had plucked from Casey's hands. "Looking for purity of a drug?"

"Or lack thereof," Viktoria said.

The woman sneered from one side of her mouth, and extended her skinny hand. "Put it here."

"Appreciate it."

"Are you going to give me any data about the sample?"

Viktoria flinched. "Would you mind keeping the specimen off the grid until we see what we're dealing with?"

She hesitated. "All right. For the time being."

"I'm Dr. Thorsdottir with anesthesia, in case you've forgotten my name. Don't call me. I'll be back."

"Not today you won't. Check with me tomorrow."

"Sure, I understand. Oh, by the way, Miss Shaw is no longer Shaw. She married Casey Johnston over the weekend."

"I heard about that wedding. Besides our Dr. Winter call room fiasco, a blurb with pictures of the wedding ceremony showed up in the newspaper today. I'm not begrudging that sweet, smart young couple but, by comparison to the apparent estate they have, the hospital must not pay me enough."

"You run a wonderful lab here and most likely have your priorities in order. Not everyone does, you know."

Viktoria felt a nervous rumble ripple through her belly as she left. She reminded herself that patient care came first and foremost over monitoring two CRNAs whom she had become increasingly suspicious about.

Another factor she needed to consider was that Casey and Jennie were well liked and advantageous anesthesia practitioners to the department. No way would she want to jeopardize the department's feedback of her services to the locum tenens agency because of her meddling in business that was not exactly her own.

The dark burgundy pickup truck pulled up in front of the second building of the Stay Long Hotel and Fred jumped out. Although he was a bit late, he was thinking clearly and in the mood to tackle the morning's work. The air was crisp and cool and, so far, there was truth to the day's forecast prediction of clear and sunny.

Ben leaned against the porch railing and Fred sat on the step, both of them milking down a cup of coffee. "You're late, you moron," Ben said.

"At least I don't show up and then take a break," Fred said lightheartedly.

"How was your weekend?" David asked.

"Well deserved." He stood by the bed of the truck and began yanking out equipment. "What's the plan today?"

"I thought David and I would work on the walls and you could replace that cabinet next to the refrigerator. You're so much better at carpentry than we are."

"I would prefer that. Where's it at?"

"Inside," he said, placing his empty cup next to the post and yanking up his pants. The two men went in and slid the new cabinet out of its packaging, and then Fred opened the old cabinet. Spaghetti noodles were sprinkled along the bottom from an open box and crumbs from an oatmeal cookie bag dotted the area. He scooted over and peered under the sink.

Fred frowned as he backed out. "Rodents. Doesn't matter which places we work at, they're ganna be around. As long as there are human beings and food to deal with."

"Quit yapping. That's nothing new."

"I'll contact the boss. Not sure if he wants to be more careful at this hotel than his other places. Maybe he wouldn't want us to spread mice and rat poison around here."

Fred sat on the floor against the counter and pulled out his cell phone.

"Evidence of rodents in building 2," he texted to their boss. *"If it's okay with you, I'll scatter Bromethalin pellets."*

Fred went outside to retrieve his tool box and, while he waited for the word from "The Man," he lit a cigarette. As he enjoyed the chemical in his lungs and the smokiness of the surrounding air, the answer to his question came bouncing back.

"Sure thing. The best time to evict those nasty mammals is when the work is being done."

Fred smiled. His boss loved that word "evict." Now he was using it on rodents besides low-income renters. He popped a thumbs up emoji on the screen, put away his phone, and grabbed two rodent killer PACS from the pail in his truck.

He decided to start outside and leave a trail of pellets along the back, side, and front of building 2. As he sucked the cigarette smoke gently into his lungs with one hand, he shook out one packet, and then a second. He crushed the cigarette butt on the ground, and brought another rodent pack inside. Leaning over, Ben busily stirred a new can of paint with a stick, and David looked over from painting the baseboard.

"You ganna get to work?" Ben asked. "How many cigarettes did you consume already outside?"

Fred reached underneath the sink, spread the pellets, and pulled back out. He scratched the scar on his cheek and stood. "Gimme a break, I'm just following orders. I'll have this new cabinet in next to the refrigerator by the middle of the afternoon while you two are still dicking around over there."

"The sooner the better for us all," David said. "We could hang out here later for a while."

"I'm game," Fred said, dragging his tools over. "As long as Mason doesn't come snooping around."

"He'll be fine," David said. "As long as there's a newspaper at the front desk and the TVs on in the background."

Going back to the OR, Viktoria went straight away to Room 3 where Casey was beginning to wake up Ashley Turner. "Breaks may be tight today," she said, sliding between the anesthesia cart and machine. "Let me take over and you go grab your morning coffee."

"You sure?"

"Don't let me change my mind." She placed her hand on the patient's LMA while she peeled off the eye tape with her other hand. The surgeon nodded and left the room as the RN secured a sterile bandage over the site.

"Record is up to date," Casey said. "I'll leave. Who knows? Maybe I'll bump into Jennie on a break, the first time as Mr. and Mrs."

Ashley's eyes opened, but she let them drift closed again. "Mrs. Turner," Viktoria said, "your surgery is all over. You did fine." With a small cough from Ashley, Viktoria carefully pulled out the LMA, and continued feeding her oxygen. Her vital signs were excellent, so she tidied up the area, and purposefully went to the red sharps' container hanging from the side of the cart. She considered that the top-level of material inside should be the latest waste from the morning. Since, theoretically, Casey had aspirated a vial of fentanyl into the syringe she had brought up to the lab, the cracked-open, empty glass vial should be evident inside.

But as far as she could decipher, there was no such Fentanyl cracked-open vial on top.

Viktoria swung around, took off Mrs. Turner's monitors, and they wheeled her over to the recovery room. After the nurse took report, she leaned over her patient. "How are you feeling?"

"Pretty good. I guess I'm all done."

"Yes ma'am"

Ashley widened her eyes further. "I'm not nauseous and, yet, I don't hurt too bad. You didn't give me any narcotics, did you?"

"I don't believe so. Today that may have been an easy request to fill." She patted the woman on her shoulder. "Be brave. I wish you lots of luck with your battle against cancer."

Just before noon, Viktoria slipped into the doctor's lounge. More doctors were there at one time than she'd seen on any day the previous week, most likely reflecting the heavy OR schedule. There was no lack of patients and cases to talk about; she thrived on the professional discussions, even if she only overheard them.

Under normal circumstances, the lunch selection of sandwich wraps and tuna salad on croissants was perfectly fine, except that it paled in comparison to the feast many people in the room enjoyed on Saturday. She made a plate and sat across from Jay Huff.

Jay nodded hello and held off taking a spoonful of soup. "I don't think I thanked you again for taking my call on Friday night. Made me more assured of showing up at Jennie and Casey's wedding not hung over without enough sleep. Of course, I feel bad for what you had to put up with."

"No problem." She cut her sandwich wrap in half. "Seems to me you were the doc pulling a lot of call last week anyway."

"Sometimes it just falls that way for each one of us. Otherwise, some weeks are lighter too."

"You were on call the day I arrived. And Wednesday too?"

"Yeah, hell. Monday, Wednesday, and supposedly Friday. But this week I only pull one night, tomorrow. Why do you ask?"

With indifference, she shrugged her shoulders. "Always interested in the mechanics of real practices. There is a wide variety to how schedules and shifts are run with each group. You must have a heavy hand in things since you are the President."

His stocky figure shook when he laughed, and he beamed over at her. "I suppose you could say that. I do plan out our call schedule, but I am fair. Each doctor can send me their requests for particular nights they may want to be on call or off call. I try my best to fulfill their needs. In addition, there's more to being the go-between between hospital administration and anesthesia services than meets the eye."

"I bet. I wouldn't want the responsibility."

"Doesn't surprise me. You're a female. Plus, you want to work a rare forty-hour-week. It must be nice."

She responded without looking at him. "You're a compulsive male. God forbid you take time to sniff the flowers."

Jay smiled, like wearing her comment as a trophy. "Not all flowers smell rosy. Aren't you aware that there are seven that are foul-smelling?" He pushed out from the table, bused his dirty bowl and paper plate to the trash can, and slipped out the door.

Viktoria ate the last bite of her sandwich, went straight to the refrigerator, and slid out her cake. The lounge had started to thin out, and she went back to her empty table. Unwrapping the plastic wrap, she smiled at the three-layered cake with raspberry filling and buttercream frosting.

"Are you going to eat it all at once?"

She continued smiling as she glanced at Jeffrey Appleton standing beside her.

"Is there any other way?"

He pulled out a chair and sat down with a look of mischief. "The only alternative is for you to share that, but I forbid it."

"Ha. Good thing."

"May I make a suggestion about where we should meet later? And would you be game for both of us to bring our dogs?"

She peeled her eyes off the cake and locked on to his amber eyes. "Buddy and I would love to meet your Golden. How old is Mattie?"

"She's three. She turns into a frolicking sack of motherly love towards dogs younger than her."

"I can't wait, but where can you eat around here where they allow dogs?"

"How about I pick you up in my dog-proof Jeep, and bring you up to the lake? You'll get out of town and enjoy the drive, which isn't really that long. My favorite, casual restaurant is up there and, yes, they have tables outside. It's called Ricky's Grill and Bar."

"Sounds too fabulous. I do have something to discuss with you."

"So you said. I'll try and get out of here on time. Pick you up by five o'clock?"

"Buddy and I will be ready. We're staying at the Stay Long Hotel."

"Yes. See you then." He fixed a cup of coffee and quickly left.

It was time to try the layered, sweet baked treat from Saturday, which did not disappoint, and practically melted on her tongue.

Bending over at the waist, Ben gathered his painting supplies in a pile. He stood straight, hoisted his falling pants, and looked over at Fred who was sitting on the floor wiping smudge marks off the cabinet he'd installed.

"Damn swell job you did over there," Ben said.

"Thanks. I should say so myself."

"Don't compliment him," David added. "It'll go to his head."

"That's all right. The three of us are skilled craftsmen and deserve credit for what we do. This kind of work is a dying art with the generation behind us. All they do is wiggle their fingers on electronic devices, play games, and watch content on their cell phones. Most of them don't even know how to interact with other human beings."

Fred uncrossed his legs and stood. "We did a day's work by two o'clock. It's time to call it quits, so I'm packing up the bulk of my stuff. I'll check that Mason is buried in the office, and bring us back a treat. I'm feeling generous, so I'm sharing today."

Ben and David exchanged glances. They had started early in the morning, and had done nothing more than eat their packed food for lunch, so they had barely taken a break. Both men raised their eyebrows, and followed Fred's lead to clean up. Fred went out to his truck, and then sneaked to the front office. When he walked past it, he glanced inside. Mason was leaning on the counter, his head resting in his hands, as he stared at a television program.

When Fred walked back to the cab of his truck, he went straight to the glove compartment. He slipped out three glass vials, as well as other paraphernalia from the console. Walking back inside, he found his buddies on the futon, one of the few pieces of furniture left while they worked, shoved up against the window area.

"I'm so damn generous," he said, handing them each a vial, a tourniquet, and other supplies for accessing their veins. They each wore short sleeve T-shirts, so it didn't take long before they each wiped a selected area of their forearm with an alcohol wipe. They helped one another secure an elastic band on their upper arms, and Fred was the first to crack a Fentanyl vial and aspirate the two ccs into a syringe.

"Here," he said, handing the syringe to Ben. His partner poked the needle into the bulging bluish vein where Fred pointed, aspirated blood, and then pushed the contents straight in. Within minutes, the three men successfully succeeded in helping each other out, and they slumped euphorically back into the furniture.

"What a beautiful way to end a work day," Fred commented blissfully.

"Not too much, and not too little," Ben said.

David spun his baseball cap to the side, and tapped Fred's thigh. "I coulda used double the dose, but who's counting when you were generous enough to treat me."

CHAPTER 24

Fred craved more. His head swam around with a great buzz as he glanced at his two buddies next to him, but today he didn't want to stop with two ccs. Plus, David and Ben had their eyes closed, and he didn't want to give them any more of his stash. He reached over to the small zippered pouch and fetched another vial, the tourniquet, and a syringe and needle. He wrapped the band tightly on the arm he had not used a little while ago, and up popped a vein right along the radial, lateral forearm. After preparing the new syringe, he stuck himself, and with little difficulty injected more Fentanyl.

After releasing the tourniquet, Fred held pressure on the site. *Damn,* he thought. *Such bliss.* He propped his feet up on the flimsy coffee table and sunk back. But instead of closing his eyes, a scary thought came to him. Earlier, when he ate his sandwich, he had grabbed a couple of gabapentin from his drug stash and chucked them down with canned soda. He didn't use the drug to relieve any kind of nerve pain, but for its calming and sedative effects. In some ways, he often thought it helped his creativity and tolerance while working.

In his cloudy drug state, he'd forgotten about that. He wished he had not injected a second vial of Fentanyl. Since he couldn't do anything about it, he closed his eyes.

A dream came quickly, so real that Fred believed it to be a certifiable, genuine occurrence. He was sailing on Lake Erie, enduring ten to twenty-foot waves and gusty winds, both of which prevented him from heading towards the shoreline. Farther and farther he sailed from the coastline until he was overcome by the peak of the storm.

Ben's skinny arm rested on the end of the couch and, in his slumber, it slipped off and startled him awake. He didn't know how long he had slept and not a peep or a snore came from Fred or David. Leaning forward, he rubbed his eyes, and looked beside him.

With a small gesture, David's hand moved on his trouser, a peaceful serenity written all over his face. Next to him, Fred's face remained expressionless, and his nose and mouth were still as stone like he wasn't even taking in air. David sat taller. His buddy's chest was damn still too.

Barbara Ebel

Ben's eyes swept over the table and another cracked vial, not there before, was in front of Fred's paraphernalia. He shook his buddy, but to no avail. His lips slightly parted, but other than that he didn't stir.

With a swat, Ben hit David on his leg. "Fred's out like a dead dog," he said.

David leaned forward, turned, and took a stab at jostling Fred as well. "Damn, he sure is. Not even sure if he's breathing." His eyes grew big as he glanced at Ben. "He's going to get us all in trouble."

"Hey, let's get out of here. We don't want any part of this."

"Let's take our used vials and only leave his stuff," David said.

The two men took the cracked glass, checked around for any remnants of their things and hastened out the door.

"I have an idea," Ben said. "Meet me across the street at the breakfast place."

They were both feeling groggy, and drove with extra caution down the road. Inside, they scurried into a booth and ordered from the "All Day Breakfasts" selection on the menu. Each of them downed a cup of coffee to work off the haze in their heads, and contemplated their dilemma.

"I'm ready," Ben said. "I'm making a call. He pulled out his cell phone, looked up a number, and dialed.

A voice on the other end chirped, "Stay Long Hotel. How can I help you?"

"Mason, hey, this is Ben. I was wondering if you could do me a favor?"

"Maybe, maybe not. Just depends."

"Yeah, well, David and I are eating breakfast food across the street. Fred lingered on the job after we left, but he still hasn't shown up, and he was supposed to join us. He's not answering his phone. Can you go tell him to get over here, that we're waiting on him?"

Mason frowned and adjusted his glasses on the bridge of his nose. "All right. Consider it done."

"Appreciate it." Ben hung up and stared at David. "This way, if Mason gets him medical care, or the cops go there, or anything, then we're not incriminated. All that drug stuff in front of him was what he did after we left him today. I don't know a damn thing and I've never touched that illegal stuff."

"I'm clueless too and have no idea where the hell he got it from," David added.

The waitress walked over, topped off their coffee cups, and both men picked at their food.

Mason walked around the counter and out of the office. There were no new vehicles pulling in with customers to register, so he felt fine leaving the front desk. Plus, Monday was their slowest check-in and out day. He strolled over to building 2 where the last workers' truck was parked.

To be polite, Mason knocked on the door. Fred, whom he remembered was the skinny one with a facial scar, didn't answer, so he turned the handle. As he entered, he scanned the fine work being accomplished, but his heart jumped when he looked to the right. Fred appeared to be out cold and suspicious materials for injectable drugs lay on the table.

Mason rushed to the couch and jostled the man as hard as he could. He was the last person to understand anything about medical matters, so with a small cry, he rushed to the landline phone which had been placed on the floor.

"911," the operator said after he pressed the numbers.

"Send an ambulance right away."

The operator waited. "Where to, sir?"

"Stay Long Hotel on north Hospital Road, near the beginning of Erie Trail."

Viktoria changed into street clothes after Dr. Nettle gave her the green light to leave for the day at 3 p.m. Mrs. Turner, her portocath patient, had successfully gone home, and Mr. Abrams was recuperating overnight on the floor with his new hip. She would see him herself the next day, and since it was Monday, she had no patients to do postanesthesia rounds on up on the floor. Any of last week's patients who'd stayed in the hospital had been discharged.

She grinned at her luck to leave on time. Now she would not need to rush a walk and playtime with Buddy, or rush to get ready to meet Jeffrey Appleton at five o'clock. She passed the women in the locker room changing shifts and headed down the staircase to exit through the ER entrance since her car was parked in the back.

Doctors, physician's assistants, and nurses were walking in and out of rooms and sitting at the main desk. Techs rolled monitoring equipment around for medical testing and a visitor rapped on a patient's room and went in.

As she passed the desk, she nodded to a familiar physician. "Mind if I grab a cup of coffee on the way out?"

"Go for it, Dr. Thorsdottir," he said.

"Thanks."

Down the short hallway to the automatic doors, she made a right turn into the small kitchenette. A pot was half full, so she filled a small Styrofoam cup and dumped in a creamer. It was the perfect temperature, fresh and strong, and she was glad for the easy access. Now her energy wouldn't dwindle for the upcoming activities she had planned.

She heard a commotion from the back door before she stepped to the doorway. When she turned around, the first paramedic was passing, so she hastened to watch. He was wheeling a stretcher with a male, skinny patient, and another paramedic brought up the rear. The second man was ventilating the patient with a mask and oxygen.

They passed in a flash, yet Viktoria squinted her eyes at the patient. He seemed all too familiar, and then it dawned on her. Was it one of the workers from the Stay Long Hotel? She could swear he was the one with the burgundy truck who smoked all the time. All she'd have to do is verify the scar he wore on his cheek.

Holding her cup tighter, she tailed them into the acute care room meant for significant emergencies coming in by ambulance. A previously alerted ER physician and staff rushed in.

A paramedic began rattling off information for all to hear. "Got a 911 call, guy barely breathing and not responsive, at the Stay Long Hotel. Some kind of worker. We found IV drug paraphernalia smack dab in front of him." He kept assisting the patient's breathing while respiratory therapy began setting up a ventilator, ready to assist.

"Here's the thing, doc," the other paramedic said. "We tried to insert an LMA, and both of us tried to insert an endotracheal tube, but he's difficult to intubate. We tried our best, but that's why we've come in ventilating him with an oxygen mask."

The ER physician gritted his teeth.

"I'm not trying to step on anyone's toes," Viktoria spoke up, "but I'd be happy to try,"

"I don't mind, Dr. Thorsdottir," the ER physician nodded. "I'm darn proficient at procuring airways, but everybody knows an anesthesiologist is the airway expert. If these two guys, who are damn efficient at what they do, couldn't intubate him, I know he's going to be a significant challenge."

"Say no more." Someone stuck out their hand and grabbed her coffee, and she stepped to the head of the table. In a flash, the airway cart was beside her.

"I'll take a size 3 curved, Macintosh laryngoscope blade, and a size eight endotracheal tube."

She checked the cuff on the tube, inserted a stylet, and signaled the therapist to stop what she was doing. With the mask away from the man's face, the last thing she saw before opening the patient's mouth was a prominent facial scar.

As Viktoria began inserting the laryngoscope blade into Fred's mouth, she recognized the difficulty the EMS providers had faced. The patient's teeth protruded and his larynx was located in an extreme anterior anatomic position making it difficult to position the blade to move the uvula up and to visualize the vocal cords to insert the endotracheal tube. With her proficient set of skills, she managed to advance the tube down and inflate the cuff. But she still could not be sure it went into the trachea and not the esophagus, so she auscultated his lungs and heard bilateral breath sounds.

The respiratory therapist hooked up tubing to the end of the endotracheal tube and ventilated with an Ambu bag. Immediately the staff saw Fred's lungs rise. She sighed with relief and securely taped the tube in place along his mouth. The ER doctor gave orders for ventilator settings and Viktoria snapped off her gloves.

"Thanks for helping out," the ER doctor commented.

"Any time," she said, and glanced at the paramedics. "I know this guy. What happened?"

"Appeared to be an IV drug overdose. We concentrated on him, but glass vials were scattered around, I bet not the run-of-the-mill cheap stuff. Cops were showing up when we left. I wonder if the matter will end up with the DEA."

"Let's get internal medicine down here right away," the ER physician said. "They should be the ones to admit him and start drug screening, toxicology, and a medical workup." He began examining the man, and meanwhile made inquiries to the ER staff going through his personal items from his blue jeans. "Anybody find any information for next of kin?"

"Not a thing in his wallet," someone said, "but we're checking his cell phone."

"He's always working with two other guys." Viktoria glanced at the EMS staff. "Were they around when you picked him up?"

Both paramedics shook their heads, and the taller of the two responded, "The guy from the front desk directed us in but, otherwise, we didn't see anybody."

The activity in the room settled down as each person continued their area of expertise. More paperwork was generated, the paramedics wheeled out their ambulance stretcher, and an X-ray technician sidled next to the bed to snap a chest film, especially to check the endotracheal tube placement. As she noticed the round wall clock, Viktoria realized that she had stuck around much longer than she wanted to. She had been useful, but now needed to hurry to meet Jeffrey Appleton on time.

As she exited the automatic back doors, she couldn't help wonder about the Stay Long Hotel laborers. Thinking back, she had seen Fred outside the breakfast diner last week. Sitting in his vehicle, he seemed hung over or too groggy. The guy had probably been a drug overdose just waiting to happen. At least, so far, he hadn't managed to kill himself.

Viktoria turned the handle to her Stay Long Hotel room to find Buddy wagging his tail and tapping his toenails on the entrance floor. Not aware that his actions qualified as a full dog trick, he spun around with delight that she was home.

Snatching the leash off the counter, she knew his bladder screamed to empty, so they went straight out. Buddy marked every tree planted in the grassy parking lot areas on their way to building 2 where one of the doors had a crisscross yellow ribbon strung across the front. Otherwise, no extra vehicles or law enforcement were around.

A brisk wind blew which caused Viktoria to button the top button on her blouse. She obliged the dog with a two-block walk and returned to talk to Mason in the front office.

"Miss Viktoria," Mason said as he tucked in his hotel shirt. "There was all sorts of excitement here this afternoon. Bet you coulda helped, you being a doctor and all, if you'd been around. One of those guys working here passed himself out and needed an ambulance. I'm going to be complaining to the management to get rid of that guy, if he lives to fight another day. I don't tolerate no shooters or spikers around here. Fred and his tourniquet and syringe injectables are not welcome here."

"I got wind of what happened because he ended up in our ER. He's in good hands and on a breathing machine."

"I wouldn't have discovered him if it weren't for his coworkers calling me to ask what was taking him so long getting out of here. He's gonna make it, huh?"

"I'll check on him in the intensive care unit tomorrow. He's not out of the woods by any means." Craving attention, Buddy gazed at her with his big brown eyes, so she crouched down and petted him.

"He's a good one. Keep telling myself I should own a dog to keep me company. Could double as a guard dog for the weirdos that sometimes walk in here."

"Yes, you should consider that. By the way, do you know where Fred's buddies are? I would be happy to give them a medical update on their friend's status."

Mason rubbed his mustache and shrugged. "Perhaps still over at the diner. Don't know."

"Okay, thanks."

Mason came around and stepped to the door behind her. He stretched out his arms and inhaled the clean, fresh air. "I should ask the owner of this joint if I can tack on a sign under the Stay Long Hotel billboard stating 'Drug-Free Hotel.'"

"Most hotels these days are tobacco free, no smoking allowed. There is merit to your idea, but don't try to ban their alcohol!"

"I wouldn't dream of it."

"See you later," Viktoria said and hurried away with Buddy.

CHAPTER 25

Half jogging with Buddy, Viktoria scrambled to the breakfast diner to scout around for Ben and David. She felt it her duty to let the men know about Fred, in case they had not yet followed up with questions after their friend's hospital admission. But she saw no evidence of their trucks, and didn't spot them near any of the window booths.

"Jiminy Cricket!" Viktoria exclaimed to Buddy. "I'm practically taking my medical job home with me, and I'm running late for dinner. No, *we* are running late because you were invited too."

Buddy sat on his hindquarters and cocked his head to the side. His tail brushed along the asphalt, but he was ready to pop up and resume their pace. She gave a tug on the leash, and they sprinted forward.

In the hotel room, she took care of her pet first and put down his dinner. Scanning down at her clothes, she frowned. In ten or fifteen minutes, Jeffrey Appleton would be knocking at her door, and she wasn't a bit ready.

Hastily, she rummaged through the top drawer and grabbed an off-white pretty top with a nautical design. After substituting tops, she hung a pair of white beads on her neck and matched the necklace with earrings.

Finished eating from his bowl, Buddy scoured the surrounding kitchen floor for any residual crumbs while Viktoria considered what she needed to bring. She had the dogs to think about and wasn't so sure that Mr. Appleton would be prepared for them, so she scooped the bowl into a canvas bag and dropped in a bottle of water. With just enough time before a knock sounded at the door, she used the restroom and ran a moist lipstick across her lips.

Buddy raced to the entrance upon hearing a car door slam outside. After one rap, Viktoria opened the door.

"Good evening," Jeffrey said. He looked fresh and crisp like he'd just showered and dressed. The sleeves of his blue and white striped shirt were rolled up and an expensive watch graced his left wrist. His tan pants fit like a charm and ended at a pair of sneakers that appeared to be brand new.

"I apologize," she stumbled. "I'm a shabby dinner mate who has run behind ever since leaving the OR."

"You may be playing catch-up, but you don't look shabby to me."

"You are too kind."

"And this must be Buddy." Jeffrey squatted and let the dog sniff him. Buddy neared the new man, gave him a nuzzle, and received a good rubbing with two hands in his furry white neck coat.

"He is a beauty, an absolute beauty." He stood, face-to-face with Viktoria.

Viktoria gulped in her air. He was flirting with her, catching her off guard. She tried not to show any embarrassment; it had been awhile since a man had complimented her in one way or another.

"Thank you. Yes, he's gorgeous, and never deserved what happened to him. Not that any dog deserves to be abused."

"An eye for an eye, they say. I believe animal abusers should be faced with the same treatment that they deliver."

"That would solve all animal abuse." She slipped on Buddy's leash, and grabbed the canvas bag and her purse.

"This place looks comfortable enough for a month's stay, but if you're missing something, please don't hesitate to ask. You're free to borrow a thing or two from me. I look after the hospital's OR staff and, personally, would love to see you comfortable."

"Thank you. If need be, I'll take you up on that."

They stepped out and Viktoria pulled shut the door. Jeffrey opened the back of his maroon Jeep and let Mattie jump out. "Better to let them meet on equal terms," he said.

A smile erupted on her face. "She's gorgeous!" The Golden Retriever's coat was picture perfect, and she was young and vibrant. "How old is she again?"

"Three, but sometimes I think she's one."

The two dogs play bowed and tugged on their leashes. There was nothing more they wanted to do but take off and run together. With the dogs loaded into the Jeep, Jeffrey Appleton took off in a northwestern direction towards Ricky's Grill and Bar.

Jeffrey pulled past the large sign by the road announcing "Ricky's Grill and Bar," and into a half full parking lot in front of a dark wooden building with welcoming steps and a porch. On the outside right side were hedges, and beyond that a patio with tables and a sprinkling of customers. Mature trees were abundant as well as several areas of perennial bushes which had lost their flowering petals late in the season.

Jeffrey tried to open the door for Viktoria, but she had already stepped out. They grabbed their respective dog's leashes and sprung the canines from the Jeep.

"Let's spin them for a walk first," Jeffrey said.

Viktoria kept from commenting on the dogs peeing ritual, but each time one of them peed, the other one had to mark over it, Buddy more so than Mattie.

"I think they like each other," Jeffrey said.

"I agree. Do you let her swim much?"

"Quite a bit. I bring her up here at least one day a week. She loves it."

"I'm not sure if Buddy likes the water or not. So far, his favorite thing is playing ball in the back of the hotel."

"That'll do. You need to keep working dogs busy. They are not your average sit-around lap dog. If you put him near cattle, he'd be herding them to the barn."

"That would be a blast to watch. Unfortunately, Long Island is overpopulated. The days of spacious farms are long gone."

They turned around, walked back to the restaurant, and opened the iron gate to the patio.

"Two for dinner and two dogs to keep you company?" asked a young woman.

"Yes ma'am," Jeffrey said.

"We usually keep customers with dogs at this end." She plopped down two menus and utensils on the nearest corner table. "Your server is Melody. Enjoy your dinner."

"Jeffrey, please pick your spot," Viktoria said.

"Right here is fine. And, please, call me Jeff." He tethered Mattie to his own chair and sat down.

"Jeff it is." Viktoria secured Buddy on the back leg of her chair and scooted in. The dogs immediately inched towards each other, tails wagging.

"There's not much not to like here," Jeff said. "I'll order some cheese sticks while you decide."

Melody arrived with a broad, pink lip-sticked smile and rattled off their specials.

"How about a chardonnay and those crab cakes you just mentioned?" Viktoria said.

The woman nodded and Jeff asked for the appetizer, a local craft beer, and a sirloin steak. "Be back in a jiffy," Melody smiled and turned on her heels.

"This is a beautiful evening," Jeff said. "How about we knock off business before pleasure?"

"Sure thing." Viktoria avoided eye contact. He was a handsome man, just her type, and she'd be better off not feeling a further attraction than she already felt.

"We didn't get too far when we were discussing anesthesia services and reimbursement. Even though the hospital is thorough and expansive when it comes to the business of billing for services, they can't double check on everything. But eventually, reimbursement should filter back to the hospital."

"I understand. At the risk of sounding like a snoop or poking my head into business I have no part in, I can't help myself. Promise me this discussion stays between us."

"We have a deal." He nodded and leaned in like they were business partners.

"Since Masonville General Hospital pays the anesthesia department staff and bills all their cases for themselves, have you ever considered that there may be double dipping going on?"

Melody stepped over and placed their drinks and appetizer down from her tray. "Can I bring you anything else right now?"

"We're good," Jeff said.

The waitress gave Buddy and Mattie a pat on the head and stepped to another table.

"Double dipping? I don't follow."

"What if the paperwork for some after hour emergencies went under the radar and never made it to the hospital's list of OR cases? If indeed that is happening, it may be a rare occurrence, and it may only involve one person cheating the system."

Jeff squinted his eyes and squirmed. "Someone is billing cases themselves?"

Viktoria twisted her lips and raised her eyebrows. She took out her cell phone and scrolled to the pictures. She found the photo she'd snapped in Jay Huff's office. "Maybe you can check if this case went through the hospital's billing network."

Jeff looked and nodded. "Forward the picture to me. Should I suspect anyone in particular, or don't you know?"

"If I were you, I would do some snooping around on Wednesday morning regarding the case load during the previous night. Jay Huff is on call Tuesday, tomorrow night."

Jeff rubbed his hand over his forehead. "I hate to hear that. Again, nothing leaves this table. You've given me more than enough to investigate this further myself."

"I'll hold you to it."

"You thoroughly withhold the Hippocratic Oath regarding the business and moral ethics of physicians. How refreshing." He edged the plate of cheese sticks toward her, and she picked one up. "

"Well, most physicians do. In this instance, I hate to be a snitch, but I got wind of a problem and I can't let my conscience just sit on it."

"Thank you, Viktoria." He picked up his beer and tapped it against her wine glass. "Now, on to the pleasure part of the evening." This time he locked onto her eyes.

Jeff slid the remaining cheese sticks to the center of the table when Melody arrived with their entrees. "Plates are hot," she said, placing them down. "Enjoy your meal."

Their forks rose at the same time and Viktoria sampled a golden-brown edge of a crab cake. "Scrumptious," she said, rolling her eyes.

"Would you like a sample?" Jeff asked.

"I'm not shy. Bring it on."

Jeff cut a quarter of his steak and transferred it to her plate while she sliced her second crab cake and slipped him a sample as well.

"Thanks for sharing," he said.

"Partners in crime," she agreed, and tasted his steak. Buddy sat attentive, his ears alert, and his eyes glued between her and the dinner plate. She laughed and looked at Jeff. "We shouldn't, should we?"

"You give him a sample and it'll be like giving a toddler one lick of an ice cream cone."

She hunched her shoulders, getting close to Buddy's face. "Did you hear that? He called you a toddler. But Mr. Appleton is correct. Your desire to have a second, and a third piece of steak will be solicitous, if not demanding."

"Smart dog. He is extremely attentive to you, besides the food. He's in love."

Viktoria straightened up. "He hasn't been with me that long to fall in love."

"Haven't you heard of love at first sight, head over heels, bolt from the blue?"

She speared an asparagus and grimaced by mistake.

"I guess not," he said with a frown.

"No, there is merit to those sayings."

"But not for you?"

"You could say that. My husband mentioned love at first sight after we met."

"But?"

"You are single. Not that this would go any further than this table, but would you like to find out my thoughts about marriage?"

"Absolutely. But I have nothing to offer in return. Seems like you are an Icelandic Goddess come to Lake Erie with words of wisdom and heretofore undiscovered business practices." He gestured with his hand and a smile to continue.

"First of all, look around at the majority of heterosexual marriages you personally know or see. I will starkly tell you the progression of the relationship over time. First, Sally and Simon are lovers. Okay, great—the blissful years. Next thing you know, they are best friends, and the lover part is sliding away over an embankment. Next, the best friend's part is losing steam and you could say that Sally and Simon can be best summed up as two roommates. And here comes the big bang. It's a matter of time before the two roommates can barely tolerate each other. And I mean barely."

Having rested his fork on the plate, Jeff stared in amazement. "Wow. I've never heard what I suspected all along to be verbalized so succinctly. The scary part is that you probably speak the truth." He furrowed his forehead and leaned in. "You seem to have this all figured out, more so than anyone I've ever talked to on the subject. So how do two people start off on a better foot or start off at all, in your opinion?"

Viktoria considered his question, not sure how much she should continue. She was no expert in relationship or marital psychology or psychiatry, but some of what she'd gleaned was from personal experience. After searching his face, she believed he was open minded and curious about her thoughts, so decided to share one more thing.

"Would you like to listen to my spiel about what to ask on a date, especially if you are searching for a true-blue partner or soulmate?"

"Please, absolutely."

"Think about how important first dates, first impressions are. You take in each other physical attributes and facial features, and launch into questions about what they do for a living, what recreational activities they like, their favorite music, places they've traveled to, etc., etc."

Jeff chewed on a succulent piece of steak, all ears.

"Asking what your date's favorite movie or restaurant is, is less important than asking this—you walk into your apartment or house after work, jacket and bag in hand, and what do you do? Walk me through it. Do you get pissed off at your dog who tinkled on the area rug after waiting twelve hours for you to get home? Do you go straight to the refrigerator for a beer and plop on the sofa for an hour to drink and eat potato chips? As the evening progresses, do you have habits that you would camouflage from the person you're dating? Do you have a stash of recreational drugs that your partner would disapprove of, so you use them on the sly? Do you gamble away a huge chunk of your monthly income, or is your down-time before retiring a long session with online pornography? You see, knowing the answers to questions like these will be the information you need to go forward or not in a relationship. At least it would be for me. Not that I followed my own advice the first time around."

Jeffrey washed down his steak with some beer. "Wow. You are so correct. When I start dating someone, I assume they don't have those negative attributes. Better to be blunt and ask."

"Otherwise, you'll find out later what was concealed from you from the get-go." She frowned and speared the last piece of crab cake.

"I don't mean to pry, but it sounds like you speak from experience."

"Ha! My directness will shock you. You could say that my participation in my own marriage is the basis of my knowledge."

CHAPTER 26

"Dinner was wonderful," Viktoria said. "You didn't need to pick up the tab."

She walked with Jeff Appleton along a sidewalk which stretched along a southern section of Lake Erie. Buddy and Mattie bobbed their heads up and down and bumped into each other along the way. Fast walkers, couples, and joggers shared the path and went in both directions. Every so often, a mist flew from the chop of the waves, and sprinkled past their faces.

"The restaurant bill will go on my expense account, so don't worry about that. We had business to discuss and you alluded to a topic that could be very important to the hospital. However, since that was a work-related issue, it means I would like to now really ask you out to dinner, not related to business, but as friends."

She slowed her pace and glanced over. He was studying her face, anticipating her reply. Needing to make a decision, she wondered how innocent his invitation was regarding going out as "friends." But she liked him, and it was not uncommon for her to eat out with male colleagues and friends without her husband, especially since she traveled.

"Sounds like another fine evening. I hate to impose on anyone, but you're my official restaurant tourist guide."

"We can go somewhere different, and we can take the dogs or not."

"If we don't bring them along, why don't we leave them together in my hotel room?"

"Or at my place. They could romp in the backyard. You could spring Buddy from the four walls of your Stay Long Hotel."

"That sounds wonderful. He's all ears." Buddy happened to glance up and Viktoria pointed at him.

"So, tell me more about Iceland. My travels outside the U.S. have been few, so I googled your country and the first advertising that showed up was for some spa called the Blue Lagoon. A tourist trap or a must see?"

"Not a must see, but a must participate. The lagoon's hype is well deserved and it is one of the country's most popular attractions. It's a geothermal spa and the water comes from the geothermal power station nearby. The water is phenomenal, a milky blue color which is due to a high silica content, and it sits in volcanic rock. It looks like something out of the movie "Avatar."

"You can't imagine wading in it in the dead of winter because the temperature of the water averages a hundred or a hundred- and one-degrees Fahrenheit. Quite heavenly. There's a soft white mud which forms on the bottom from the silica and people rub it on themselves because it's healthy for your skin. In addition, it has proven health benefits."

"With your medical knowledge, is that really true?"

"Yes, that's how it all started. A patient with psoriasis bathed in the runoff water from the power plant years ago and discovered that his skin condition markedly improved. Studies confirmed the water's beneficial effect and the Blue Lagoon became a company and opened facilities. If you decide to test your travel legs and set off for the country where the sun never sets, then be sure to prebook your ticket. You can't just walk in there and take a dip."

"So, I can't be a procrastinating tourist. Isn't it too cold in winter? Aren't there far more tourists in the summer?"

"For sure. And you would experience Iceland's nightless sky. Instead of setting, the sun scoots across the horizon. Not that I'm prejudiced, but the country, in my opinion, is the most unique continent in the whole world. One which is the most other-worldly, like it is the diamond in the rough of all countries."

"Sounds fantastic. You are giving me a bug to travel, or at least, to check out places in Iceland."

Viktoria nodded as a sea mist came their way. It made Buddy frisky and he picked up his pace. "Maybe we should turn around. I am not a night owl and by the time we get back to Masonville, I'll be ready to turn in. My specialty dictates getting up way before sunrise and going to bed when people are just finishing their dinner."

"I hear you. I am fortunate that I really don't have to start work until eight o'clock."

They turned and a silence filled the air. The seconds stretched into a minute, but a feeling of comfort grew along the way. They both held their dog's leashes and took in the scenery of the husky trees, the great lake, and their four-legged friends leading the way.

Jeff opened the back of his vehicle when they returned to the restaurant's parking lot and the dogs jumped in. At the Stay Long Hotel, he let Buddy jump back out and Viktoria left him off leash. She petted Mattie on the head. "Nice to meet you, girl."

"I'll see you at the hospital," Jeff said, closing the Jeep door. "How about we touch base and see which day would work out best for both of us to grab dinner again?"

"I would like that. Thanks for the fine meal and for Buddy's opportunity to make a new friend—a girlfriend."

Jeff's eyes met hers. "You're welcome. My pleasure."

Jeffrey pulled away from the hotel and peered back in his rear-view mirror as Viktoria disappeared into her room. As he drove along Hospital Road, his thoughts were stuck on the female Icelander who was the most distinct and interesting woman he had ever met who was also close to his age.

He wondered if the attraction he felt was solely due to the allure of her background. He'd been to numerous big cities, including the Big Apple; and Canada, the Bahamas, and Newfoundland, but he had never traveled anywhere else. Her country appealed to him, although he practically knew nothing about it.

But there was more to her than her country of origin. She was damn independent and brave to be on the road herself and to work in a totally new hospital where she was an outsider. For her job, she needed to adapt to a new environment where she was essentially in charge of patients' lives. He imagined a person needed guts to subject themselves to that.

And her attractiveness. She had a rugged, earthy appearance which he found totally enchanting. No woman he ever dated came close to her figure, looks, or intelligence. There was a magnetism about her.

He pulled into the driveway of his single-story ranch with a fenced-in backyard, let Mattie out in the garage, and opened the door into the kitchen.

"I hope you liked your new friend," Jeff said, letting his Golden retriever go in the house first, "because I really like Buddy's mom. Too bad she's married."

As she drove to the hospital on Tuesday morning, Viktoria's thoughts jumped from one thing to another. On the plus side, she had thoroughly enjoyed her evening with Jeff Appleton the day before and hoped she would more regularly bump into him at work—which could not be that often since most of her time was spent in the OR.

There were other things to attend to as well, such as checking on Fred, the worker from the hotel, especially since she wondered if he had been regularly doing drugs at the worksite. How could his co-workers not have known? How could they not have stopped him? He could have died, or perhaps he passed away overnight. And how on earth were IV drugs like that accessible to someone like him? Was there some underground drug lord in this small town keeping people hooked and stocked with potent drugs that should theoretically only be used by, and in the hands of, anesthesiologists and critical care physicians?

Secondly, did Evie, the laboratory director, finish the mass spectrometer reading of the drug syringe she had brought her yesterday from Casey Johnston's case? Did she verify its content—supposedly fentanyl?

And thirdly, she was way too curious what the results of Jeff's investigation would be regarding the reimbursement-slip, cell phone picture she forwarded to him. What if there was double-dipping going on? The thought repulsed her.

Albeit, physicians work very hard for their salaries and deserve their income, but she knew all too well that some of them become greedy and no amount of money was enough for them. Medicare fraud by doctors and overcharging in other ways was not an uncommon occurrence. Why the hell they did that, she had no idea. What benefit would all that money be to them if they ended up behind bars? Were they bad people to begin with starting out in medical school, or did the comfortable salaries turn them into crooks later on? On the other hand, some doctors worked grueling hours with heavy responsibilities and made a lot less than veterinarians and even CRNAs. She frowned at the discrepancies, and realized how important some specialties were to allow a physician a more balanced life when it came to responsibility, hours, and income.

Viktoria changed in the locker room still mulling over these thoughts and hoped she would be assigned to supervise CRNAs for the day. That would make it easier to be flexible to step away between cases and check off her tasks to do outside the OR. It was Jay Huff's day on call, so he would more than likely be the one running the schedule. After her discussion with Jeff last night, his record of cases tonight, and how the reimbursement tickets would be handled would also be under scrutiny. *Heck,* she thought, *she felt like a potential whistle blower.* Hopefully, she was off base and totally wrong about the President of the group.

She slipped out of the locker room in fresh scrubs, clogs, an OR jacket, and cap, and walked up behind Jay Huff standing at the schedule board, his shoulders sagging as if under the weight of being in charge. He spun to the side.

"Miss Viktoria. Welcome back. I'm assigning you an ortho room and the eye room—bones and eyes. Ready for another day at Masonville General Hospital?"

"Absolutely. I'm looking forward to an in-depth day. Nothing's going to hold me back."

"Glad to hear it. Your patients are ready to be seen in the preop holding area."

Parting the curtain in the holding area, Viktoria found a man and a woman, their eyes glued on her arrival. "Good morning. I'm Dr. Thorsdottir, the anesthesiologist."

"I was waiting on you," the man on the stretcher said. "Not you in particular, but the anesthesiologist—who happens to be you."

"Bobby," the woman next to him said, "quiet it up and let the lady talk."

"Mr. Glade," Viktoria said, "the preliminary notes in my hand indicate you're a healthy seventy-two-year old. Any medical problems I need to know about?" She figured he was active for his age. Trim, with good muscle tone, he filled the stretcher's length with a full six-foot-one frame.

"Except for occasional indigestion with those greasy burgers at the golf course club house, my handicap is seven. So, I'm healthy."

His wife rolled her eyes. "Bobby lives on the golf course. That's why he's finally having his knee replaced, because his arthritic knee is causing him to shoot like someone his age. God forbid."

"Now, now," he said. "A man has to have a pastime besides his spouse."

"Yeah, but you'll be taking your hat off from the putting green to show respect as my casket goes by the golf course in a limousine."

"Honey," he said, "I'll be there for the most important part. After the funeral procession passes, I'll catch up for the preacher's remarks when they lower you in the ground." He laughed, blew her a kiss, and patted her knee.

She gave him a scowl. "Stop and consider that you'll pass away first. Your ears will be ringing when I throw a celebration party."

"Ouch," he commented, not patting her knee this time.

Viktoria stepped up and interjected before they theoretically took out and signed divorce papers right in front of her.

"Mr. Brady, have you experienced problems with anesthesia in the past?" she asked referring to his record. "For your appendectomy or neck surgery?

"Nope. I go to sleep like I do at home, where I don't know anything until the sun comes up."

"For this surgery, I'd like to suggest an epidural. I would insert the catheter into your back through a needle and then medication would be infused which keeps you numb from the waist on down. We would also make you sleepy with IV drugs."

"As long as I don't stay numb forever, like the people who get paralyzed from spinals."

"Spinal paralysis is like fiction, mostly a myth."

"All right then, doc. Short term pain for long term gain. I agree, because I want my golf score to be as good as my age." He settled his hand on the top of his head. Inching his fingers to the back and left, his hair moved with them.

Viktoria finished asking him questions and telling him what to expect. She paused and asked, "Your toupee may be safer left with your wife than wearing it back to the OR."

"I guess so. The adhesive has come to the end of its lifespan and my hairpiece is due for maintenance. I shouldn't have worn it." He pulled it off carefully and handed it to his wife. "Do you mind?"

"No. I told you to take it off."

"You were right, dear. Like always."

Instead of parting the curtains, Viktoria thought it best to give Mr. Brady a touch of midazolam. She brought out the syringe from her pocket and gave him one cc. Closing his eyes as she left, she figured the sedative would do wonders for their marriage before they wheeled him back to the OR.

Her other patient, Viktoria discovered, was late to arrive. "Go get a cup of coffee," Jay told her. "The OR staff needs to resterilize a piece of equipment for Bobby Glade's case, so both of your cases are delayed."

"Holler if you need me." But instead of going to the lounge, Viktoria had other plans. The convenience of a block of free time hastened her steps, and she soon boarded an empty elevator up to the medical ICU.

Exiting the elevator, she walked past the wall divider and the plastic ivy potted plants between the hallway and the waiting room and crossed her fingers that Fred had made medical progress overnight and maybe was off the ventilator. From what she'd heard, the internal medicine service in the hospital had a fine reputation and, hopefully, Fred was on the road to a full recovery.

The ICU doors slid open and she padded in. Heading towards the desk to inquire about Fred's whereabouts and condition, she nevertheless glanced into the rooms to her right. Arriving at the next doorway, she stopped short. Two uniformed men stood inside, as well as a nurse, and Fred was in the bed, the endotracheal tube jutting from his mouth with the mechanical drone of the cycling ventilator, and his vitals prancing across the monitor above.

The man standing at the foot of the bed glanced her way and the man in front of her, facing the other way, turned around. Noticing that she wore scrubs and a white coat, he frowned.

"I was hoping you were some sort of family member, not a doctor," he said. "Nothing personal." He was a tiny man whose uniform would fit someone half her size, and he stepped to the side thinking she needed to be next to Fred's bed. "Are you the doctor taking care of him? When can we talk to him?"

Thinking they were regular police officers, she discovered her supposition to be inaccurate. The emblems on both their uniforms said

"DEA."

"No, I'm not," she said. "I'm an anesthesiologist. I happen to know him from the hotel I stay in while I work here as a locum tenens doctor—a doctor working for a service that provides temporary coverage to a health care facility."

"We've contacted an out-of-town sibling half across the country and found out his father has dementia, so we're striking out. Anything you can tell us about his job. Apparently, he was on a job site at the Stay Long Hotel when EMS brought him in. Is that where you know him from?"

"Yes, and I've talked to him a few times as well as his co-workers."

"Co-workers?" The man at the bottom of the bed chimed in. He was the older of the two with a serious mustache and large hands, one of which stayed hooked to his belt. "Apparently they found him working by himself."

"Nope, there are two other guys. One seems to be their senior, wears a black baseball cap, and the other one had a purposeful habit of wearing his pants too low. I can't tell you much more than that, but I tell you who can. The manager in the front office, Mason, should know about them. Was your division called in for a particular reason? All I know is that he had a drug overdose."

"That information should help because, yeah, we were just given the case and haven't been over to the hotel yet. This guy's drug screen was significant for 100% pure fentanyl, not like the doctored-up stuff we find on the street."

The nurse emptying Fred's Foley catheter bag nodded in agreement and said, "You'd think an anesthesiologist like you had given him the pure potent drugs that were swimming around his veins when he got here."

CHAPTER 27

The little DEA officer glanced at Viktoria and the nurse. "Can either of you guess when he's going to be able to answer our questions?"

"The internal medicine service will be doing rounds shortly," the RN said. "I'd stake a bet it will be sometime today after he wakes up."

Viktoria nodded. "If he has no medical complications, that's a strong possibility."

"Fine then," the officer said. "By the way, I'm Buster, and he's Patrick. And here's my card." He handed one off to both of them and faced the nurse. "Please call us, Miss, when he has that tube out or ask the doctor in charge to call us."

They sauntered out and the RN grinned. "Buster?"

Viktoria chuckled. "Yeah, a big name for a tiny guy."

"It must be a nickname that stuck."

Casey Johnston slapped an OR bonnet on his head and entered the anesthesia office where CRNAs and anesthesiologists were buzzing in and out. He went to his second locker outside of the male changing room and grabbed a fanny pack which he had recently started wearing. Small and unobtrusive, he slung it around his waist under his scrub jacket. It provided extra storage; another place besides the pockets in his jacket which needed the necessities of the day's schedule, pens, hard candies, drug syringes, and drug vials. The fanny pack often secured the vials which he was confiscating out of the OR.

A few steps behind Casey, Jay Huff bounced into the office full of energy and made clear to the anesthesia staff that he was in charge of the schedule and was the doctor on call for the day. "Casey, you're the floater today, the primary person in charge of breaks and lunches. If cases are delayed, etc. etc., I'll have other free people help you out." He turned and popped back out the door.

Jennie Shaw patted the top of the table for her husband to take a seat. Sipping black coffee from a foam cup, she slid another full cup to him.

"Here you go, slow poke. How come we come in together and you're always slower changing into scrubs than I am?"

Leaning in from the same table, Susan Rust eyeballed the two of them. "Now, now, leave the marital individuality alone. If you both do things the same way, your marriage will get stale."

"Yes, Mom," Jennie said.

A cell phone rang and Casey fumbled in his jacket. Pulling out his iPhone, he squinted at the number, and looked with concern at his wife. He leaned into her. "Ben is calling. He knows not to bother me at work."

"It must be important." She waved her hand below the table, signaling him to go take the call. He nodded and exited the OR.

In the hallway, Casey hurried and stopped between the doctor's lounge and Jay Huff's office. He leaned against the wall and slid his finger across his phone to accept the call.

"Ben, this better be important."

"You want to know about this. First of all, Fred overdosed on narcotics late yesterday on the job. David and I got out of there, but had Mason immediately check on him, so he'd call 911. He's at Masonville General Hospital. So, he's out of commission as far as work.

"Secondly, David and I are in the Stay Long Hotel parking lot. We pretty much finished up the room we were working on yesterday, but came back this morning to sweep and tidy it up. See if we'd left anything. However, cops have yellow ribbons over the door. So where do you want us today?"

Casey felt his blood boil because Fred's hospitalization was a significant problem. Would there be questions asked as to where he got the drugs to OD on? He thought about it quickly. Maybe health care workers would just treat his overdose and not dive into his personal drug use. However, if cops had been at the scene, that was the scary part.

"What a screw up." Casey tried to keep his voice low, but it wasn't easy. "Get out of there then. There are two units at the low-income housing project on the other side of town right now that need to be cleaned out— furniture, personal items etc. Both renters left without a trace. Glad I got a month's security deposit out of them to cover the month's rent. Anyway, you know what to do. Keep what you want or move what you don't want to consignment or Good Will and keep any proceeds as part of your salary. Then, give me your input about what else needs to be done—carpet cleaning, walls painted etc. I'll try to look them over in a day or two as well.

"And Ben, no more screw ups. Here's a new rule. No drugs on the job. Shoot up at your own residences from now on."

"I'll pass it on. Sorry boss."

Casey retraced his steps back to the anesthesia office. He made direct eye contact with Jennie when he entered and shook his head. Pulling out the chair in front of the computer, he sat and looked up Fred's whereabouts in the hospital. His name didn't come up on a regular floor, but popped up in the medical ICU. Casey lowered his head and cursed under his breath. He swiveled the chair and whispered to Jennie. "I have bad news. Horrible news. I'll tell you later."

Susan Rust sat across from Jennie and pushed back her chair. "See you later when I need an old woman's bathroom break," she said to Casey. "I think the OR is finally ready for my knee replacement case. I'm going back. It'll be a nice day, I hope. Dr. Thorsdottir is my staff."

"Okay, I'll break you out first," Casey responded.

Casey left after giving Jennie another concerned look. He had time before starting morning breaks, so he sneaked back out of the office. In the elevator, he hit the button for the ICU. He had to visit Fred and absolutely take a peek at his chart to find out how much was known about his overdose.

Passing the plastic plants and the waiting room to the automatic doors upstairs, the ICU doors opened before him. Two officers, like two mismatched tinhorns, swaggered out. He stepped straight past them, his heart taking a knocking against his chest when he saw "DEA" on their uniforms.

Could their presence have something to do with Fred? The possibility was highly likely, more than highly likely. He gulped the lump in his throat as he went straight in. At the nurses' station, he glanced at the board for Fred's room number and grabbed his chart.

Casey stepped around the counter, aiming for Room 3. The RN came out, and they smiled at each other, but without any forewarning, he almost bumped into Dr. Thorsdottir, who rounded the corner after her.

"Casey," Viktoria said. "What are you doing up here?"

At a loss for words, he wanted to ask her the same thing. Why would she be visiting Fred? He was not a surgery patient from yesterday needing a postop anesthesia note. Her being in his room was disconcerting.

He thought fast. "Dr. Huff sent me to find you. Your knee replacement patient has gone back, and they're almost ready for you."

"Thanks," she stammered. "I was on my way back down." She hastened away, but she stayed perplexed the entire way to the OR. How did he know where to find her?

In the OR Jay Huff stared at the board, tapping his pen on top of the main desk, as Viktoria approached him. "Thanks for sending Casey to get me."

Jay gave her a blank stare. "I didn't send him anywhere. He must have done it on his own. Susan Rust is probably ready for you."

Viktoria nodded. Casey clearly lied, but what provoked him to step into Fred's ICU room? She had no answers, but ever since the beginning, she didn't trust him or his wife, and now she was clearer with that fact. As she walked back to her case, however, it was strange that she suspected them of shorting patients of their intraoperative narcotics and the man Casey just visited came in with a drug overdose. She couldn't make the connection, but it was strange nevertheless.

She pushed aside her concerns for the moment. It was time to insert Bobby Glade's epidural for his knee replacement surgery.

Buster and Patrick left the hospital and headed up Hospital Road to the Stay Long Hotel, but not without Patrick breaking down and veering into a drive-through fast food lane. The rest of the drive, he chewed on a takeout breakfast sandwich, and Buster sipped coffee from a go-cup.

Patrick's cell phone, mounted on the air vent, buzzed, and he answered hands free. "I have your home search warrant for the drug overdose user," someone on the other end said. "Swing by the office when you can."

"Thanks," Patrick said. "We're stopping by the hotel, and we'll be by next." He made a left and eased their vehicle to a spot in front of the hotel's front office. He crinkled his sandwich paper in a wad, placed it in the bag, and threw it in the back seat.

The two men entered Mason's office where the middle-aged man was sitting in the back room, legs crossed on the stand in front of him. The DEA officers took in the view of his brown, old-fashioned laced shoes and

Buster hit the ding button on the counter.

Mason's shoes dropped to the floor, he hung up his call, and he came out. "Back again so soon?"

Buster jutted out his square chin and spoke before Patrick. "We came back to ask you what you know about the two other workers who work with Fred Stowe. Names, addresses, whatever."

"I've got their names and phone numbers, but their boss, my boss, would have more details. He's the same guy who owns the hotel. They call him "The Man.""

Buster yanked a notepad from his pocket and placed it on the counter. "I'm ready."

"Ben West and David Bidwell." He rattled off their cell phone numbers and paused. "And the owner is a guy named Casey Johnston. Actually, he owns it with his wife. A woman named Jennie. I heard they just got married."

Patrick took his hands off his thick waist and tapped on Buster's piece of paper. "You never know. Give us a number for this "Man" in case we need it."

Mason added the number to Buster's note and wrote down Casey's name. "Anything to help. My boss is not going to be happy with what happened yesterday. I haven't called him yet. I put that task on my back burner for this morning."

"Thanks for your help," Buster said. "We'll be getting out of your hair. Mind if I fill up my go-cup with some of your coffee?"

"Help yourself."

As the officers left, Mason slipped his hand under the counter, and pulled out his daily newspaper.

After stopping at the office and picking up their search warrant, Patrick put the car into drive and the two DEA officers followed the GPS to a trailer park southwest of the city. Trash cans dotted the entrance where the smooth road turned into gravel and tree limbs arched over the lane in a lazy fashion. After trying to make sense of the addresses, Patrick came to a stop.

Buster tossed back the last few ounces of his coffee and both men scrambled out of the vehicle.

"This is so small-time," Buster said. "It's like we're wasting our man-hours on an insignificant user, not a dealer."

"On the contrary," Patrick said, "our low-key little town is doing well after that meth facility entrapment two years ago. That's what we want, isn't it? And besides, sometimes a little drug bust leads to a bigger drug deal or more significant stash camouflaged behind it."

Buster glanced sideways with a nod and Patrick knocked on the peeling trailer door. Since Fred was in the hospital, the bigger agent figured no one else was about and, with little doing, he unlocked the flimsy lock.

For some light, they left the door open to see the narrow unit not as unkempt as they might have thought. At most, Fred was clearly behind on his dirty laundry pile thrown on the flimsy futon. Buster set out peering into the kitchen cabinets and Patrick headed to the bedroom.

The unmade bed housed more dirty clothes. He checked the side tables which were full of key chains, old wallets, and photographs, and then the narrow dresser. Most of the top drawer held a tidy shoe box. Patrick pulled it out and took off the top. The box had jostled, so some vials had tipped over, but the man's neatness was apparent with his stash of drug vials.

There were 2 and 5 cc solutions for injection but, in addition, 20 cc vials. Patrick's eyes widened. He had never seen the chunky fentanyl size before. Then he spotted the more potent narcotic than fentanyl. The drug hoarder had confiscated vials of sufentanil citrate injection, a potency of 50 mcg/cc, and they were stashed in 1, 2, and 5 cc glass ampules. The CRNA also had a neat pile of 5 cc vials in packages of ten.

Patrick whistled out loud, knowing the opioid analgesic was ten times more potent than fentanyl and should only be used by persons trained in their use, and only if an opioid antagonist, oxygen, and resuscitative and intubation equipment were readily available.

Buster showed up and glared inside the box as well.

"High grade stuff," Patrick said. "This isn't something he got off a street corner. This is some kind of a direct-access, inside job."

CHAPTER 28

After Susan Rust gave Bobby Glade two ccs of midazolam and one cc of Fentanyl, he was barely bothered by the epidural Viktoria inserted in his back for his knee replacement. She taped down the catheter on his back, he lied back down, and the nurse began to prep his knee.

"My legs are starting to go numb," the elderly golf player said. "That's kind-of scary."

"That's because I'm injecting local anesthetic into that catheter," Viktoria said. "You're doing fine."

Bobby slipped his hand up and tapped the OR bonnet they'd put on his head. "Damn good thing you put this hat on me after making me ditch my hair piece. I wouldn't want any of my girlfriends to see me like this."

Susan smiled at Viktoria and secured her patient's arm to the arm board. "Does your wife know about your girlfriends?"

"Nah, I'm only kidding." His voice trailed off as Susan fed him another cc of fentanyl.

Viktoria scanned the work area and Bobby's vital signs one more time. "Looks like we're ready to go."

"Thanks, Dr. Thorsdottir."

"I'll be back." She scooted out of the room and, with a break in the action, headed for a quick cup of coffee.

Jeffrey Appleton sat down at his desk, and leaned forward over his computer screen. He had a pile of work to dive into on Tuesday morning, but there was also the priority of Dr. Thorsdottir's anesthesia billing slip that she had found in Jay Huff's office, a copy of which she had emailed him yesterday.

He opened up his hospital Gmail account, printed out two copies of the email and, without delay, went to the corporate offices on the top floor of the hospital and waltzed into the billing office.

Jeffrey knocked on the department manager's open door as the woman looked up and waved him in. He always figured Sarah Wentworth's sculpted breasts were the work of a plastic surgeon. He approved of her professional attire—her tailored beige skirt and jacket were more upscale than most of the women's attire in hospital administration.

"Good morning, Sarah."

"Jeffrey, to what do I owe the pleasure?" She stood and undid the breast button on her jacket, revealing a silky white blouse. As she pointed to the chair in front of her desk, she wore a full smile.

Jeff's light brown eyes acknowledged her as he remembered her often flirtatious behavior when they met. He wasn't in the mood nor was he interested, but he didn't want to be discourteous either.

"Perhaps you can help me out with this anesthesia record for billing," he said, handing over the copy and declining her chair. "Was it filed with the outside anesthesia billing service for payment? Can you check for me?"

"It must have been a long, involved case for you to show interest. We try to leave no bill unpaid, so I hope to inform you that reimbursement was fine."

"I don't doubt you do an excellent job. I'm actually wondering if somehow the charge slip was lost in a shuffle between the OR and your office, which means it never went to the outside agency."

Jeff didn't take a seat, so she stayed standing and glanced at the sheet.

"I will find out immediately. As soon as you leave, I'll fax this over to the person-in-charge to investigate. After all, if one billing slip fell through the cracks, who knows how many more do the same thing?"

"Precisely, that's what I'm worried about," he said with a frown and turned. "You have my number."

Sarah's gaze followed him out the door. She wished she could use his number for something other than business.

Jeffrey went back to his office, returned phone calls, and dug into one small pile of work. An hour elapsed before he felt the need for a second cup of coffee, so he stretched and headed to the doctor's lounge. Several physicians were at the tables and counter and the television played the local weather.

With a couple of nods and "good mornings," he poured coffee into a hospital mug and spotted Viktoria in a soft chair. The surgeon she'd been talking to got up and left, so Jeff walked over.

"Dr. Thorsdottir, may I?" He pointed to the empty chair.

"Of course."

"Did Buddy sleep as well as Mattie last night?"

"Based on the number of twitches in his sleep before I fell asleep myself, I'd say so."

Jeff placed his cup on the side table between them and rolled up his sleeves. "Ha. Mattie jerks around in her sleep like she's got firecrackers going off in her legs."

"That sounds disruptive. How is your day going so far?"

"Fine, but you're the one with the more important responsibility of putting people to sleep and waking them back up again. If you do something wrong, it can be catastrophic. If I goof up with something on my agenda, no one will be paralyzed, narcotized, or not wake up because of it."

"I've had lots of training just like you in your current business profession which hinges on your clinical years. And as you know, I don't always render general anesthetics. Right now, a man is having his knee replaced under an epidural. It's the perfect anesthetic for the case." She smiled and nodded.

"I take it you enjoy doing regional anesthesia. You don't smile a lot, and you just expressed your pleasure."

"Don't smile a lot?" She tilted her head, and knew that to be true, but wondered how he would respond.

He widened his smile and took a few seconds to consider her. "In my opinion, you are not an unhappy person. However, you carry a serious expression on your face quite often. Maybe you adopted it during childhood, from the rugged environment you grew up in."

"I never break down with laughter like some folks do, and I certainly worked hard as a child. Not unlike some kids in the U.S. who grow up on farms and ranches and get their hands dirty on a daily basis. You're right, though. I only hope I'm not too staid or gloomy."

"I bet your husband doesn't think so." He raised his coffee cup and took a sip.

"Often his perception of things is altered, so I don't know."

He wondered what she meant, when his cell phone rang. With a nod, he waved his finger in the air, acknowledging a call he was waiting for. "Sarah," he said, "anything to report so soon?"

"Of course. I tracked that anesthesia slip down pronto. But, in other words, there's no record of it being submitted. It was never sent to billing."

Although he suspected the news, he still gritted his teeth at the truth. "Nice work, Sarah."

"You're welcome. They are also going to go ahead and bill for that case."

Jeff peered over at Viktoria. "I can tell you the results. It won't get paid because it's been sent in for payment already."

"What? By whom? Jay Huff?"

"Give me a few days, and we're going to have to put our heads together about this. I may need to bring this to the attention of Cathy Banker."

"If you're talking about bringing this to the attention of the CEO, then I'm with you."

"One shady 'lost' reimbursement is one thing. I'm going to follow up with you again tomorrow about the possibility of more."

"I was hoping we could work closer together," she said, her voice flirtatious.

Jeff frowned, his brown eyes still on Viktoria, and he ignored her remark. "Talk to you tomorrow."

"Was that about what I thought it was about?" Viktoria asked.

Jeff leaned over, and lowered his voice. "Yes. The billing office checked on the information you sent me. They have no record of that case being submitted for payment."

"I hate to hear that. I was hoping it was not true. Means we should check on what happens with the case slips tonight."

"Exactly."

The door opened, Jay Huff strutted into the lounge, and veered straight for the donuts.

"Buddy gets his stitches out today," she said, changing the subject. "I am like an excited kid wanting him to earn a clean bill of health on his back leg. He's become so important to me. I should have had a dog before now."

"But then you wouldn't have had Buddy. Specific dogs come into our lives when and how they are supposed to—when we both need each other the most. And you have been a God-send, caring for him the way you do."

Viktoria became emotional. She nodded and took a big breath, clearing the sentimentality she felt for the dog.

"Thanks, Jeff." They both rose and, carrying his coffee along the way, they parted outside his office.

The first person Casey earmarked for a morning break was his own wife. Most surgical cases were underway, and without a prompt from Jay Huff to begin breaks, he went straight back to the OR rooms.

He slipped into OR 9, where Jennie was settled at the head of the table with a general anesthetic underway for a lower leg debridement of a diabetic. The surgeon was engrossed with removing the dead skin and tissue and chatted with the tech about the little care his patient had taken to prevent the infection in the first place. He wiggled between her and the anesthesia cart and crouched down.

"I came to give you a break first," he said softly.

"Being married to the floater has its advantages," Jennie joked. "What did you find out in the ICU about Fred?"

He gave a disapproving shake of his head. "That damn idiot overdosed on our drugs. He's on the ventilator, and it gets worse than that. Two cop types with 'DEA' on their shirts came walking out of the unit when I went in."

Her smile faded. "Perhaps that's just a coincidence and has nothing to do with Fred."

Casey looked at her like she had three heads. "Are you injecting yourself with drugs too?"

"Shh. Just keep your cool. Why don't we lie low for a while while this blows over?"

He grimaced and rose. "Give me the rundown about the patient and take your break."

Jennie rattled off the pertinent information about her fifty-eight-year-old diabetic and his anesthetic care. Casey studied the syringes and vials on the top of her cart.

"What can I take from here?" he whispered. He picked up a 2-cc vial of fentanyl and a 2-cc vial of midazolam.

"Are you crazy? Didn't you just hear me?"

He didn't like her telling him what to do. It was his original drug operation and scheme to pay the low life's working at his rental properties with IV injectables and the left-over furniture and remnants from abandoned units instead of cash or salaries. Most of his workers used the drugs themselves, but if they were secondarily passing them on or selling them, it didn't matter to him.

Besides, he thought, many of them didn't know his real name or that he worked in an OR—which was the source of the pure, non-doctored drugs that he paid them with. His actions were too slick. He received a chunky big salary as a CRNA, but his sideline because of that profession, in essence, paid him even more. Double dipping was the way he saw it and, to qualify, he had only needed to graduate from nurse anesthetist school.

Jennie bumped his elbow, waiting for a response. She was adamant about him not continuing to pocket drugs until the heat of the situation went away.

He glared at her and became increasingly annoyed. Many of the fine things in her life were due to his illicit dealings.

"Go," he said. "Take your break before I change my mind and go give someone else a break."

"You wouldn't dare." She grabbed her cell phone from the cart, stuck it in her pocket, and eyed the drugs before stepping away. *There was a strong chance her husband was going to steal them anyway,* she thought, *and realized he was more addicted to the art of robbing sedatives and narcotics than his workers were hooked on the substances he provided.*

Viktoria went into her total knee replacement room where the orthopedic surgeon was full swing with tools and implements over the patient's bent knee. She swiped her eyes over the surgical field to evaluate the patient's blood loss, and found it to be minimal because of the adequacy of the tourniquet on Bobby Glade's upper leg.

"How's he doing?" she asked Susan.

"Very well. He's healthy for his age which helps enormously."

"Why don't you go take a morning break?"

"Are you sure? Casey Johnston is the floater. He may be by soon, especially since I'm the oldest CRNA in the group, and he knows my bladder doesn't last like the rest of them."

"I'm free at the moment. Please, go ahead, use the restroom and grab a drink and a bite to eat." If she could, she wanted to give her own CRNAs a break and keep Casey out of her rooms.

"All right, Dr. Thorsdottir. Appreciate it." She ambled out of the OR and Viktoria turned her attention to her patient. Mr. Glade was nicely half sleeping with the nasal cannula oxygen in his nostrils and unaware of the major work being done on his knee.

After five minutes, Viktoria sat down. Her phone had dinged earlier, and she checked to make sure it wasn't work-related. A message had come in from Rick, only letting her know that he was potentially doing something.

"Someone contacted me and is sending pictures of three pricey paintings for my upcoming online art auction. I should make a pretty commission on them! Insurance business slow the last two days. How are you and how's the dog?"

She never, ever answered personal text messages while caring for a patient, so she put her phone back in her pocket. Rick knew that as well, and, for sure, he didn't necessarily expect an answer. *He was just letting her know that he was doing a half hours' worth of work today,* she thought, *and grimaced.*

Susan Rust came back in another ten minutes and Viktoria left with only one thing on her mind. It was time to find out if Evie, the laboratory director, had the results of the syringe's contents she had left with her the day before.

CHAPTER 29

The clicks and buzzing of machines in the laboratory reminded Viktoria of cicadas rubbing their wings deep in the forest. She looked up and down two aisles and found no employees. Finally, she heard a voice.

"Dr. Thorsdottir," Evie said. She approached from the side and pushed back her streaked gray hair. Her expression stayed serious as she shook her head.

"Now I understand why you wanted the fentanyl syringe evaluated. There's not a trace of narcotic in it. The syringe contained Lactated Ringer's solution, your OR standard fluids."

Even though Viktoria anticipated the result, she shuddered. Her heart thumped against her chest thinking of the sheer devilishness of diverting pain relief away from a patient for some sinister, narcissistic motive.

"I wasn't ready to hear that."

"Who would be, if I'm assuming someone is playing tricks in the OR?"

"Can you please document our encounter? It may serve as some kind of record that I at least came to you for an analysis."

"Sure. Give me your email address and I'll send you what transpired between us."

"Appreciate that." Viktoria turned on her heels and left, but outside in the quiet hallway, she leaned against the wall. Casey Johnston was a thief and, quite possibly, so was his wife. It was one thing for a person to steal something they shouldn't, but in this case, it had a direct bearing on patients. People who put their utmost trust in an anesthetist while they are unconscious and undergoing a surgical procedure. Someone committed to the Hippocratic Oath to 'do no harm.' Someone who must uphold the highest moral standards while caring for someone totally dependent on them and everything they do during that critical time.

Casey's patients were unaware of their blind faith in him. The more she pressed back against the wall, the more her blood boiled. And what was he doing with the drugs he was stealing? In her opinion, he and Jennie never seemed to exhibit behavior that would hint at being high or sedated with drugs.

His presence at Fred's bedside, however, was strange. Her instinct told her his overdose and Casey's drug confiscations were related. The little DEA man had given her his card, to call if she had any information. Would she be a pest or an inappropriate whistle blower if she called and gave them Casey Johnston's name along with her suspicions?

Where she came from, if a person inappropriately cries wolf to a law enforcement agency, they deserve the reputation of a rat—a very contemptible person. She bit her lip, too hard for her liking.

Damn, she mumbled, before realizing that she was in the perfect position to say something, if something should be said at all. She was an outlander, not part of the anesthesia group, and the worst that could happen to her was a bad review to the locum's agency. There again, the agency would understand her moral dilemma, and her speaking up about the corrupt goings-on would have nothing to do with her fine anesthesia skills. She was also on fine terms with Regina, the woman in charge.

Screw it, she mumbled for a second profanity in a row. She slipped out the DEA agent's card and placed the call on her iPhone.

"Buster here."

"Hello again. This is Dr. Thorsdottir. We met earlier today in the ICU at Masonville General Hospital."

"Yes, ma'am. What can we do for you?"

"I hesitated to call for several reasons. My imagination may be working overtime, and I may be wasting your time. I also may be out of line in telling you this."

If Buster had learned one thing on the job, it was that a piece of information thought by someone to be frivolous could be the key to a puzzle. "Please, Doctor, I'm all ears. You won't be out of line, not with me anyway."

Viktoria flexed her knee, and put her foot against the back wall. "I am a temporary doctor at the hospital, so I am not a local who's been working with the OR staff here for a long time. Certain codes of conduct exist for practicing anesthesia regarding the use, accounting for, and disposal of sedatives and narcotics. Working with one or two of the nurse anesthetists, I have had reason to question their behavior."

"You have my attention."

"From a case yesterday, I had the lab analyze one of these CRNAs syringes which was labeled as the narcotic fentanyl, but the analysis turned up no narcotic at all, only regular IV fluids. The implication is that narcotics are being diverted away from patients and stolen. On top of it, and perhaps an unattached coincidence, this anesthesia nurse seemed to show an interest in the ICU this morning in the drug overdosed patient you visited."

"What's his name?" Buster asked, glancing at his partner.

"Casey Johnston."

Buster pulled out the name that Mason had given him earlier. "How do you like that? The hotel manager also mentioned him this morning. A jack of all trades."

"What do you mean?"

"He owns the Stay Long Hotel and employs the handymen doing the work, including Fred, the man on the ventilator. Who, by the way, has a stash of drug vials in his trailer. This Casey guy is also a slumlord, and owns lots of low-income housing projects outside of his nine-to-five."

Dumbfounded, Viktoria dropped her leg to the floor. "Like vials from the OR?"

"We assume so."

"You could talk to the anesthesia tech in the OR who does the ordering. Lot numbers are stamped on vials purchased and you could compare them with the ones you confiscated."

"Perfect. Text me the direct number. In the meantime, we'll be getting a search warrant for this Casey nurse."

"It's becoming clearer how he affords the house and property he owns with his new wife, the other CRNA."

"In Masonville?"

"Wait until you see. I'm from Long Island where there are politicians and actors' estates to the east and their places aren't even that gorgeous."

"Sounds like we're in for an eye-opening visit. Is this couple at work in the hospital today?"

"Sure are. You'll have the place to yourself."

"Can't wait," he said and laughed. "We'll be in touch, and thanks so much for your help."

"Would you mind keeping my name out of this?"

"Don't know what name you're talking about."

They ended the call and Viktoria took a big breath. Her arms quivered as she put her phone away. Sooner or later, the vibrant, successful newlyweds were going to get what they deserved.

For the second time that day, Buster and Patrick held a search warrant. Their GPS took them down a long, beautiful street that they never knew existed in Masonville. As Patrick drove, he gulped down the coffee he'd bought at the drive-through window, while Buster still blew on his to cool it off.

"I don't get it," Buster said. "How you finish drinking down steaming hot coffee while I haven't even started mine. Is your mouth immune to heat, like a heat-resistant thermos or something?"

"My oral mucosa is normal. Your mouth is what's sissified."

"Sissified? What the hell is that supposed to mean?"

"Girlish. You've got a prissy mouth."

"Damn. Good thing we're partners and get along, except for our stark difference in the ability to consume coffee, otherwise I'd pull my gun out at you."

Patrick shrugged and then grinned at Buster. The DEA officer pulled forward to the first visual of Casey and Jennie Johnston's home and the two officers exchanged glances. Patrick whistled.

"I smell a drug bust," Buster said as they parked in the circular drive, and set foot between two manicured areas of knockout roses. Patrick took the steps first and rang the doorbell on the great door.

"They're at work," Buster said, still nursing his coffee.

The door opened to a chunky woman with love handles testing the sewing job of her black top. With a look of surprise, she stared at Patrick's DEA emblem.

"Ma'am, are the owners home?" Patrick asked.

"No, can I give them a message?"

"If you would like. However, we came with a search warrant and would like to come in. We are Drug Enforcement Agents here to do a job." He showed her his paperwork. With skepticism, she narrowed her eyes.

Buster opened his wallet and showed her his official badge. Then he pointed to the judge's signature on the warrant. "This is official ma'am. Here is the presiding judge's signature for us to come in and take a look around."

Fidgeting with her hands, she stepped back and allowed Patrick to enter and go his own way. She hurried back to the kitchen, wanting to use the landline phone to call Jennie.

The sound of the agents' footsteps echoed in the foyer. "My first choice is to check the office over here," Patrick said. "Why don't you go search the bedroom?"

Buster nodded, knowing his partner may not be skilled at drinking coffee, but he was aware of the likely places that crooks stash their loot. He stared at the artwork on the wall on his way up the circular staircase to the second floor. *Although the stuff must cost a fortune,* he thought, *there was no accounting for taste.*

Entering the master bedroom, the king bed was unmade, so he figured the housekeeper had not made up the room yet. He began opening closets and drawers, and peeked behind art on the wall for any wall safes. Nothing suspicious turned up, so he sat on a cozy armchair and scanned the room visually again.

His eyes locked on the platform-style bed. He stepped over and held up a corner of the mattress. Sure enough, there was no box spring, just a full board underneath which the mattress rested on. Which also meant he couldn't see between the board and the carpet underneath. The oak base of the bed wrapped around the entire bottom periphery of the bed, but that didn't stop him from investigating.

On his hands and knees, Buster evaluated the side board closest to him—all one single solid piece of wood. Nothing unusual. He crawled around the corner to the bottom where he noticed the pane split into two. Putting his fingers under the oak in front of him and prying, it was solidly in place. He scooted over to the other side, and wiggled his finger between the board and carpet and pulled forward. The pane raised with a smooth motion, a clever mechanism in place on both upper corners.

Buster wiggled his hand into his pants pocket for the light on his key chain and shined it into the dark space. What he saw looked like a large plastic shoe organizer for underneath a bed, so he frowned with disappointment and pulled it forwards.

He sat back on his haunches to see his hunch was correct. It was a shoe organizer with twelve adjustable dividers and a zippered closure with a semi-clear window. His cop instinct ramped up because he detected no bulkiness or unevenness to whatever shoes were inside.

Starting from the side, Buster unzipped the organizer and peeled back the cover. *Some shoes!* he thought, allowing a smile to light up his face.

Instead of twelve pairs of shoes, the almost three foot by three-foot container held high-end narcotics and sedatives. Even propofol vials.

"Bingo!" Buster exclaimed. "Straight from the operating room!"

Jennie's housekeeper, Marybelle, positioned herself by the kitchen wall and picked up the landline phone. Working for the Johnston's for one year, and being severely devoted to her successful, rich employers, she could not fathom why two law enforcement men had come in with a warrant to search the couple's home. Jennie and Casey were totally fair and appreciative bosses, always empathetic if she came forward with a special request for a day off or a last-minute emergency. She had also agreed, when they had made the request, that she should contact them if ever anyone showed up that seemed to have no business being there.

She had a stronger bond with the female of the house, so she dialed Jennie's cell phone number, something she rarely did. Her employer answered immediately.

"Marybelle," Jennie said with dread in her voice, "is everything alright?"

"Two men are here at the house. They showed me a piece of paper, a search warrant. I let them in because it appeared to be genuine."

Jennie gasped into the phone while her heartbeat galloped faster than her monitored patient stimulated by surgery. She held the phone tightly trying not to sound alarmed. "Are they cops?"

"Drug Enforcement Agents. This is crazy. Why would they be here?"

Jennie stared at her patient under a general anesthetic and wished she were unconscious like her patient. The reality of what her housekeeper just said was unbearable. She was always the one a bit leary of the "business" she and Casey ran on the side but, nevertheless, she had participated of her own free will. The idea of those guys at her house was damn scary. Yet, were they as smart as Casey to discover his hiding place for drugs?

Marybelle was still on the line, as Jennie also realized for the first time that the DEA could use drug dogs when and if needed. Could their trained dogs detect drugs that came in glass vials? She shivered realizing that she knew nothing concrete about the law enforcement or legal aspects of what they had been doing. Certainly, they'd be in trouble and their jobs would be in jeopardy, but it was not like they were street drug pushers jeopardizing the lives of young people.

"Marybelle, try not to worry. They must have made some kind of mistake. Please text me soon with any developments at all. Like if they are taking anything out of the house, or if they say they're finished. Anything at all. I'll let Casey know what's going on."

Jennie gave it another thought. "Where are they right now?"

"One of 'em is upstairs and one of them is down here. But the one in the master bedroom just called for the other one to go up there to see something."

Jennie thought she'd stroke. A crushing pain enveloped her head, and she gritted her teeth. "I better let you go," she said, "text me instead of calling."

She ended the call and immediately scrolled to Casey's number and hit "message." At one time, they had discussed an emergency text to use for each other. Although she had never had an occasion to use it, she went to numbers and typed "7777." The lucky numbers were an alert, warning Casey that she meant just the opposite of a lucky situation. He would understand that something was terribly wrong.

Patrick stood over the couple's drug loot that Buster had pulled out from underneath the master bed. He lowered himself on the mattress and looked up at his partner. "People's ingenuity ceases to amaze me."

"Yeah, but we've got them red-handed. This'll be a damn quick closure of a case if we acquire more definitive proof about these drugs. I'm good for working straight through this evening. We can bring the rich Masonville couple in before they try something stupid. How about we split up? One of us should go to the Hospital's OR. Follow up on what Dr. Thorsdottir mentioned checking vial lot numbers with the technician there. That way, when we bring them in, we practically have all the proof we need. A lawyer can hardly help them weasel out of this one."

"I'm in. Nice work finding this stuff." Patrick took out a notepad and began writing down at least one vial number of each lot housed in each shoe section. "I'll go to the hospital. You call the office and ask for help to confiscate all this stuff."

"Sure thing. Plus, I have to scout around for other drug paraphernalia. My take on this is that the owners of this house are pretty smart. They avoided doing drugs themselves, and unloaded them on other sorrowful souls who sought to ruin their own lives in a cloud of amnesia and mental impairment. Wasted enough to need life support on a ventilator."

Patrick nodded. "They weren't smart enough to not get caught. However, I wish it had been sooner." He turned and checked out the walls again. "They do have decent taste in artwork."

"I wouldn't hang this stuff in my house if my life depended on it."

"Artwork is in the eye of the beholder. You need your vision checked."

"Says you," Buster said, getting in the last word as his partner left.

Downstairs, Patrick stopped in the kitchen and ran the faucet for a glass of water. Marybelle sat motionless on a stool, one hand gripping her iPhone resting on the counter.

"Have you contacted them?" Patrick asked.

The housekeeper's eyes widened. "Surely I had to. If I hadn't, they could fire me for letting strangers in, cops searching the place, without telling them. You must understand, I am a faithful employee, and this job is what pays my bills."

Patrick gazed into her eyes as her face scrunched up like she was ready to cry. He put his hand on her shoulder.

"Your employers may have a rocky time of it in the near future. I would start looking for another job if I were you."

CHAPTER 30

At three o'clock, Viktoria reported her cases in progress to Everett Benson, who was the late doctor of the day behind Jay Huff's night on call. She checked on Bobby Glade as the orderly began steering him out of the recovery room.

"Hey, doc," he said. "Nice job with that anesthesia. Can you believe it? My leg is still a little numb and I don't feel any pain!"

"That's the beauty of an epidural. Not only does it work for surgery, but it can continue postop pain relief. I'll be by personally to check on you upstairs tomorrow."

"My hair will be back on, so look for the handsomest male patient on the orthopedic floor."

"I'll remember that."

Viktoria shook her head as she passed the front desk where Jay Huff sat discussing after hour cases with the head nurse. "Enjoy the evening," he commented as she paused.

"Many add-ons for the evening?"

"An emergency burr hole and two orthopedic cases so far."

"Hope your night is manageable."

She went straight to the locker room where she changed into street clothes. An RN wished her a pleasant evening, making her grateful that the hostility she felt the previous week had somewhat diminished.

Wearing tan cargo pants, blue sneakers, and a smart polyester blouse, she set off for the hallway, heading for the elevator.

Patrick had no use for hospitals. Splitting up with Buster to go to Masonville General Hospital was a fine idea, however, he wanted nothing to do with sick people. When he entered the lobby, he went straight to the information desk where a woman sat wearing a pink volunteer smock. "If I need to speak to someone in charge associated with the operating room, but without subjecting myself to patients, where should I go and whom should I talk to?"

The elderly gray-haired woman stared at him for a moment—official uniformed men were a rarity at her counter. "See Mr. Appleton, the Director of Surgical Services. His office is in the hallway on the second floor before you get to the OR."

"Thank you." Patrick rode the elevator dodging the scrutinizing glances from fellow riders. On the second floor, he took off down the corridor and easily found the nameplate on the wall for Jeffrey's office. The door was slightly ajar, so he rapped lightly and peered inside.

Jeffrey glanced up from his desk, his countenance changing when he saw the man in a uniform, and he stood up. "Come in."

"Patrick McCormick with the Drug Enforcement Agency." He grasped Jeff's hand and shook firmly. Each man stood over six feet, but Patrick was built like a heavyweight boxer compared to Jeff's trim physique. "The volunteer at the information desk downstairs suggested I start with you."

Jeffrey furrowed his brow and tilted his head to the side. In the hallway, Viktoria passed, but she stopped and peered back into his office. "I don't mean to interrupt," she said to Jeff, "but have a nice night."

Patrick spun around. "Well, if it isn't Dr. Thorsdottir."

"You two know each other?" Jeff asked.

Viktoria stepped into the office. "I met Patrick and his partner up in the ICU."

"I wouldn't be here if it weren't for this astute doctor's lead. There's a problem, Mr. Appleton, and I'm here to track down drugs believed to be stolen from your operating room. This young doctor suggested we check lot numbers from the anesthesia technician. What she doesn't know is that we've confiscated a pot of gold—fentanyl, sufentanyl, midazolam, and propofol—at the home of two people who apparently work here."

Speechless, Jeffrey let his jaw drop. He looked back and forth between Patrick and Dr. Thorsdottir and then settled his gaze on Viktoria. "You've been figuring this out in addition to the most-likely reimbursement scam?"

She grinned and nodded. "I suppose so."

"What reimbursement scam?" Patrick asked. "Is that something the DEA or cops need to know about?"

"We'll keep this problem internal," Jeff answered, "but thanks for asking."

"Suit yourself. Would one of you mind pointing me in the correct direction and introducing me to the anesthesia technician, so I can begin asking her or him questions?"

"I'm out of scrubs," Viktoria said, "but we can access the anesthesia supply room from a back door not through the OR."

"Viktoria, are you sure?" Jeff asked. "Aren't you on your way out? I could show him."

"I'll get the ball rolling. I must tell you something on my way back out, but maybe you can check on Mr. McCormick here in a few minutes to make sure he's getting everything he needs."

"Okay. See you shortly."

Viktoria led Patrick through the hallway and a non-sterile area. The door to the workroom was open. She was glad she guided him back so as not to prance him through any of the main areas where word would be out that the DEA was in the OR. She wondered if Jennie and Casey would think about why the DEA man was there. If the couple made a connection to their anesthesia drug activities, would they be a flight risk or make every effort to cover their tracks?

The anesthesia tech was not present, so Viktoria texted her number and asked her to stop by the workroom. Soon an animated young woman with a long ponytail scrunched under a bonnet came strutting in. Nervously, she put her hand over her mouth upon seeing someone official-looking in her work space.

"Tina, this is a DEA officer, Patrick McCormick. He has some questions to ask you. His visit is also okay with Mr. Appleton, but don't gossip about this to anyone in the OR. What he needs to ask you is confidential and important."

"Okay, Dr. Thorsdottir. I'll help in any way I can." She straightened her shoulders, now feeling extremely important.

"Thanks," Patrick said to both of them.

Viktoria shuffled out, straight back to Jeff's office. Once inside, she pulled the door fully shut. "I can't afford for anyone to overhear me."

This time, Jeff came around and leaned against his mahogany desk. "Viktoria, I am overwhelmed by your moral standards and am shocked over what I just heard."

She nodded and frowned. "McCormick is talking to Tina, so be sure and follow-up back there."

"As soon as you leave."

"I can't stay long. I need to spring Buddy from the hotel room to walk him, and bring him to the vet. I'm like an over-concerned mother until his stitches come out on his back leg."

"I'm sorry you have been delayed. Our pets are family to us and you are closer to that dog in less than two weeks than some long-term pet owners I know."

"Thanks, Jeff. There are three add-on OR cases already which will not be found on the printed schedule from this morning. One is a neurosurgical burr hole and the other two are orthopedic cases. You know what to do with that information, which did not come from me."

"I will check myself for those anesthesia reimbursement slips which should go to billing in the morning, as well as any other add ons I find out about. Jay Huff is still the doctor on call, correct? That has not changed?"

"Still the same."

Jeff pushed off from the desk, which put him and her close. Very close.

Viktoria took a deep breath as her heart thumped against her chest. His soulful eyes were searching her, making her feel like a schoolgirl, a young girl being flirted with by the male class dreamboat. *It was stupid of her,* she thought, *she was beyond such feelings.* After all, the most important man in her life was her hugest disappointment.

"Thank you again for going out on a limb for this hospital." He inched his hand forward, wanting to take hers, apparently for a handshake.

Viktoria slid her hand into his, but he gently clasped it and raised it to his lips. He closed his eyes for a moment, making the gesture more personal.

The silence of the room closed in on them like they were in a remote, private bedroom, like lovers getting away from it all. They both put their hands back to their side.

"Please go take care of Buddy. I'll text you later. I'd love to know how he fares at the vet, and I'll let you know any developments from the DEA officer's visit."

"With a clean bill of health, he and Mattie can have another romp."

"For sure."

Viktoria turned, but looked back from the door. "I must shake the feeling that I'm a traitor-like whistle blower reporting such incidents from an anesthesia department."

With a stern expression, Jeff shook his head. "Your situation is ideal. You are practicing excellent anesthesia, but are in no way an employee here. If you hadn't followed up on the things you were suspicious of, no one else would have, even if they'd gotten wind of what was going on. They would have been too afraid. Your presence was meant to be. In addition, I personally love you being here and wish you could stay."

"All right, then. Talk to you later."

Viktoria left with a slight smile. In the car, she popped a chocolate licorice into her mouth before heading up the road to the Stay Long Hotel.

"Buddy!" Viktoria exclaimed as she pushed the door open to her hotel room and dropped a few things on the counter. "Let's go for a walk and a special appointment for your leg." He licked her hand and furiously wagged his tail until it settled down to a slow spin. She responded by holding his head and dropping kisses on his forehead. After slipping on his leash, they headed for a walk and then loaded themselves into her Honda.

It was one of a dog owner's pleasures, when at all possible, to have a back window partially open and to see your dog's pleasure in sticking his head slightly out the window, sniffing the fresh air, and letting the wind blow on his face. It was dog ecstasy, and she glanced over several times to watch her Border Collie's sheer joy.

After the hospital, she made a right turn and was soon at the Masonville Animal Clinic. Going inside, they went to check in.

"Howdy, Viktoria," Linda said.

Surprised, Viktoria responded, "I forgot you worked here part-time. Guess you have off from the coffee shop today."

"Yes, I'm here today. I like the variety of having two jobs. Coffee and pets, two things I'm passionate about."

"Bet you can't wait to be a vet yourself."

"So true." She pulled one of her double braids in front and toyed with the end. "This must be Buddy's big day to get his stitches out. Dr. Price can see you right away. We were super busy before, but things have calmed down."

"Appreciate it."

Linda walked them back to a room and fetched the veterinarian, who limped in with a suture removal kit. Linda helped hold Buddy's leg while

Dr. Price evaluated it. "Leg looks dandy," he said as he already started snipping out a stitch. "And you have a fine and cooperative Border Collie here. They are fine animals and you two are going to have a solid relationship for a long time."

Viktoria nodded as the vet finished up and Buddy looked no worse for wear.

They walked out and Linda spoke up, "No charge today for taking out what we already billed you for."

"Thanks so much, and I'm sure glad I met you at the coffee shop and you steered me to the right vet."

"Me too. I'll see you soon."

"Bye."

Viktoria enjoyed the slower traffic trip back to the hotel. More cars were on the road from late day workers heading home, and Buddy had more window time.

At the hotel, she grabbed a ball from the room, and brought him out the back-sliding glass door. The late afternoon weather was stellar for a game of catch, and in the security of the grassy area between the building and the back woods, she unleashed him, put a distance between them and threw the yellow tennis ball.

With a fine toss each time, Buddy caught the ball with almost every throw. The more difficult chore for Viktoria was getting him to unclasp it from his teeth for her to throw it again. "Buddy, drop the ball," she announced every time.

Finally, she sidetracked him to the room and grabbed a few tiny biscuits to lure him to drop the ball in lieu of a treat. As they went back out, she noticed one of the two squirrels who hung around. He stood by a tree, his other squirrel buddy nowhere to be seen. Buddy veered off to the back of the next two buildings, sniffing and trotting along. His head dipped low several times, obviously into something.

Viktoria let him wander a bit and, after calling him a few times, he finally stopped chewing, finished whatever he'd been eating, and trotted over.

"These dog cookies are going to be tastier than the grass or whatever you were eating over three. I promise. Still interested in playing?" She tossed the ball in the air and Buddy made a full leap with a solid catch. His interest and energy level stayed steady, and she kept the game going for another half hour before bringing him in and setting down his dinner.

Jennie Shaw pulled her elegant vehicle into the three-car garage and immediately closed the door with her remote. She sprung out of the car and into the kitchen door to find Marybelle wide-eyed and nursing a glass of water at the counter.

"You're here past three o'clock," Jennie said.

"I had no choice but to let those men in here. I feel so bad. Something's not right. I wanted to stay to let you know more men came and took some stuff out of your house."

Jennie twirled a clump of her long black hair so tight in front of her chest that she thought it would rip right off her scalp. "Where from?"

"Upstairs. I'm pretty sure from the master bedroom."

Jennie slumped over the coriander counter and put her head in her hands. Looking up, she said, "Thank you, Marybelle. You can go."

"Will you be okay?"

Jennie wanted to nod, but she couldn't. "Time will tell."

Marybelle grabbed her purse from a nearby chair and glanced back at her employer. "Good luck." She approached the front door. "Casey's home too. Just pulling in."

The housekeeper left as Casey pulled into the garage and came barging into the kitchen. Jennie's large, alert eyes settled on him. "We're in big trouble," she said. "Better go check the master bedroom. Marybelle said stuff was confiscated."

Casey clamped his teeth, and held the pressure the whole time he flew up the stairs. Jennie followed.

"Shit," Casey said. The board to the bottom of the bed was upturned and, with a peek underneath, the couple could tell from the darkened space that it was cleared out. Not a trace of their shoe storage drugs.

Jennie sat on the bed. She always knew deep down that their antics were, or bordered on, being criminal, but she kept denying it. She mostly believed her husband that confiscating the anesthetic agents secretly and methodically from OR patients the way they did it, they would not get caught. But now they had. What would happen to her? She began to cry, tears welling in the corner of her eyes without any control. Sobbing, she wiped her hand across her cheek.

Casey paid little attention. He circled the room like a large cat in a cage and fidgeted with his hands. "We better call that lawyer we've used for evicting tenants. We need him in our back pocket."

Jennie continued crying. She started out the day happy to be putting a patient to sleep under anesthesia and now she needed legal representation. Maybe to keep her out of jail.

CHAPTER 31

Viktoria held a grilled cheese sandwich and slid onto a stool as her cell phone rang. Glad to see the caller ID, it was Regina from the locum tenens agency.

"Dr. Thorsdottir, how is Masonville General continuing to treat you?"

"That's a loaded question. A better question would be how am I handling them instead of them dealing with me."

"Don't think I'll get into that one. Did I catch you at a bad time?"

"Not at all. I'm ready to tank down some orange juice, a grilled cheese sandwich, and a scoop of cole slaw. My Masonville dog, Buddy, is panting at my feet."

"Not much of a fancy dinner."

"It'll suffice. Sometimes avoiding restaurants is the healthier alternative."

"I thought I'd run this by you regarding your next assignment. Even though you enjoy other locations, a hospital on Long Island is looking for anesthesia coverage starting the week after you finish there. You could stay home for a change."

Viktoria frowned and locked eyes with Buddy. She did prefer not being around her husband, but being in her own home for a change and letting Buddy romp in a fenced-in yard while she was at work, sounded like a fine idea. A month at home. On the weekends, she could take Buddy to the beach, and they could walk on the boardwalk.

"Same pay, same hours as now," Regina interjected. "No night call unless you feel so inclined. Mostly bread and butter stuff and some OB."

"Yes, I'll take it. Sounds fine. Email me the paperwork and my electronic signature will be on it in a flash. My dog will love me for it."

"Perfect. Guess I don't need to tell you the hospital or anything. I'll shoot the info up there as soon as we hang up. Enjoy the rest of your meal."

"Thanks, Regina."

Viktoria finished eating, rinsed the dishes, and sat on the couch with a paperback and a bag of cookies at her side. After reading one chapter, she closed the book and called Rick.

Her husband took the last hit of weed from the joint he was smoking, and grabbed the call before it slid into voicemail. "Viktoria, how's it going?"

"Not too bad, but I'm knee-deep in this anesthesia department's affairs. Practicing medicine anymore isn't only about rendering health care. Issues that pop up on the side are important too."

"Seems to me knocking people out and waking them back up is *the* priority."

"So true. Rendering safe anesthesia is number one, but preventing corruption in the OR is pretty vital too."

"Whatever you say. How's Buddy? I can't wait to meet him."

"You will. I just signed on for my next assignment, a local position on Long Island. We can both bond with Buddy because he'll be there."

"You're staying home?"

"Yes, for at least one month."

"Maybe we can do some things, like go to the movies, and I'll mow the backyard for the dog if the grass needs cutting."

"All right then. I better give Buddy his last walk and get ready for bed. It's later than I like."

"Sweet dreams."

Buddy jumped up when Viktoria rose. She slipped on his leash, and they used the back door. As opposed to being at her Long Island home, she could make out the stars on the clear night, and the half-moon managed to reflect light brightly around it. They walked straight over the grass where they played ball, and to the edge of the woods. Buddy sniffed and lifted his leg on a clump of weedy bushes.

Behind the ground foliage, Viktoria strained her neck upon making out something in a lump. Buddy slunk forwards, trying to decipher it as well.

"Oh, no," Viktoria muttered. It was a motionless squirrel, his tail and body as still as the dirt. His eyes were slightly open and death had taken hold. *What a shame,* she thought, *and assumed it was one of the squirrels she had not seen earlier with his partner.* The two rodents had seemed young and spirited, so she stood perplexed over this one's death.

Viktoria and Buddy stepped back into their room as her phone rang again, this time from Jeffrey Appleton. "Hello?" she said.

"How is Buddy? Did his stitches come out?"

"They sure did. He's as good as new."

"Mattie will be happy to know," he said, and chuckled.

"Thanks for asking. I took him for a spin just now, and we found a dead squirrel. Not a pleasant way to end the day."

"I suppose not. Don't fret about it. Maybe it was his time to go. And listen, with all that's going on in the OR, I still can't thank you enough. I have a feeling tomorrow will bring the department some closure. Perhaps more than I care to think about."

"I agree."

"See you soon..." he said and hesitated, "both professionally and personally."

Low overhead lights were on in the DEA office as Patrick sauntered in and found only a janitor hauling a trash can and Buster sitting on the top of his desk, his feet planted on the chair.

"What'd you find out in the OR?" Buster asked, pausing before taking another bite out of a thick granola bar.

"That doctor was right. We've got a match on lot numbers with what you confiscated from the couple's home."

"Doesn't surprise me." Buster nodded and waved the snack. "We've stopped a harmful, deceptive scheme. I wouldn't want to be a patient in that OR and have either of those two give me an anesthetic. You trust caretakers to do what's right. Imagine being put under the knife while someone is holding back the pain medicine that is rightfully yours."

Patrick shuddered. "Gives me the creeps. I mean, what is anesthesia all about, except to prevent pain? I hope a judge throws the book at them."

"But being asleep and not knowing what's going on is important too. At least I don't want to overhear what the surgeon and the anesthesia provider is doing or saying. How about we do one more thing in the morning and check on Fred Stowe in the ICU? Hopefully, he's off the ventilator, and we can question him. He's gonna talk, which will cinch this case up like a hangman's noose."

"Then we'll go arrest Jennie and Casey Johnston. Right out of the OR."

Buster took the last bite and tossed the wrapper into the adjacent can. "This is a new one for me—perps getting married, followed by their arrest."

Wednesday morning, it wasn't only the DEA agents that wanted to visit Fred Stowe in the medical intensive care unit. Viktoria stayed conscientiously attached to the welfare of any patient she had a direct relationship with, and in Fred's case, she had inserted his breathing tube, and had had multiple personal run-ins with him in and about the Stay Long Hotel. With time to spare, she carried her to-go cup from the coffee shop up the elevator and into the unit.

Reeling back when she entered, she was the fourth person to step into Fred's room. A male RN hovered over chart work and the two DEA men were already there, making her reconsider that anesthesiologists are not the only people who start work at the crack of dawn. Still dressed in a hospital gown, the workman nervously swung his leg while sitting in a chair.

Everyone turned to Viktoria, but she focused on the patient first. "I guess this answers my question whether or not you were extubated and are doing better."

"You again," Fred commented. "You seem to show up when it's important."

"Happy to help," she quipped.

"Internal medicine took him off the ventilator late last night," the RN said. "He was more than ready."

"We were just asking Mr. Stowe about his drug habit," Buster said, "and where he got the drugs he used to overdose on. Not only do we have a wrap on the persons providing them, but his two buddies receive anesthetic drug payments as well. Two CRNAs downstairs pay their employees very creatively."

Viktoria widened her eyes. "I'm sorry to hear the truth. I wish it were a different story."

"Us too," Patrick added a firm nod. "We'll be going straight down to the OR. Ever see an arrest in the surgical suite?"

She shook her head. "Assignments are probably made out already for the morning cases. Hurry down before the cases start. The anesthesiologist in charge can reassign people to take the place of the two you are hauling away. We don't want patients to suffer any kind of delay or rescheduling of their surgeries based on the history of these two narcissistic individuals."

"We'll be following up with you," Patrick said to Fred, and then turned to Buster. "Let's follow her advice."

Viktoria patted Fred on the shoulder. "Glad you're doing better, Mr. Stowe, but get yourself into rehab, and drop the drug habit."

"Yes, ma'am."

Viktoria followed the uniformed men out the automatic doors straight to the OR.

Of course, it was not Jay Huff making out the day's assignments since he was postcall and had already left the hospital, but Phillip Nettle. The DEA men asked for Viktoria's assistance, so she settled them in the doctor's lounge with a cup of coffee while she changed into scrubs.

Viktoria poked her head back into the lounge. "You ready, guys?"

"You doctors sure drink lousy coffee from here," Buster commented as they strolled through the hallway.

They passed the Director of Surgical Service's office as he just arrived, and Jeff turned to spot the three of them on their official mission. "I'm coming too," he barked out the door.

All heads at the front OR desk turned when the OR doors slid open and Viktoria, Jeff, Buster, and Patrick stood in front of the surgical scheduling board. Phillip turned, his jaw dropped, and he squinted through his thick glasses.

"These gentlemen need Casey and Jennie before they start any assignments you've given them," Viktoria said.

Phillip stared at Buster's patch on his breast pocket—"DEA." He took a gulp. "Okay, they should both be in the preop holding area."

"I'll go," Viktoria said, "subtlety and without fanfare." She hastened next door and signaled Casey away from a patient and Jennie away from a chart at the desk.

"There's been a scheduling change," she told the couple. "Let's go back to the front desk."

Jennie thrust her lips out in a sullen expression. In no way did she want any unexpected happenings in her forthcoming day. In full denial of what could happen to her during the day, she wanted to start her assigned case for a tonsillectomy on a child and get on with anesthetic care. She reluctantly followed Casey and Viktoria.

"No way," Jennie blurted out as she stepped through the automatic doors. It was horrid enough that two men stood there in official uniforms, but when they turned, and she saw "DEA," her OR clogs froze to the hard, cold floor.

"Oh, shit," Casey spoke aloud. He righted his crestfallen face and put on his charismatic expression, albeit with a slight tremble.

"Are you Jennie and Casey Johnston?" Patrick asked.

Casey nodded, but Jennie still stared like a deer caught in headlights.

"Then let's not make a scene," Patrick said. "We have your drugs from your house, we've matched OR vial lot numbers, we've got one of your worker's statements, and enough evidence has been gathered to throw you in the slammer for a long time."

Casey wanted nothing more than to leave and be spared the pairs of OR workers' eyes that were adding up and viewing the scene by the minute. He locked his hand around Jennie's forearm and tugged her along.

As the two CRNAs passed through OR double doors for the last time, Buster glanced over at them. "That elegant Hollywood mansion of yours is gonna be headed for the auction block."

"What the hell was that all about?" Phillip asked dumbfounded.

"They've been stealing anesthetic drugs," Viktoria whispered, "and distributing them to their own employees."

Dr. Nettle stared deep into Viktoria's eyes, not believing what he heard. She stared back and nodded.

Jeffrey leaned in. "Dr. Nettle, we have an OR to run. Better make the necessary adjustments now that you're short two CRNAs."

Phillip twisted his mouth in a lopsided frown.

"You can put the CRNA that was going to give breaks into Casey or Jennie's case," Viktoria said, "put another anesthesiologist in a room, and I'll supervise more cases. In addition, you and I can give breaks and lunches."

"That's a lot on you," he said.

"I can handle it."

Jeffrey smiled and patted Viktoria on the arm. "I'll talk to you later about the other problem, after I investigate it this morning." Jeff parted from their threesome and weaved his way out the door between onlookers.

Phillip sighed deeply. "Even though he's at home sleeping off a call night, maybe I should call Jay Huff about the CRNA problem. This is a major development in the department."

"I believe Jeffrey Appleton will be calling Dr. Huff about more than your nurse anesthetist coverage."

Phillip stared after Viktoria as she hurried off to see patients in the holding area. He rubbed his glasses with a lens cloth and stuck them back on. How come this outlander from Long Island and Iceland knew more about what was going on in the department than he did? Especially after she was given the cold shoulder and no benefit of the doubt as to her clinical abilities when she arrived?

CHAPTER 32

Jeffrey slipped between more onlookers as they speculated over the scene they had just witnessed. Two of the OR employees most charming coworkers had just been led out by officers. Most people loitering about had witnessed the couple's wedding but three days ago, where they had attended the most prestigious event in all of Masonville. Being able to say that you'd been inside the home of Jennie and Casey Johnston was high on the city's social bragging rights.

Mr. Appleton ignored the speculation, realizing it would sweep through the hospital and be reiterated in the President's office within no time. It made his next chore that much more critical, with a need to be expeditious. He did not want to waste Cathy Banker's time by telling her one huge debacle, but he wanted to bring both issues he suspected right to her great mahogany desk at the same time. *Kill two birds with one stone*, he thought.

First, at the OR front desk, he closed the door and sat close to the secretary. She smiled, and tugged on the dreadlocks from an extension hair piece clipped to the back of her hair.

"Miss Lamont, I don't only want a copy of yesterday's printed schedule, but handwritten adds-on through the evening and night on every single case that went in and out of the OR receiving anesthesia services."

"It was busy last night," she said, and went about preparing his request.

Jeff studied the sheet when she was finished. The add-on cases Viktoria had told him about were there as well as some more. "Thank you so much."

Luckily, he knew how things operated and poked into the anesthesia office. The pile of billing slips from the day before were already missing, carried off by the mail department and headed to the billing office. He headed straight upstairs and wanted to avoid Sarah Wentworth, but knew she would be the most capable person to help him out.

"Sarah, I am here to bother you again about billing slips." He stood inches from her desk and handed over the personalized OR schedule he had brought.

Looking up, her face beamed with enthusiasm, and she managed to slide the V-neck collar of her blouse aside to expose more skin. She extended her hand and took the sheet. "Anything for you, Jeff. Is this all of yesterday's?"

"Yes, please compare it to the anesthesia billing slips which I hope have been deposited up here."

She rose and walked slowly and closely past him. "Might as well come with me."

Between the open room of workers at their desks, they came to a file cabinet with all the early morning inter-departmental mail stacked in piles. They both began sorting through until they found the OR slips they desired. With heads bent together, they compared the slips with the cases done.

Jeffrey raised his head with a thrust. "Three slips are missing."

"I agree. Healthy tickets for reimbursement too. An emergency burr hole, a long hand case, and a facial fracture from an MVA."

Jeff clenched his teeth, angry at the skulduggery of it. It was straight out-and-out double dipping by the President of the group, who was in charge of the department and entrusted with a moral code to be expected from someone in his position. Why did the anesthesia providers at Masonville General Hospital need to be making extra money outside their normal work salaries? Greedy and immoral, that sums them up.

He shook his head while Sarah tapped on the sheet he held. "Nice detective work. We should get together and celebrate our discovery!"

"Umm... some other time. My damage control is just beginning." Jeff made haste to leave and headed straight for the office of the President.

Cathy Banker rose and closed her office door with a loud click after Jeff walked in. "Jessy Winter's suicide in our hospital was enough big news for a year, but this takes the cake. What the 'f' is going on in that OR you're in charge of?" She stormed back to her side of the desk and turned to him abruptly.

Her anger surprised him, especially since it was directed at him. "As I imagined, you heard the news. The two newly wedded CRNAs have been hauled off by the DEA, no doubt guilty of stealing anesthesia drugs from the OR."

"Probably for some time!"

"Ma'am, there are checks and balances for signing in and out of the narcotic machine, but then there is the human element of anesthesia and OR providers to not scam the system. These two were skillfully milking the records to indicate that the drugs were given, and then taking the vials home themselves. It could have happened anywhere."

The tension in her lips subsided, but Jeffrey knew he had to forge ahead. "This is not the only scandalous news I have this morning. Jay Huff, the President of the department, has been making off with charge slips, billing separately for cases which are rightfully to be reimbursed to the hospital."

"What? Are you sure about this?"

"Beyond a shadow of a doubt."

She took her fingers and thumb and rubbed them across her eyebrows, then she threw her hands in the air. "I'll call an emergency board meeting. It won't be solely up to me, but what do I want? Fire the whole GD department."

"I understand and agree," Jeff said timidly.

"Go back downstairs and try the hell to put a lid on the gossip that will be flying out of that OR. Have a meeting or something to stem gossip." The thin woman grabbed her chair first before lowering herself. "Don't think that your job, however, is secure, Mr. Appleton."

Jeffrey's heart pounded as he left the top floor of the hospital. He had not considered it, that his own job was in jeopardy. So much for doing the correct thing.

The pace was steady and almost too much to handle. Viktoria started a case with a CRNA, and checked her watch. The time had flown, and she had not hydrated during the last few hectic hours, nor had she had the opportunity to talk with Jeffrey Appleton.

She scurried out into the hallway where she noticed Jeff in front of her, turning into the lounge. Making the same right turn, she sidled next to him at the food counter.

He glanced over. "You eat lunch yet?"

"No. But it'll be an eat and dash."

He nodded to the one empty table as they both quickly grabbed the chef's sandwich of the day. Jeffrey poured two coffees, and they sat across from each other.

"I'm dying to know," Viktoria said, leaning in.

"Jay Huff kept the slips from last night's neurosurgical burr hole case and two others. I already reported his actions to Cathy Banker."

"That must have gone over like catching dead fish. Did you tell her about the CRNAs?"

"She heard about that already. I corroborated the rumor. She's calling an emergency board meeting. More than likely, they will fire the whole department." The spark in his brown eyes faded as he frowned. "That will make it almost impossible to provide anesthesia coverage and to keep the OR running like usual."

"You will see to the manpower and run it as efficiently as possible."

"That is, if I still have a job at the end of the week."

"Oh, no." Viktoria took a deep sigh. The last thing that should happen is that Jeff ends up the fall guy. She slid her hand forward close to his. "Hopefully, it won't come to that, Jeff."

They each took a bite out of their panini sandwiches and thought about the current situations.

"You can contact my locum tenens agency if the need arises. Regina does a fine job of finding quality health care providers."

"Yes, I may have to. Thank goodness you're at least here for another two weeks."

Two internists passed their table, chatting about the arrest in the OR. Jeffrey shook his head.

"Say, why don't we go out for dinner this evening? Get our minds off our work. Take the dogs. There's a picture-perfect lighthouse in the area where we can walk them before hitting the nearby restaurant."

"That's the most sensible thing I've heard all day."

"I'll pick you up. We'll throw the dogs in my Jeep."

Since arriving in Masonville, Viktoria dolled up more than usual, even more so than for the previous weekend's wedding. As she fastened her favorite necklace around her neck, she wondered why. She deserved the effort on herself for a change. After all, she took care of other people all day long. But she also admitted to herself, in a short time, she would be sharing a few hours with a man whom she'd grown fond of. Very fond of.

Like a mini-dermabrasion, she scrubbed her face with a polishing cream, and added more highlight to her dark eyebrows. She moistened her wide, full lips with lip gloss, a deep autumn rose color. Throwing some clothes on the bed, she chose a casual, sporty outfit—crisp, wrinkle free, smart black cargo pants and a shiny white blouse which would flutter in the wind. She changed into the different set of clothes and surveyed herself in the door mirror. Pleased, her eyes settled on Buddy lying behind her. For late afternoon, he seemed more tuckered than usual.

Viktoria scooped out Buddy's dry dog food and placed it in his bowl on the floor. His usual warped speed inhalation of his dinner was less robust than normal. Without his finishing every kibble, she finally picked up his bowl and washed it.

A knock sounded at the door and Jeffrey Appleton stood there with a glow like a teenager on his first prom date.

"Dr. Thorsdottir, you are a wonderful sight after such a shaky day."

"Likewise, Mr. Appleton."

Viktoria patted her thigh, Buddy followed her, and jumped into the back of Jeff's car. For a moment, Viktoria rustled Mattie's coat, and then slid into the passenger's seat as Jeff held the door open.

"How about we eat first and then stroll by the lighthouse?" Jeff asked, putting his vehicle in drive.

"Yes, especially since I'm hungry. There was no time for munching after that lunch we had."

"I'll try to steer away from all that happened today, but for an update, the President and the board is meeting as we speak."

"It scares me to imagine what they are thinking after one OR event which will be hard-pressed to stay out of the media and a billing, financial scam all in one day. How will the hospital save face with its shareholders after news like that?"

"We both know heads will fly. They must purge the riff-raff. I believe more and more that they'll can me."

"Don't worry about it tonight. You will find out soon enough."

They silenced as Viktoria scanned the countryside, for the first time gazing out at the Pennsylvania orchards she previously heard so much about. Set back from the two-lane road, apple trees lined both sides of the street, and before long, pear trees took their place.

"Too bad you're not staying longer," Jeff said. "The fall markets and seasonal get-togethers are magnificent. Us northern Pennsylvanians throw parties geared around fruit, such as all-things apples."

"Every place has its attributes. Maybe I should bring a basket of fresh apples home to Long Island."

Jeff frowned, sorry to contemplate her eventual departure. Before long, they parked in the lot of another of Jeff's favorite eateries. A wooden deck surrounded the building and customers dotted the aluminum table sets. They asked the inside maître d' for a table outside and tethered the dogs to the railing.

With menus in hand, Viktoria settled on grilled salmon and Jeff ordered a prime rib. When the waitress returned, she placed garlic bread and two glasses of wine on the table.

"To a fine dinner and fine company," Jeff said, raising his glass.

"I second that notion."

Their glasses clinked together and over the next hour and a half, Viktoria and Jeff grew more immersed in their conversation and less strained from the day which faded behind them. They both waited for dessert—a bourbon bread pudding which they decided to share.

Mattie and Buddy remained patient and yet alert to the customers who went up and down the porch stairs. The golden retriever stood quickly when an old sedan's engine rattled laboriously from the parking lot. Buddy stayed down and hardly flinched, but a few moments later, he stood and arched his back. Retching forward, he vomited to the side, as far away from his spot as his leash would allow.

"Buddy," Viktoria said, and rose. She took a paper napkin and cleaned up the compact mess and laid it off to the side for disposal later, and moved Buddy a foot over while Jeff did the same with Mattie. "Are you okay?" She looked the dog over, but other than his vomiting and being less peppy than Mattie, she could see nothing else wrong. The area on his leg previously cared for also appeared to be fine.

"I hope he's okay," Jeff said.

"Maybe he caught a stomach bug."

The dessert arrived and Jeff picked up a spoon. He extended his utensil over to Viktoria's mouth with a scoop of the soft, bourbon y pudding. She obliged and opened her mouth.

"You're stunning in the outdoor light, you know," he said.

Viktoria closed her eyes, savoring the taste, and opened them. The handsome man across from her, the wine's enhancement of her mellowness, and the loving dogs beside them were blissful. Her heartbeat pattered along with a slow, steady rhythm of contentment.

"Thank you, and this pudding is irresistible, like you."

Jeff leaned further in. "So why resist?"

She again closed her eyes. Yes, why resist him? She could not remember having such a wonderful evening with a man in years. At home, she rarely sat with her husband for meals anymore. She had grown weary and intolerant of him scrolling through his iPhone, reading a magazine, or checking out what was on television in the background while they ate. And his actions were independent of his mental status, whether he was high or not.

She gasped for a breath of air; Jeff had such an effect on her. "Yes, why resist," she said softly.

Jeff held the spoon steady. "Come back to my place tonight."

"I would love to. Believe me, I would."

He silenced and gazed down.

"I'm sorry. Perhaps I'll change my mind before I leave. You have a deep understanding of what women, or I, want. Yes, the thought of sex with you is totally inviting, but the attention you bestow on me is worth more frolics in the sack than you can imagine. Many women my age would tell you the same thing. And because of my current marital situation, your attention has made my anesthesia coverage here that much more rewarding and satisfying."

Jeff smiled. "You are so direct. I love that about you. Miss Viktoria, if you change your mind or not, I hope we can stay close friends. I've never met an Icelander quite like you."

"That's because you've known no other Icelanders," she said and laughed.

He laughed along with her and added, "and if I were to see you regularly, I would shower you with the attention that you deserve."

After they finished their dessert, they walked the dogs around the lighthouse, and drove back to Masonville. At the hotel, it took all of Viktoria's will power to spring out of his vehicle and not go home with him.

CHAPTER 33

Jeff's office phone rang, and he hesitated to answer. Most of his Wednesday morning calls so far came from reporters. Not only had the Masonville newspapers and television news stations contacted him about the scandalous drug bust related to the hospital, but news-gathering sources were contacting him from all over the state. He shuddered to think about how many calls may be flooding into administration upstairs. And surely, they would be none too happy.

Since he expected a call from Cathy Banker any minute, he answered. "Come up to my office right now," she said, without so much as a hello.

Jeff huddled in the back of the elevator and thought ahead, anticipating his defensive answers if she suggested the board's decision to terminate him. All told, they needed him now more than ever for damage control and for his people skills when it came to employee disruption.

He knocked on the CEOs door and walked with confidence into her office.

"Sit down," Cathy said.

Jeff obliged. On the side of the desk in front of him was a box of cinnamon-apple donuts, the smell wafting by his nose. The distraction was welcome and calmed his nerves.

She perched herself against the front of the desk and crossed her legs at the knee. "Last night I thought the board members were going to roast me in a fire. Luckily, they made decisions which everyone could live with. We will obviously be conducting an investigation of how the present system failed us, and how both grave misconducts occurred right under our noses. Not just one illegal act, but two.

"We are firing the entire anesthesia department. We're going to call that locum tenens agency to help us out in the interim. More permanently, you and I will contact full-time physician service companies that are known to put entire hospital professional departments together, such as anesthesia, pathology, or radiology. We'll let them put together our department, and they will be paid handsomely for their services. Let's make sure that woman visiting anesthesiologist, Dr. Thorsdottir, stays on board through her contracted tenure and, if possible, longer than that."

"She's leaving in two weeks and has her next assignment thoughtfully lined up. But she's a great asset in the interim."

"Yes, and we owe her a lot professionally and personally. Do you think she'd mind being in charge until she leaves? Do you have a good relationship with her?"

"I believe so, and she's a born leader. She will take charge if I ask her."

"Talk to her, and tell her to visit me about all of this at her convenience. When and if she pops in, I will drop whatever I'm doing to make her acquaintance and assure her we are thrilled to have her here."

Cathy turned to the side and held out the donut box. Jeff shook his head. "No, really," she said and took one herself.

Jeff selected one and took a bite.

"We're fine," she said. "The board believes you are a valid asset and will steer the OR and this anesthesia department problem back on track. We all believe it won't be easy, but we trust you. Let's stress to the agencies that we insist on a new group with individuals who hold the Hippocratic Oath and integrity as important as the anesthesia skills that they provide."

Unaware of the tension he'd brought into the room, Jeff felt a pent-up strain dissipate from his muscles. The rich flavor of the donut did him good, and he smiled. "I will be happy and ever so dedicated to be putting our OR back on track."

"Go talk to that Dr. Thorsdottir and get on the phone with the locums agency. After lining up at least half the coverage, fire the department. They don't have a leg to stand on. If we are short of anesthesia providers for a short time, we will run fewer rooms. The board supports that decision."

They both finished their donuts, comparable to sealing their discussion and the decisions made.

Jeff hopped into the elevator, the doors snapped shut, and he headed downstairs to inform Viktoria.

In the preop holding room, Viktoria squatted in front of a little girl who twirled with one ponytail dangling from the side of her head. The youngster's parents watched with relief as Viktoria eased the little girl's nervousness about having her tonsils removed.

"You are the prettiest patient I've had all day," Viktoria said.

"I am?" The preschooler asked.

"Yes, and I bet you love stories in books, which makes you smart too."

The little girl grinned. "I do. My favorite is Chester the Chesapeake. I love all the dogs."

"Dogs are wonderful. I have a dog named Buddy."

The curtain parted and Viktoria turned. Jeff nodded. "When you have a moment ..."

"I'll be back," Viktoria said to the girl and her parents. "We'll talk more about anesthesia."

Viktoria stepped out, and Jeff waved her behind the empty desk. They stood huddled next to the wall where he spoke softly. "The board and CEO made their final decision to fire the department. I'll be talking to your agency, getting interim help, and using a physician full-time recruitment company to hire a whole department. We would like for you to take charge of running the department with additional compensation. I'm firing Jay Huff by the end of the day. Any chance you could stay beyond your two remaining weeks here?" His eyes sunk into hers, a personal as well as a professional request.

Viktoria let the words sink in. She glanced past him and frowned. "I will step up in the interim." Her eyes moistened. "I'm sorry. I better not stay on. After much soul-searching in the past, I made the decision to work in different locations and practices. I'm not ready to renege on that promise."

Jeff waited a second while a nurse picked up a chart on the way past the desk. He leaned his shoulder against the wall. "I understand. I wish I could change your mind, but if that were the case, then you wouldn't be the most interesting and unique person I had the opportunity to meet and spend time with."

"Thank you for understanding, Jeff."

The curtain parted and the little girl fixed her eyes on her anesthesiologist, waiting for her return. Viktoria sauntered back over, and by the end of the day, she was overseeing the next day's printed surgery schedule with ideas about how to use the anesthesia personnel available to her most effectively.

Viktoria anticipated Buddy's greeting at the end of the day, especially after the stressful day at Masonville General Hospital. In eight hours, she went from being the outlander, temporary anesthesiologist, to running the schedule and being sought after to stay on permanently. It warmed her heart to be wanted and appreciated, but now she wanted to show her affection for Buddy and spring him from the confines of the hotel room.

Inching open the door, she spotted him at the end of the couch. She went in, only to step over a small mound of brownish-red soft material on the floor. Her guess was that he had vomited again, so she went straight to him, curled up in the corner by the armrest.

"Buddy, what's wrong? Is your stomach still upset?"

The dog raised his head and responded to her touch. She rubbed his head and his belly, and looking him over, she didn't see any areas of concern on his body. "Let's get you out for a walk and then I'm going to call the vet."

Viktoria leashed him and they proceeded outside. It was a sullen, cloudy day, and she didn't miss the bright sunshine for their walk. By the time they reached the first trees out front, however, she wondered if his hind limbs were walking with difficulty, as if they were trying to seize up and quit working.

"We're going to skip playing ball," Viktoria said after she kept the walk to a minimum and brought Buddy back inside. He settled on an area rug and with his head flat on the floor, peered up at her with his big, dark, eyes. She frowned as they lacked their usual gaiety and alertness.

At the counter, Viktoria scrolled through the numbers in her phone and called Masonville Animal Clinic. "Hello," she said, "this is Viktoria Thorsdottir and I'm calling about Buddy. Do you have any openings before you close today or late tomorrow? He's had one or two bouts of vomiting and I could swear his hind legs seem impaired."

A young woman, not Linda, responded. "Dr. Price is booked today. We can fit you in at five tomorrow."

"Yes, please, put us down."

When Viktoria hung up, she placed Buddy's kibbles on the floor, but he showed no interest in eating. She had contemplated going to the nearby restaurant for breakfast food, but decided against it. After making a sandwich with the little turkey and cheese cold cuts left in the refrigerator, she sat next to her four-legged friend and stroked him with one hand while she ate with the other.

Buddy showed no improvement with his lethargy on a simple last walk before bedtime. When coming back inside, the dog sipped some water, and for that, she was grateful. She changed into pajamas and slithered under the bed sheets by 9 p.m. Lying on one side, she watched the dog on the floor. He was stretched on one side, his eyes closed, his shiny black and white coat draped over his belly.

Viktoria dozed off to sleep. The day had been so packed with mental stimulation, that she slept deeply, exhausted with the weight of the outcome of the anesthesia department's corruption and her poor dog not feeling well.

At midnight, little did she know that Buddy's muscles first showed muscle tremors, but soon he twitched and jerked in a full generalized seizure. The seizure tormented his agile body like a twisted pretzel, and as the dark hours of the night passed, his central nervous system became more and more depressed.

Buddy's breathing slowed. The grateful, renewed life that Viktoria had given him, ebbed away slowly, and the beautiful border collie took his last silent breath.

The alarm sounded, startling Viktoria straight out of a bizarre OR dream. She propped herself up on one elbow and opened her eyes. Buddy was on the floor near the bed, pretty much the same spot where he went to sleep, which was not his norm. Customarily, he would change location, even so much as to bed down on the couch.

She swung her legs over the side of the mattress, and leaned forward. "Buddy?"

Remembering the stiff movement of his hind legs, she gazed directly at them. Now they even appeared to be stiff. "Buddy?"

The dog didn't stir. Viktoria jumped up and fell next to him on the floor. Fearing the worst, she stroked him. She moved him by his upper body onto her lap, but his head dangled along with the movement, without any purpose.

"Oh my God. No!"

Viktoria showered. Showered to let the tears wash away down her face and down the drain. She could barely stand it, that her dog was dead in the other room, taken too early, and after escaping one close call with death before. It wasn't happening. It was unfair. The dog didn't deserve death. The two of them were to go on and enjoy at least twelve more years together.

She stepped out, dried, and got dressed. Before she left the room, she gently wrapped Buddy in a spare, light blanket she found in the closet, and left a message with the vet.

Stepping out of the elevator, Viktoria's thoughts exploded with the task at hand to run an anesthesia schedule and thwart the pessimism of the anesthesia providers who were on the schedule for the day. Above everything that was occurring with personnel and politics, the safety of the patients was her primary concern.

And she needed to stifle her sadness over a dog that had stolen her heart. She guessed correctly that Jeff would be coming to work in the near future earlier than normal, so she headed to his office before the locker room.

His door was slightly ajar. "Jeff," she said, poking her head in.

He finished taking a swig of coffee and waved her in. "Good morning. Or is it?" The cheerfulness in his voice left as she approached, and he sensed her despair. "What's the matter? Not one more thing?"

Her emotions grabbed the best of her, and she couldn't talk for a moment. "It's ... Buddy. I don't know what happened. He passed away. He's dead in the hotel room."

"Oh my God." In a flash, Jeff was next to her, holding her in an embrace. "I'm sorry. So sorry."

For an eternal minute, she let herself be held. She closed her eyes and breathed slowly and deeply. Tears welled in her eyes, and she brushed them away as her head rested on his shoulder. "Thank you."

Viktoria straightened herself. "I'm going to bring him into the vet's office at the end of the day. Maybe the vet will have some answers for me. Maybe I'll have him cremated."

"May I come with you?"

She nodded.

"It's going to be another tough day in the OR, but I'll do my best."

"I'll be back and forth and help out in any way that I can."

"You were amazing today," Jeff said as he drove Viktoria and Buddy to the vet's office before they closed. "With the manpower we had, and the slightly curtailed OR schedule, you ran the schedule efficiently and I heard not one complaint."

"It's easier than you think. Everyone is simply too busy gossiping about Jennie and Casey Johnston being drug crooks and the President of the group being an embezzler." She tried to smile. "Any doctor filling in after that mess is going to be a hero."

"You qualified as a hero even before filling the shoes of Jay Huff. And a hero to that wonderful dog." He put the car in park at the vet's office, and opened Viktoria's door for her. Then he went to the back of his Jeep and scooped Buddy up in his blanket and carried him inside.

After Linda escorted them back to an examining room, Dr. Price ran his hand through his gray hair, and stepped back away from the examining table where Buddy had been lain.

"I have my suspicions, especially based on the history you told me. I see it several times a year, especially from dogs brought in from around the low-rent housing district." He arched his eyebrow and Viktoria waited with bated breath.

"Rat poisoning. Bromethalin ingestion. It's not uncommonly sprinkled around by workers in housing units or landlords to keep their units rodent free. Strays or household pets don't know the difference in eating that poison, and its toxicity makes them severely ill or kills them. Where did you say you've been living?"

"At the Stay Long Hotel. Construction men worked over there fixing rooms; they ended up in their own trouble. But come to think about it, Buddy was busy a few days ago eating something outside and behind the

241

units they were servicing."

Dr. Price frowned. "I'm sorry. I think you have your answer as to how Buddy died."

Viktoria rested her hand on Buddy's torso. "Can you cremate him for me?"

"Yes, we have a service here. We'll call you in a few days when he's ready."

Jeff started the engine. "May I take you for a bite to eat? This is a sad day, but you still need to eat."

"I don't know if I can eat a bite, but that's sweet of you. I feel devastated. I've lost my best friend."

He didn't put the car in drive, but waited for her to agree. "How about something light? Like scrambled eggs?"

"How did you know? Standard breakfast fare is what I fall back on in a pinch. Okay, we can stop at the diner restaurant down the block from the hotel."

"I would be honored to bring you."

Viktoria chose the booth when they arrived and as they waited for their order to arrive, she dug into her purse and dragged out a small bag.

"We do a lot with licorice in Iceland. I never shared my favorite treat from there with you." She picked out a candy and placed it in his hand. "It's a Sukkulaoihjupaour lakkris."

"Ha, what did you call it?"

She repeated herself, he smiled, and popped it in his mouth.

"Suck on it. Let the outside candy part melt in your mouth."

"Awesome," he said. As he swallowed the last of it, their scrambled eggs and bacon were set down.

Outside, they slid into the Jeep, and he turned to her. "I'm going to miss you when you leave. In the meantime, I'll savor your friendship until you go. Remember, you are welcome to my home any time. Mattie would love to see you too."

This time, Viktoria didn't hash through the do's or don'ts of the situation. She glanced sideways. "Jeff, let's go back to your place."

He squeezed her hand which rested on the console and smiled.

EPILOGUE

It was far from pitch dark when Viktoria climbed into her Honda at 4 a.m. on Saturday morning after her month's assignment at Masonville General Hospital was finished. The half moon and stars were crisply clear to her naked eye, and she hated that would not be the case back home on the populous island she called home, full of man-made light that blared into the sky regardless of day or night.

She started the engine and tipped her head toward the front office, steering away way before Mason would be reading his newspaper. When she checked out the night before, he reiterated again his condolences about Buddy, and wished her good luck. He felt partially guilty that Casey Johnston's workers had spread rat poison around the hotel grounds, especially since the facility allowed customers to bring their pets.

Used to long interstate trips, Viktoria drove several hours before the need arose for gas and a bathroom break. By then, driving conditions had changed. More cars joined the road, and the sun cascaded up the horizon. She turned off her headlights and entertained herself with talk shows and streaming music apps.

Her last day at the hospital the day before had been difficult, and for the last two weeks, she held together a dying anesthesia group and began building a new, vibrant one. Her deeds were not left unnoticed. Even though staff filtered in and out during the day, they managed to set up a thoughtful and vibrant going away party for her in the nurses' lounge, complete with helium balloons announcing Bon Voyage.

In the middle of the day, Cathey Banker also called her up to administration to personally thank her for being the catalyst to overturn the corruption in the OR, and to present her with a $1,000 check from the hospital as a "thank you" and a retribution for any hardship she may have endured.

But the most difficult person to say good-bye to was Jeff. In such a short period of time, they had become more than close friends. Intimate discussions between them lasted for hours, as well as the attention they bestowed on each other. By the end of the last week, she had spent half her nights at his place. She would miss his attentiveness, tenderness, and lovemaking.

She did further heavy thinking and reminiscing. Her primary plan to stay on Long Island for her next job assignment had backfired. Buddy had been her main concern--she wanted the energetic, smart dog to learn about his true, real home, and backyard on Long Island, and partake in a routine that placed him solely as a family member in a two-person household. She thought this despite the fact that she and Rick qualified as less than a true family.

With sorrow, she kept glancing to the passenger seat, at the white plastic container that held Buddy's ashes. Not right away, but maybe she would find herself another dog, one who would slip into Buddy's role of what she had envisioned—to be best buddies and to keep each other company during her anesthesiology assignments.

Viktoria made two more stops, including a fast-food drive-through for a late lunch. Late in the afternoon, she reached her final major road change and merged into the buildup of traffic on the Long Island Expressway. Time to call Rick, she thought, and allow him to clean up his act before she walked in on him, if that was even a possibility.

"I'm on the L.I.E.," she announced. "I drove straight through."

"That's a long haul. You're crazy, and I don't know how you do it, but glad to hear you're almost home. See you soon."

"I could use some help to unpack the car when I arrive."

"Sure thing."

They ended the call, and Viktoria focused on watching out for the Long Island sliders who cut drivers off when going from the fast lane all the way over to their imminent exit lane.

At home, Rick pocketed his cell phone. He slowly savored the joint he was smoking, licked his thumb and forefinger, and doused what was left of the weed. He dropped it in the ashtray in front of him, and wafted his hand around the table to clear the air. In the hallway bathroom, he emptied the joint end and ash down the commode, and flushed. Back in the kitchen, he rinsed out the ashtray.

He stared out the kitchen window. He'd been contemplating it while his wife had been away, especially since she must have gone through a hard time with that dog she'd saved. Buddy's dying was a bummer. Perhaps he would try to give up his drug habit and go to some kind of therapist or rehab. He was married to a wonderful woman, and he knew he appreciated her and treated her a lot better, when he was straight. It was worth a try, so he committed himself to the idea.

Within two hours, Viktoria pulled into the driveway of their North Shore home. She could smell the salt air not far off. It reminded her of the great body of water, Lake Erie, and the surrounding area, where she experienced meeting a loving border collie and a fantastic man who didn't do drugs.

End

FROM THE AUTHOR

If you'd like a release alert for when Barbara Ebel has new books available, sign up at this site: http://eepurl.com/cKrn0D   This is intended only to let you know about new releases as soon as they are out.

Barbara Ebel is a physician and an award-winning and *USA TODAY Bestselling Author*. Since she practiced anesthesia, she brings credibility to the medical background of her plots. She lives with her husband and pets in a wildlife corridor in Tennessee but has lived up and down the East Coast.

Visit or contact her at her website: http://barbaraebel.weebly.com

The following books are also written by Dr. Barbara and are available as paperbacks and eBooks:

The Outlander Physician Series:

Corruption in the O.R.: A Medical Thriller (The Outlander Physician Series Book 1)

Wretched Results: A Medical Thriller (The Outlander Physician Series Book 2)

EBook Box Sets:

The Dr. Annabel Tilson Novels Box Set:
Books 1-3 (The Dr. Annabel Tilson Series)

The Dr. Annabel Tilson Novels Box Set:
Books 4-6 (The Dr. Annabel Tilson Series)

The Dr. Danny Tilson Novels Box Set:
Books 1-4 (The Dr. Danny Tilson Series)

<u>The Dr. Danny Tilson Series: (Individual paperbacks and ebooks):</u>

Operation Neurosurgeon: You never know… who's in the OR (A Dr. Danny Tilson Novel: Book 1).

Silent Fear: a Medical Mystery (A Dr. Danny Tilson Novel: Book 2). Also an Audiobook.

Collateral Circulation: a Medical Mystery (A Dr. Danny Tilson Novel: Book 3). Also an Audiobook.

Secondary Impact (A Dr. Danny Tilson Novel: Book 4).

<u>The Dr. Annabel Tilson Series: (Individual paperbacks and ebooks):</u>

DEAD STILL: A Medical Thriller (Dr. Annabel Tilson Novels Book 1)

DEADLY DELUSIONS: A Medical Thriller (Dr. Annabel Tilson Novels Book 2)

DESPERATE TO DIE: A Medical Thriller (Dr. Annabel Tilson Novels Book 3)

DEATH GRIP: A Medical Thriller (Dr. Annabel Tilson Novels Book 4)

DOWNRIGHT DEAD: A Medical Thriller (Dr. Annabel Tilson Novels Book 5)

DANGEROUS DOCTOR: A Medical Thriller (Dr. Annabel Tilson Novels Book 6)

<u>Stand-alone Medical Novels:</u>

Outcome, A Novel

Her Flawless Disguise

Nonfiction health book:
Younger Next Decade: *After Fifty, the Transitional Decade, and What You Need to Know*

Children's book series written and illustrated by Barbara Ebel:
Chester the Chesapeake Book One
Chester the Chesapeake Book Two: Summertime
Chester the Chesapeake Book Three: Wintertime
Chester the Chesapeake Book Four: My Brother Buck
Chester the Chesapeake Book Five: The Three Dogs of Christmas

Made in United States
Orlando, FL
21 January 2022